UTTERL

PAULINE MANDERS

Published in 2022 by Ottobeast Publishing
ottobeastpublishing@gmail.com

Cover design Rebecca Moss Guyver.

ISBN 978-1-912861-15-6

A CIP catalogue record for this title is available from the
British Library.

Also in the Utterly Crime Series by Pauline Manders

Utterly Explosive
Utterly Fuelled
Utterly Rafted
Utterly Reclaimed
Utterly Knotted
Utterly Crushed
Utterly Dusted
Utterly Roasted
Utterly Dredged

To Paul, Fiona, Alastair, Karen, Andrew, Katie and Mathew, and a special dedication to Vigo.

PAULINE MANDERS

Pauline Manders was born in London and trained as a doctor at University College Hospital, London. Having gained her surgical qualifications, she moved with her husband and young family to East Anglia, where she worked in the NHS as an ENT Consultant Surgeon for over 25 years. She used her maiden name throughout her medical career and retired from medicine in 2010.

Retirement has given her time to write crime fiction, become an active member of a local carpentry group, and share her husband's interest in classic cars. She lives deep in the Suffolk countryside.

ABOUT THE UTTERLY CRIME SERIES BOOK COVERS

REBECCA MOSS GUYVER

Rebecca is a painter-printmaker who exhibits regularly in East Anglia and London. She lives next door to Pauline Manders and has produced all the covers for the Utterly Crime Series. Occasionally Pauline and Rebecca walk their dogs, Lyra and Otto, around the fields near their home.

ACKNOWLEDGMENTS

My thanks to: Beth Wood for her positive advice, support and encouragement; Pat McHugh, my mentor and hard-working editor with a keen sense of humour, mastery of atmosphere and grasp of characters; Rebecca Moss Guyver, for her boundless enthusiasm and brilliant cover artwork and design; David Withnall for his proof-reading skills; Andy Deane for his editing help; the Write Now! Bury writers' group for their support; Sue Southey for her cheerful reassurances and advice; and my husband and family, on both sides of the Atlantic, for their love and support.

CHAPTER 1

'So tell me again; why do we need to be here this morning?' Clive asked as he stood with Chrissie on the edge of a loosely-knit group of people, all of them dressed in work clothes or overalls.

'Because....' The words died in Chrissie's mouth, as reasons jostled for priority. She drank in the heady mix of excitement and anticipation, took a deep breath and gathered her thoughts. 'Look; even Ron is here,' she said.

Clive raised a hand in greeting, and smiled at Ron Clegg, an elderly furniture restorer, Chrissie's mentor and business partner. 'Good morning, Ron,' he called, but before he could say more, a hush descended as a middle-aged man strode through the gathering.

'I have the keys to the Poachers Basket! The pub is ours!' the man shouted like a captain rousing his team.

Cries of 'At last!' and 'Good on ya, Steve!' greeted the announcement.

'That's Steve Corewell,' Chrissie said, felt stupid for stating the obvious, and moved closer to Clive.

'If anyone wants to have a look around the pub before we start work, now's your chance. But first you'll have to wait a minute while I open the main door. It's secured with the old bolts, so I'll have to slide 'em from the inside.' Steve marched to a side entrance set into one end of the pub. He fumbled with a key and disappeared into the building.

While they waited, Chrissie took in the flaking window frames and rotten sills. First-floor windows peeked from under a low thatch roof, its ridge pattern slipping and moss covering one end. Stuccoed walls once painted in Suffolk pink had weathered, fading into a mottled carapace. The unloved exterior and boarded, ground-floor windows made it obvious to everyone - the pub was closed for business. It had been closed for eighteen months.

'You can't really tell how old it is from the outside. I'd say anything from one hundred to three hundred years old,' Chrissie said, more to herself than Clive.

'It's a bit out of the way for a pub.'

'You're forgetting the Second World War. They extended the airfield, and it swallowed the road at this end of the village.'

Scraping and thuds sounded through the heavy front door as bolts were drawn back. Someone shouted, 'Finally!' The door juddered open. Clapping rippled through the group.

A couple of men edged forwards. Chrissie, sensing the movement, craned to get a better view.

Steve stumbled from the doorway, his broad face ashen and his jaw slack. He started to work his mouth, but there was no sound.

'Stop fooling around,' someone shouted.

'Is he having a stroke?'

'What the hell?' Clive pushed through the group. Chrissie followed close on his heels.

'Is something wrong? Are you OK?' Concern cut through Clive's words as he reached Steve and grasped his elbow to steady him.

Chrissie, a step behind, saw the horror in the man's eyes. Instinctively she looked past Clive. She strained to get a view beyond the doorway. It took a moment for her eyes to adjust. Then she saw it. A dark mound lay on the floor. She traced its outline; picked out shapes at one end. They seemed pale, familiar. What was she seeing? A human foot? No, a pair of feet. God!

'Clive, I-I think there's someone on the floor. They don't seem to be moving.' She barely managed a whisper.

He must have heard because she sensed him tense. 'OK, everyone; let's give Steve some space.' And then to Steve, 'Did you see a body – someone - in there?'

Steve closed his mouth and nodded.

'OK, do we have lights? Is there any electricity yet?'

'Not until I've turned on the mains.' His voice sounded hollow, broken.

'Right, everyone stay out here with Steve. I'm going to take a look inside. Ron, will you come with me? You probably still remember the layout and where the fuse box and mains are.'

She waited for Clive to include her, but instead he simply headed into the pub without a backward glance. She sensed the change in him. Her relaxed live-in partner had morphed into Detective Inspector Clive Merry. The rest of the group must have picked up on it as well. Their silence said it all.

Chrissie felt torn between an overriding urge to see what Steve had seen, and the instinct to avoid the nightmare it might fix in her mind. She loved the way Clive had taken control, and she understood why everyone else should stay outside. But since when had *she* been "everyone else" as far as Clive was concerned? And besides, if she moved slowly, would anyone notice? She only needed to get a tiny bit closer and she'd be able to see so much more.

Ron limped past and she drifted behind him. By the time he had crossed the threshold, she stood unnoticed in the entrance.

She peered in. Natural light shafted through the doorway. Everything beyond its reach was shrouded in gloom. The air felt chilly; several degrees colder than outside, now bathed in the weak September sunshine. And it had a whiff about it; the unmistakeable smell of damp, mould and decay with the faintest hint of ammonia. But there was nothing animal, nothing fetid, thank God; only the musty scent of rotting wood and plaster.

Clive crouched next to the heap, partly caught in the natural light. His mobile phone's torch highlighted the rough weave and leather panels of a black donkey jacket, the shape of a body lying on its side, the height of a shoulder, the gentle slope from chest to hips, and the sprawl of legs and arms. A glimpse of matted hair, dark in the gloom, and the back of a head; it was all too human. Chrissie dragged her eyes away from the head and concentrated on the feet. From the size of them she guessed it was a man.

'Is he dead?' She shivered.

'Yes. There's an empty bottle of vodka by his hand. It's odd he's not wearing shoes or socks. Can you stay there and stop anyone coming in? Oh, and may I borrow your phone?'

'My mobile? What for?' she bristled.

'It has a torch as well, Chrissie. We need more light in here. Otherwise Ron and I'll break our bloody necks finding the fuse box. God knows what other surprises are lying around.'

'Oh right, well let's hope there're some bulbs in the sockets and some of them work.' Her words sounded tetchy, even to her own ears. The shock was playing havoc with her nuance and tone. 'I'll put the torch function on.'

'Thank you, Mrs Jax.' Ron stood beyond the range of

4

Clive's beam, his face shadowy, his manner controlled and formal. She guessed Clive had picked him for his calmness.

She was tempted to suggest it was about time Ron succumbed to 21st century technology and got a mobile phone. But she didn't; it was an old chestnut. And besides, he'd called her Mrs Jax. It made her feel professional.

'Is anyone going to call an ambulance?' Ron asked, his voice barely audible.

'I'll make the calls in a moment, Ron. But this is for the police doc and a coroner, not an ambulance to A & E. Right, let's see if we can get the lights working. Chrissie. Keep people out and ask Steve to send everyone home will you? This could be a crime scene. We're not going to get any clearing up done today.'

'OK, but I don't think they'll want to leave yet, Clive. Not before they know what's happened and who he is.'

It was a relief to have a task, something to stop her looking at the body. Hell. It had to be easier to face the group outside than stare at those pale feet.

She stepped outside into full daylight, and drew herself to her full five foot two. Everyone looked at her, questions breaking on their lips. Except for Steve. He sat on the ground, his head in his hands. She took a deep breath.

'Clive, that's DI Clive Merry, says we should all go home,' she began. No one moved.

She cleared her throat and tried again, 'We should all go home,' she repeated, a little louder.

Silence greeted her words. She'd have to elaborate.

'There's a man lying on the floor in there and… it's pretty obvious he's dead. We don't know what's happened, so the police and coroner have to be involved. Clive says it would be easier if we went home now because there's no way we can sort through all the old furniture, and clean up today. We'd have to keep traipsing through… and well, we can't - not if it could be a-a crime scene.'

'A crime scene?' a voice piped.

'But who is he? And how did he get in there?' Steve asked. He straightened his back; once again the group's natural leader, despite his position on the ground and the wobble in his voice.

'Sorry, I-I don't know. But we'll be in the way out here once the police and forensics arrive. Clive said to ask you to send everyone home.'

'Did he, now?'

'Yes. Sorry – I should have said that first.'

'I s'pose we're forgetting he's a detective inspector.'

She nodded, and stopped herself from adding that it was his weekend off. It would have sounded peevish. Instead, Chrissie stood in front of the doorway, blocking it for anyone brave enough to take her on. She was aware she looked elfin, with her short blonde hair and petite build, but her blue-grey eyes were like steel. And for once her age helped. At mid-forties, she was a force to be reckoned with.

No one tried to pass her, and the group milled around outside, only drawing further from the door when a police car arrived, blue lights flashing.

Chrissie, and a slowly recovering Steve, retreated to wait and watch from one end of the front of the Poachers. They sat on a two-foot-high brick wall, where Ron soon joined them. There was no sign of Clive.

They were too lost in their own thoughts to say much while more police arrived, along with the forensic physician, or police doc, as Clive preferred to call him. Any remaining view was blocked by the influx of the SOC team and their van, with FORENSICS written along the side.

'I hope Clive hands this over to the duty DI,' Chrissie sighed.

'My guess is he'll want to see it through, Mrs Jax.'

'Jax?' Steve cut in, his animated manner almost fully restored. 'Of course! The old barn workshop on the airfield boundary lane. Right?'

She nodded, picturing the sign: *Clegg & Jax. Master Cabinet Makers and Furniture Restorers.*

'I'm sorry if I'm being a bit slow, Chrissie. But stumbling over that man was a shock. I must say, though, it's good of you to turn up here on a Saturday morning. Especially when you don't even live in the village.'

'But our workshop counts as Wattisham.'

'And you're forgetting I live in Wattisham,' Ron added. 'I've enjoyed a pint in this pub for nigh on fifty years. When I was a young'un, I even helped with repairs in the bar. I reckon it might've been what got me into carpentry.'

'Yes, we decided as a business it was important to support the local community project,' Chrissie added. She realised her words sounded pompous, and bit her lip.

'You know the owner closed the pub because he wasn't making enough money from it? He reckoned he'd get more if he sold it as a domestic dwelling.' Steve almost spat the words.

'Then I guess he was pretty hacked off when his application for *change of use* was opposed by your action group,' Chrissie said, her mind racing in a new direction.

'Surprised, more like. I don't think he expected us to raise enough money from selling community shares in the pub.'

'Well you did. And you've won,' she said, raising her

hand as if raising a glass.

'Yes, for now, Chrissie. But we've only got two years to get this up and running and meet costs. Otherwise it's back to the owner and–'

'Wattisham loses its pub forever?'

'Yes, unless we can get more backing from somewhere. And you can see how this… this man found dead in the pub….well it could put us back; stop essential repairs before the winter sets in.'

'I doubt he died in the pub on purpose,' Ron said quietly.

'Are you suggesting the owner was somehow responsible, Steve?'

'No, of course not, Chrissie.'

A policeman strolled over and took their names and contact details, but it was another twenty minutes before she watched a black body bag being wheeled out on a gurney and loaded into an unmarked dark grey van. It struck Chrissie as strangely sad and final, but at least it was a signal for the group to start drifting away.

Clive was one of the last to leave through the side entrance. Chrissie caught the weariness in his tone as he said, 'Steve, we can lock up now. Can you give the police a key in case they need to come back again?'

Steve nodded.

'Good; so for the moment the pub stays closed. No one is to enter.'

Without a word, Steve got up from his perch on the low wall, locked the door and handed over the key.

Chrissie shivered, despite the weak sunshine. 'Can we go home now, Clive?'

Behind him, a uniformed policeman strung blue and

white striped tape across the pub's front and side entrance doors. The words *Police* and *Keep Out* were printed in bold letters on the tape, like credits at the end of a rolling film. She tried to read Clive's face but it gave nothing away.

'Don't worry, Steve. We'll have the key back to you and everything opened up here as soon as possible. Do you know how many people have keys?'

'No. I collected this one from George, this morning. He's the Friends Committee Chairman. He said he'd had more keys cut, so he's the one to ask.'

'Right, and the last time you went into the pub?'

'Wednesday, with George. I'd seen the surveyor's report a while ago, but I wanted to take another look before deciding on a work schedule.'

'Right.'

'As you know, today was meant to be for sorting through what's in the pub. It needs to be cleared and made ready for redecoration.'

'Yes, I was in the work party, remember? Can you give me your number, and also George's if you've got it? I know you've given it to the constable, but it's Saturday and I'm not sure how soon I'll get to the station.'

Clive smiled at Chrissie, as if he'd only just noticed her. 'Sorry, Chrissie; I'll have to go into Bury, but it can wait an hour or so.'

'You mean there's time for lunch?'

'And possibly a half pint.' He smiled again and this time she noticed the crease lines reached his eyes. He'd returned to off-duty Clive.

CHAPTER 2

Chrissie sank into the passenger seat of Clive's black Ford Mondeo.

'I thought we were never going to get away. How can it take so long to process a scene as small as that?' she asked.

'A small scene?' Clive said, nuancing his words as he manoeuvred the car off the grass verge near the pub. He drove slowly to the main road and past the tiny green, its village sign depicting a red coat of arms on a white shield.

'That wasn't a small scene, Chrissie. The body was lying on the floor inside a locked pub. Furthermore, it's a pub which has been boarded up for well over a year. Before you dismiss him as some unfortunate vagrant who probably died from alcohol, hypothermia and whatever else he'd taken, you have to ask how he got in there.'

'So are you saying he was squatting in the pub and no one noticed? The pub's in a village; someone must have seen something.'

'We checked all the rooms and there were no signs of anyone living there. There's no indication of how he got in, and interestingly, we couldn't find his socks or shoes.'

'So....' She let the word drift. A thought took shape as they followed the road out of Wattisham.

'His feet,' she began, 'or rather his bare soles, looked very pale. If they were so clean, then he couldn't have walked there; at least not without socks or shoes.

'Are you suggesting he was carried in? Or are you saying they were removed while he was lying on the floor?'

'I don't know, Clive. It's just that I mostly only saw

his feet. I can still see them now if I close my eyes. And if they'd been dirty, they couldn't have looked so pale, right?'

'But blood doesn't circulate when you're dead. Skin can look paler than normal, simply because the blood settles where gravity pulls it. And of course it depends how the body is lying. But lips, hands, extremities can look bloodless while other areas are darker or bluish-purple. It's called lividity; or *livor mortis*, as the police doc calls it.'

'Lividity? Well I guess you'd know. You've come across enough dead bodies in your time.'

The car ran smoothly, soothing her restless mind as Clive concentrated on driving. Her eyes wandered over fields of wheat and rapeseed stubble as they snaked down the long incline into Bildeston. It was a village nestling in a shallow valley cut by a tributary of the River Brett.

'Do you want to drop in at the pub?' Clive asked as they turned into the narrow high street.

'Yes, let's; I could do with a drink.'

Clive parked near the war memorial in a small square in the heart of the village. Chrissie got out of the car and ambled to a waste bin.

'Are you thinking what I'm thinking?' he said as he caught up with her.

'I doubt it. My thoughts are just helter-skelter.'

'Well that's nothing new.' He peered through the opening into the heritage-style bin. 'No shoes,' he laughed.

'Now you're making fun of me.'

'Not at all. I'll ask my DS to check the area outside the Poachers Basket and the bins in Wattisham for shoes and socks. But I don't think we need to take it as far as a county-wide search.'

'Now you really are making fun.'

He took her hand by way of an answer, and together they crossed the quiet street and walked along a pavement squeezed in front of a row of 17th century houses. There was something comforting about the feel of his hand. It transmitted sureness; a kind of *I've investigated so many deaths, and this is how it is, right at the start when we've only a few facts to go on. Relax, Chrissie; we'll get to the bottom of it soon enough.*

She increased her pace to keep up with his stride. Sunshine caught his short auburn hair and he smiled in his easy off-duty manner as they negotiated the double doors into the Princes Feathers.

The smell of ale and warm pastry greeted them. Light streamed through sash windows, bringing the old floorboards to life. It wasn't a large space, but it felt welcoming.

'It's a bit different to the Poachers Basket,' she said.

'Well for a start, there's no one dead on the floor.'

'I didn't mean it like that, Clive.'

'I know what you meant. Now, what will you have? Ginger beer?'

'No, a glass of white wine, please.'

Chrissie headed across to the open fireplace. It stretched most of the length of one wall and bore the scars of centuries of use. The soot-stained bricks radiated antiquity and permanence, while an oak beam running above the open hearth spoke of the past with a wormed face and tallow scorch marks. The most recent addition was a wood burner, installed to replace the need for an open grate.

'Does the Poachers have a wood burner?' she asked when Clive carried over a glass of sauvignon. She eyed up the darkish brew in his other hand as she added, 'Did you get the lights working?'

'Yes, to a wood burner; yes, to the lights; and yes, in answer to your next question.'

'My next question?'

'Yes, I thought I'd try their Crowdie. It's their oatmeal stout.' He set the glasses on the low table and sat down.

'An oatmeal stout? That's a bit different for you. Hmm, so the Poachers has a wood burner. I assume you looked in it for any sign of shoes or socks?'

Clive reached for his glass and took a mouthful. 'Yes, this'll go nicely with the steak and ale pie.'

Chrissie bit back her frustration. She had lived with Clive for long enough to guess where this was leading. Obtuse answers and stopping for a reasonably-sized lunch meant only one thing. He wanted to relax and clear his mind before a long afternoon working on this new case. And the long afternoon would likely spread into the evening. It had happened more times than she cared to remember. Well, he might want to clear his mind but she wasn't ready to clear hers.

She tried again. 'What was the pub like inside?'

'Not as bad as I was expecting.'

'Meaning?'

'It's crying out for a refurb and decoration.'

It wasn't the answer she was after. She wanted to know what, besides an empty vodka bottle, had been in the saloon bar with the dead man; and then after that, the layout of the rooms, upstairs and down. She craved details and specifics, not generalisations. But before she could reframe her question, Clive asked, 'Have you chosen what you want to eat?'

'What? Well I suppose it rather depends on whether you think you'll be back in time for Nick's gig at Frasers this evening?'

'Well I hope so Chrissie, but–'

'No that's OK, if you're still working on the case,' she said a little too fast. 'But if it's only me eating at home this evening, I'll have my main meal now.' She squinted up at the menu board, 'Yes, I'll have the *Broccoli and Stilton Bake* and a side order of chips. Then I'll only need a snack this evening.'

He made a move as if to get up, but stopped and frowned. 'Tell me, why were you so insistent we join the work party at the pub this morning? I know you're as nosey as hell, and remarkably intuitive, but even you couldn't have guessed Steve was going to find a dead body today.'

'Well no,' she said, ignoring the slightly negative inference in the *nosey as hell* bit. 'I was hoping for some free advertising. I thought, once we got the furniture out and assigned it for storage or the dump... well, there might be some tables and chairs I could repair at the workshop. Just think; repairs and restorations by Clegg & Jax - ones that people will sit on, or rest their drinks on in the new bar. They'll say it's great and we've done a fantastic job for nothing, or rather nothing but community spirit!'

'So why didn't you say at the time?'

'It might have sounded calculating... and I haven't run it past Ron yet.'

'Ahh.'

She sipped her sauvignon and savoured the ambiance while Clive gave their lunch orders at the bar. A pair of cyclists made a blustery entrance, the cleats on their cycle shoes tapping a percussive rhythm on the wooden floor. Their noisy disruption and colourful gear reminded her of her friend Sarah. Maybe she'd ask Sarah if she wanted to come to Nick's gig?

'So what will you do this afternoon?' Clive asked when he sat down again.

'Well, I'll text Sarah and then I might drive over to Bury.'

'For the market?'

'It depends on what Sarah's doing, but I thought I'd combine the Bury market with dropping round Nick's before I came back.'

'Won't Nick be busy?'

'Maybe, but band practice will've been this morning and I want to see his Polyphon.'

'His what?'

'Polyphon; it's an old type of musical box. It plays metal discs - so you can change the discs and get different tunes. I looked it up on the internet. The discs make it look a bit like a record player; one I could imagine Leonardo da Vinci inventing in the fifteenth century.' She sipped her wine. 'Apparently it dates from the late 1890s. Needless to say, twenty-five, thirty years later, it was superseded when they discovered how to record and reproduce sound waves.'

'I never had Nick down as a collector of old musical boxes.'

'He's not. At least I don't think he is. His parents found it when they were clearing out his grandmother's house and because he's musical, the family wanted him to have it. I suppose it's a kind of heirloom from as far back as his great-grandmother's generation, or even earlier.'

'Well, Nick is full of surprises.'

CHAPTER 3

Nick hurried down the narrow stairs and opened the front door. 'Hi, Chrissie.'

He smiled, pleased to see her. She was like a big sister and friend rolled into one. She might be twenty years his senior, but time spent on the same carpentry course had made her the trusted anchor in his hectic life.

'Hmm, what a wonderful smell of fresh-baked bread,' she said, by way of a greeting.

'That'll be the baker's shop. You get used to it after a while. Come in.' He led the way up the staircase, leaving Chrissie to close the front door and follow.

'So am I above the bread ovens?' She stood at the head of the stairs.

'They're at the back of the shop and it faces St Andrews Street South. So yeah, I'd say you're on one of the hot spots when they're baking.'

'Great! It's nice you're in the centre of Bury. I take it you're still happy with the flat? Are you all set for the gig tonight?'

Nick heard the breeziness in her tone but noticed her tension. Something was wrong. He waited to see if she was going to say more. The sound of an electric guitar reverberated through the ceiling and broke the moment.

'Jake's playing around with a new song we've been working on.' He let the notes drift for a moment before adding, 'We've come to an arrangement with the bakery. When they're open, we try to keep the sound down, and Jake uses his small speaker up on the top floor. But when they're closed, we let rip down in here with the main amp and big speakers.' He walked into the living room.

'That sounds unusually thoughtful. Hey, let me guess; there's a payback. You get the pick of their throwaway cake and bread at the end of the day.' Her words were almost lost as she followed him into the modest-sized room spanning the front of the building. It was dominated by a pair of large suitcase-sized speakers, a sofa and a double futon folded to make a chair.

He drew back shabby curtains, and sunlight filtered through a pair of narrow but elegant sash windows. 'How did you know about the cakes and bread?' He didn't get a chance to add, *I s'pose Matt told you* before she was speaking again.

'Well, it was a safe guess, and knowing you, you'll have chatted up any girls working down there.' Chrissie glanced around. 'It looks bigger in the daylight. And it's better now you've got a proper sofa in here.'

'Yeah, we nearly didn't. It got stuck at the top of the stairs. So – do you want to see the Polyphon, then?'

She nodded.

'I'll bring it down for you. If you want something to drink, there's beer in the kitchen... or make yourself a coffee or tea.'

He left her and took the steep flight of stairs up to the top floor. This time he remembered to duck his head where the stairwell cut through the ceiling. His bedroom was next to Jake's, squeezed under the slope of the roof. He made straight for two wooden boxes one stacked on top of the other, along with a pile of metal discs the size of dinner plates. The collection stood just inside his doorway.

The existence of the Polyphon had been a complete surprise. He knew about early gramophones playing cylinders and flat discs, made from shellac and vinyl. But mechanical musical boxes playing changeable metal discs? It was news to him.

Unbeknown to him, his grandmother had squirreled away her own mother's 1910 Polyphon. However, it came with its own mystery. Over a hundred years ago the Polyphon mechanism had been removed from its original manufacturer's wooden case and remounted in a plain homemade box. But why? And why then keep the empty original? It made no sense to Nick.

He had reckoned Chrissie would love the brainteaser of it all, except... today, her cheeriness seemed artificial and she wasn't quite her usual self. He decided the puzzle could wait for another day, and only carried the plain wooden box, and a couple of discs down to the living room.

He found Chrissie sitting on the sofa. 'Didn't you want anything to drink then?' he said as he placed the box on the floor, centre stage in front of her.

'Not for the moment, thanks. So this is the Polyphon.' She got up from the sofa and knelt in front of the box. 'I've had a look at some online, and they all seemed to have the name Polyphon and fancy designs on the lid. This one seems unusually plain. Can I open it?'

'Yeah, go ahead.'

'So... it looks like stained beech and turn of last century.' She lifted the lid on its hinges. 'Isn't the inside of the lid usually decorated as well?'

He watched her peer in and touch the oblong metal plate spanning the box, about a quarter of the way down.

'Wow! Well at least this has Polyphon embossed on it,' she said.

'Yeah. The trouble is, it's set in that blond oak and it

kind of closes off the rest of the box. You can't see what's underneath.'

'Ah yes; I read it's called the bedplate.'

He crouched beside her and held one of the metal discs for her to inspect.

'See how the spikes on the underside of this disc have bent ends? When the disc rotates, the spikes catch on those wheels, there.' Nick pointed to a gantry of star-shaped wheels on the bedplate.

'I read something about star wheels. When they turn, they pluck the teeth on the steel comb. I'd have expected the disc spikes to pluck the comb direct.'

'Yeah, I reckon it's because the star wheels are a good place to attach the dampers.'

'Dampers? Don't mention dampers. I gave up reading about it when I got to that bit. Too complicated.'

Nick grinned. 'At least it's easy to see the steel comb. It's awesome how it can make so much sound.' He indicated the single steel comb screwed to the bedplate.

'I get that; it's all about the lovely blond oak soundboards.' She tilted the box to get a view of the base. 'Come on then, get it going!'

'Sure.' He wound the handle on the front of the box, slipped the metal disc onto the central drive post, and clipped the pressure bar over to hold the disc in place. 'OK, ready?'

'You bet.'

He pushed the start lever back and the disc began to rotate. Sweet sound tinkled from the box, slightly slow and with an occasional discordant note. He pulled a face as he adjusted the speed regulator lever. The tune played a little faster and he settled onto the floor.

Chrissie's frown melted and her earlier brittle cheeriness seemed to soften. She moved her head to read the disc as it rotated. 'It says *Love's Old Sweet Song* on the disc.'

'It was either that or *Home Sweet Home*. It's an awesome bit of kit, don't you think?'

Chrissie appeared entranced as the box jingled the melody. In the background, Jake's guitar riffs clashed. A mechanical clunk sounded from inside the box and the disc stopped abruptly. *Love's Old Sweet Song* had played out, but Jake's guitar played on.

'Do you know, it feels kinda cool to own this.'

'It's a piece of history, Nick.'

'Yeah, from the era of tuned metal vibration.'

'Tuned?'

'Well, more or less in tune.'

'You know these joints aren't factory-made. What happened to its original box?' Chrissie asked, her manner changing.

'I've got it upstairs. It looks perfect, so I don't know why anyone bothered to mount it in this homemade one. Any ideas?'

'Me have ideas? I don't think Clive was too impressed with my ideas today. Did you hear the clear out at the Poachers Basket was cancelled this morning?'

'No. Why?' He couldn't help but smile. Chrissie was starting to sound like her normal self.

'We found a dead man on the floor in the saloon bar.'

'What?' The words took shape. 'Dead? How long had he been there?'

'I don't know. He was just… lying there.'

'God, that's….' He read her face. 'Are you OK?'

'I suppose so. No one seemed to know how he came to

be there.'

'It must have been horrible. Are you sure you're OK?'

'Yes, while I block it out it. But in the background, it churns in my mind. It's going to be a police and coroner's case, so I'm not supposed to talk about it, even to Clive. But you know me; always asking questions. I want to know the *why* and *how* of it.'

'So Clive got irritated with you, right? I take it he was with you when this man was found?'

She didn't answer.

'Well....' He groped for something soothing to say, anything to distract her. In his experience, there was little to be gained from going over and over a painful memory. He didn't want to visualise the body, and he doubted if Chrissie would be helped by seeing it in her mind again.

'Why don't you distract yourself by... by working out why there are two boxes for one Polyphon?'

'What? Investigate the Polyphon? You can't compare a Polyphon to a human death. Where's the intensity or drama in a wooden box?'

'Or the horror.'

'True.' She nibbled her fingernail.

Nick watched her for a moment; it was her left index finger. He'd seen the signs before. Didn't they all have their own ways of coping when the stress got too much? If it was him, he figured he'd have penned the first few lines of a song by now. The words *waiting at the bar so long I died* sprang to mind, along with the phrase *saloon floor crawl*. But music was his way of getting by, and this was Chrissie; it was her shock and her drama.

'I tell you what,' she said, interrupting his train of thought, 'why don't you bring both boxes round to the workshop? Ron is brilliant at looking at furniture and seeing its whole history unravel in every tack and nail hole.'

'But what can Ron say that I don't know already? I'm a carpenter too, Chrissie. I can tell if something's been made by hand or a machine. I'll look stupid.'

'Possibly. But he's full of surprises. And you'll get a mug of coffee as well. Anyway, it's up to you. The answer will lie with your great-grandmother; you could get Matt to do a family history search on her.'

'What? Ask Matt to nose around my relatives? You're joking.'

'You've got a point, but Matt does come up with interesting stuff.'

'Hmm.'

CHAPTER 4

Matt stared at the Monday lunchtime newsfeed filling his screen. *Man Found Dead in Boarded-up Pub in Wattisham.*

He read on: *A man was discovered dead on Saturday, September 13th inside Wattisham's Poachers Basket, a Suffolk pub recently rescued from permanent closure by a community initiative. The Friends of the Poachers Basket group made the discovery when they entered the pub to begin repair and refurbishment work. The dead man has been named as Jason Brookford, a 34-year-old thatcher and resident of Sutton. A police spokesman said the cause of death was unknown and the case has been referred to the coroner. Post-mortem results are awaited.*

Jason Brookford was last seen alive leaving his thatching work in Bildeston on Friday afternoon, September 12th. The police are appealing for information from anyone who may have seen him between Friday afternoon and the early hours of Saturday morning. It is hoped that any sightings of him may help to build up a picture of his last movements.

'Jason Brookford? Don't I know 'im?' Matt skimmed through the article again.

'What's up?' Damon asked behind him.

Damon Mora, of Balcon & Mora, was his thirty-year-old boss and always had his administrator's view of Matt's computer screen displayed alongside his own. Matt couldn't see Damon without turning round, but he didn't need to. He already knew he'd be sitting at a trestle desk, eyes darting between his own work and Matt's.

'It's the bloke named in the newsfeed; the one found

dead. Dint we search for 'is contact details a few weeks back?' Matt said, his Suffolk accent pushing through.

'You mean Jason Brookford?' Damon's voice sounded sharp.

There had only been one name in the short article and Matt felt momentarily confused. 'Yeah, Jason Brookford; there aint no other name mentioned.'

A sense of unease took hold while he waited for Damon to search the Balcon & Mora People-Tracing Agency files. Botnetting mega pixels! What if Damon discovered Matt was a close mate of one of the work party at the Poachers Basket? But how could he? Not unless Matt let slip about Chrissie being there, and he wasn't going to do that. But what if Damon could somehow see it in his face; read him beneath his scrappy beard, and know?

He pictured Damon going ballistic, his pasty complexion pinking up as he blustered *you better not have shot your mouth off to your mate*. And then there'd be the lecture, *if word gets out we haven't kept our traces confidential, we'll lose our clients. And if it's a police case and you've been poking around, we could be in trouble with the law. The names aren't for public consumption; got it?* Matt *got it*; he knew the routine. It was the same every time anything remotely risky or police-related reared its head.

'Hey, you're right, Matt. You found the latest mobile phone number for a Jason Brookford back in August.'

'Yeah, I thought I knew the name.'

'Right. Keep your mouth shut and don't even think about sniffing around.'

'Yeah, yeah, I know. Anyway, you've got it password protected.' Matt didn't bother to add there was no need for the file or passwords. His photographic memory gave him instant recall of the information. But there was something more urgent on his mind.

'D'you s'pose he died coz of somethin' I found out about 'im?'

'You only found his new mobile number. How could that have killed him?'

'No....' Matt drew out the vowel in his Suffolk way. 'I did a bit of phonin' round; askin' the people who'd had him thatchin' their roof. You know the kind of thing. Is he any good? How can I get hold of 'im? One of 'is satisfied customers gave me the number.'

'It sounds pretty tame.'

Matt pushed his plastic stacker chair back from his table against the wall and repositioned himself to face Damon. A heavy silence filled the space between them, only broken by the whirring of fans cooling the hard drives. The sound of the Bury St Edmunds traffic and life outside drifted through the open sash window, but the turmoil in Matt's head distanced him from it all. His guts twisted. His words came in a rush.

'Yeah, but Damon; what if the credit card client put the squeeze on him so bad, he killed his self? I-I'd be responsible, right?'

'No, Matt. It'd be down to whoever put the squeeze on him. And there's nothing in the newsfeed about him topping himself.'

'No...,' he drew out the vowel again, 'but that don't mean....'

'We've been through this kind of thing before, Matt. If we hadn't done the tracing, a rival agency would have done it. So one way or another, Jason Brookford's new number was going to be found by someone. Look, if the bloke had creditors, they were bound to catch up with him sooner or later.'

'Yeah… but–'

'But if there's a connection then it's police business, not ours. So, don't go shooting your mouth off to your mates or poking around on the net. And remember, the names of the people we trace are confidential. They aren't for public consumption.'

'Yeah, I know that, Damon. You keep sayin'.'

'Right.'

'So do you s'pose there's a connection? Should we check if our client really were the credit card company? Will you tell the police?'

'I don't know. I have to think about it.'

Matt was pretty sure what Damon would do, just as he was sure he'd played his own part in the whole sorry tale. First he'd traced the man's number and now, he'd recognised the man's name. It was all down to fate, sequences and patterns of behaviour for all of them, and Damon, true to form, would be working his way through an algorithm; Damon's risk-averse *I don't want to get on the wrong side of the law* algorithm. It was what he always did. He was bound to contact the police.

Damon's predictable nature was strangely comforting to Matt, and the tightness in his guts began to ease. He touched his face and rubbed the hairs of his sandy beard between his fingertips, a nervous habit before smoothing his tee-shirt over his ample belly. Perhaps the tightness rooting through his guts was down to hunger? He let his mind drift onto food and by association, the previous day's continental food market in Woodbridge.

He still bore the mark of a potato fritter stain mid

chest, right down the central white panel of the Italian flag design printed across the front of his tee.

'Il Tricolore,' he murmured, relishing the Italian name for the flag, and then, 'Raggmunk.'

'What are you on about, Matt? Have you remembered another name?'

'Nah, raggmunk is a kinda Swedish potato fritter. They fry it like a pancake. I tried some yesterday. It were awesome. Maisie dint like it, so I got to eat 'ers too.'

'What? You two went to Sweden for the weekend?'

'Nah. I aint been further north than Norwich. This were in Woodbridge.'

'Right. So there's no Mr Tricolore Raggmunk. I might have guessed your mind would be on lunch.'

'Yeah, I think I might drop by the bakers on St Andrews Street.'

'The one your mate Nick lives above? Do you get a deal on everything?'

'Sausage rolls an' doughnuts. I aint asked for nothin' else.' Matt didn't add that he hadn't thought to branch out. Lunch items had a routine; they offered comfort through certainty.

Something occurred to him. 'I were thinkin', Damon. When... sorry, *if* you contact the police, do you s'pose they'll want the bloke's old number an' old mobile service provider. He could've had a different network operator to the one now.'

'When I call the police, I'll give them the bare minimum. Let them ask if they want to know more.'

'Right. So you're goin' to call 'em?'

Damon nodded. 'Yes, bare minimum. Hey, no longer than forty minutes for lunch. We've a lot of names to trace this afternoon.'

Matt didn't wait. He'd learnt from the past that Damon wanted him out of the office when he called the police. Without bothering to grab his denim jacket, he lumbered out of the cramped office, down the narrow stairs, and out into a back alley behind the Buttermarket.

If finding Jason Brookford's new number had led to Jason's death, then he knew he should try to make up for it by doing the right thing *now*. The police had to know everything, not just the minimum.

He fired off a text message as he headed for St Andrews Street South.

Hi Chrissie. Just caught newsflash naming dead man in Wattisham pub. Is Clive leading the case?

CHAPTER 5

Chrissie sat on her work stool in the Clegg & Jax old barn workshop. Egg and cress sandwiches beckoned from her unopened lunchbox, and a mug of tea waited beside them.

Ping! She reached for her phone and frowned as she read Matt's text message.

She looked up to catch Ron glancing away, as if he'd been watching her face as she read. 'It's from Matt. They've just named the dead man in the Poachers Basket. Apparently it's all over the news.'

'So who is he, Mrs Jax?'

'Well, that's the thing. Matt hasn't said. I guess he thinks I've seen the newsflash, but I bet he's forgotten how weak our internet is here.'

'Or he thinks you already know from Clive.'

'Clive doesn't talk to me about his cases.' She studied her phone and tried not to give herself away, only for a vision of the dead man's soles to crash into her mind.

Damn! It was so like Matt. Why hadn't he put the name in his text message? The rush of her frustration cleared the image of the feet.

'Matt wants to know if Clive is leading the case. Why would he ask that, do you suppose?'

'I don't know. Is Clive leading the case?'

'Yes; at least he was when he left this morning. Don't you want to know who the dead man is, Mr Clegg?'

'Yes, but I can wait. I didn't care to look too closely at him when he was lying on the floor, and I'm not expecting to be any the wiser after I'm told his name.'

Chrissie looked up at the wormed beams spanning the

lofty roof space above and took a deep breath. The scent of wood dust, linseed oil and beeswax hung in the air. She closed her eyes and for a moment let the fragrances focus her in a way that emptying her mind couldn't.

'Just think, Mrs Jax. We'll get on with a lot more work this afternoon if we don't know who the man is. It's waited all weekend; a few more hours won't make any difference.'

'I know, but that's not the point.'

Ron had been her trainer when she was a raw apprentice, and his steadying words had curbed more of her impulsive need-to-know quests than she cared to remember. His calmness was the key to their partnership, along with his need to teach and hers to question and explore; his need to stay firmly rooted in the past, and hers to bring in her accountancy skills and push their business into the 21st century.

'OK, I'll send Matt the answer; but no questions.'

As if to make good her promise, she read out the words as she texted, '*Hi Matt. Yes, Clive is leading the case.* How's that, Mr Clegg?' Then she added Clive's mobile number in case he didn't have it.

'Spot on, Mrs Jax.'

'Good. Now if we can't spend our lunch hour chewing over the dead man's name, why don't you tell me about the old days at the Poachers Basket instead?'

'You really want to know?'

'Yes, I'll let you know if I'm getting bored.'

She reached for her mug of tea and smiled at his amusement.

'Where do you want me to start?'

'How about when you were a boy, doing the repairs

there?'

'Hmm, that'd be back in the sixties. It was known as "the friendly pub". There was a room out the back for paying guests to stay. And as it was so close to the airbase, there was always a steady trickle of visitors coming and going. You know; reps, or engineers, or even girlfriends coming to stopover. It was more private, or should I say more discreet, than staying on the base. And the publican could always be relied on to keep his mouth shut. No doubt his visitors slipped him something extra.'

'It sounds rather mysterious and fun.'

'Yes, I suppose it was. And I reckon you could describe the fight as colourful.'

'A fight? What kind of fight? Were you involved?'

'Slow down, Mrs Jax. I didn't see the fight but I helped repair the damage in the bar and guestroom afterwards. Just me and the barman. I must have been around eleven at the time; it made me think carpentry was rather exciting.'

'Was anyone injured or...?' She let her unspoken word hang in the air.

'I don't know. There was blood on a door where the panel had split, and the visitor was never seen again.'

'Really? So was the place crawling with police?'

'There weren't any police. It was all hushed up. That's why I was roped in to help. They reckoned I'd be too young to guess what was going on.'

'And that you'd keep your mouth shut.'

'Yes, that as well.'

'But how exciting! And no police... I wonder if it was related to the airbase.'

'Now don't you go getting any of your wild ideas, Mrs

31

Jax. It's more likely a travelling salesman was caught cheating with someone's wife.'

'But come on, Mr Clegg; it was the time of the Cold War. Even at eleven you must have wondered about the aeroplanes on the base... and spies and the Russians. And if not the Cold War, you must have been into boys' adventures and all that kind of thing, surely?'

'If I had, then I might have signed up for the RAF instead of carpentry. The airfield was right on our doorstep.'

Chrissie bit into her sandwich, her thoughts filled with the mysterious missing guest and the blood splatter on a split door panel. Would searching through the newspapers of the 1960s turn up a local report covering the story?

'What year was this, Mr Clegg?'

'I can't be sure, but I'd say 1961, or thereabout.'

'I can't wait to take a look round the pub. Will I be able to see where you mended the split?'

'You'll have to tell me, Mrs Jax.'

Ron seemed reluctant to say any more about the incident, despite Chrissie's coaxing. Instead, she was left to weave her own tale around the supposed travelling salesman of 1961. But it lightened her mood and pushed the pub's most recent shock from the front of her mind. The rest of the lunch hour flew.

'How's that early Georgian side table coming along?' Ron asked as she tidied away their empty mugs.

'There's more work to be done than you'd imagine. It's only got the one drawer, but it's in a sorry state.' She walked over to a workbench where a wide, shallow, mahogany-fronted drawer sat in solitary splendour. The side table stood a few feet away on elegant cabriole legs, but the empty aperture for the drawer gaped at them like an open mouth. 'Mr Croft, that's the customer, told me the drawer got pulled out and... well I guess it fell on this front corner.'

'Ah, that's not good. I'd have expected it to fall on one of its back corners.'

'Yes, I suppose you're right. Anyway, the mahogany on the front here has cracked, and some is missing where it extends beyond the face of the drawer.'

Ron limped over to look more closely.

'Don't forget to check the runners and stops.'

'Yes, of course. And there's a split in the drawer's base boards.'

'Hmm, it'll be the central heating; the modern scourge of antique furniture.'

'I know; you keep saying, Mr Clegg. But you can't blame people for wanting to be warm and comfortable, and at least it brings plenty of repairs our way.'

Her thoughts flew back to her East Anglian childhood winters; the need for vests and long socks in her early schooldays, the electric storage heaters promising so much but always disappointing in their warmth; chilly air in her teenage bedroom, and outside - the constant wind.

She pulled her mind back to the present and examined the length of mahogany she'd salvaged from a discarded table in the storeroom. 'I thought I'd use this. But now when I look at it, I'm not so sure. There's a ripple in the grain.'

'I reckon Mr Croft's side table is Cuban mahogany. It might be worth taking another look for some in the storeroom, Mrs Jax.'

She left Ron to his restoration work on a customer's set of six Ball Back Suffolk chairs and headed outside. She hugged her short sleeve blouse close and hurried across the corner of the courtyard to a single-storey brick building that housed their wood store. A quick glance over her shoulder, and she couldn't help thinking how the old barn workshop seemed to dwarf everything.

She loved the barn, with its black weatherboarding and all the bends and imperfections in the old wooden beams. She hadn't expected to become so attached, but over the years it had worked its way into her heart. She supposed it was the same for the Poachers Basket and all those Wattisham residents who had propped up the bar for so long.

What a pity the outside of the pub hadn't a lot going for it. But to Chrissie's way of thinking, its very ordinariness made it all the more likely to be hiding a secret. In that moment she knew she had to find out more; not just about the Poachers Basket of today, but also of the last half century.

***

It took Chrissie until Wednesday evening to find a suitable opportunity to ask Clive about Jason Brookford, the man found dead in the Poachers Basket. She had cleared away their meal of lightly fried fishcakes, quickly thrown together from leftover salmon fillet, fresh ginger, lemongrass and coriander. It had turned into a rather filling supper when served in burger buns with a sweet chilli sauce and salad. The mood was mellow as Chrissie set two mugs of freshly brewed coffee on the low table in front of the sofa in her living room.

Clive sat, legs stretched out and head thrown back against a cushion plumping the back of the sofa.

'You look comfortable,' Chrissie said as she settled next to him.

'Hmm… I was thinking it's a pity we can't fit a larger sofa in here.'

'We could if we got rid of the rest of the furniture.' She didn't bother to add that the living room had been considered an adequate size for a terraced cottage back in 1876, the year it had been built.

'And that's assuming we'd be able to get it through the front door and hallway,' he added.

'I know, but I like this room the way it is. The rug and floorboards make it look bigger, and you'd lose the effect if it was filled with a great block of leather or velvet.'

They fell into a relaxed silence while Chrissie regarded the narrow Victorian fireplace and the rug's geometric patches of burgundy, midnight blue and beige.

'Do you know when the Poachers Basket will be opened for repairs?' she asked, dropping the question lightly, as if barely interested.

'I should think by the end of the week.'

'Steve Corewell will be pleased. It'll mean he's only a week behind schedule.'

'Hmm.'

'So did you find that poor man's shoes? Were they in the saloon bar's wood burner?'

'No, I'm afraid they're still a bit of a mystery.'

'But you know how or why he died?'

'Yes and no; it's complicated. I was talking to the forensic pathologist about it today. The man had enough alcohol in his blood to make him crash out on the floor.'

'Well you said he had an empty bottle of vodka next to him.'

'Yes, and his blood alcohol level was above 300mgs per 100mls, which is high, but not enough to inevitably kill him.'

'So what happened?'

'The pathologist thinks the cold helped him on his way. He found signs consistent with hypothermia.'

'Hypothermia? Inside the pub at this time of the year?'

'Yes. But when he died sometime last Friday night or early Saturday morning, the temperature had fallen to a low of 10°C. And remember there's been no heating in the pub for months. There's a tiled floor in that part of the bar, and he'd wet himself, so he was lying in clothes soaked with urine. He'd have lost heat very quickly.'

'And his feet were bare, Clive.'

'I know. It's bugging me. Did you know hypothermia victims occasionally undress? Evidently, despite the cold, they can suddenly feel warm and illogically strip off their clothes... except with our man in the pub, it was just his shoes and socks that came off.'

'Which you still haven't found.'

'Quite. So my question is; did he die from hypothermia or did it only contribute to his death?'

'Does it matter?'

'Yes. It makes a difference. If the alcohol would have killed him anyway, then the cold simply sped things up. But, if he only drank enough to give himself a nasty hangover and nothing more, then the cold tipped the scales and that's what caused his death. In other words, if somebody locked him in the pub overnight, then it's manslaughter or... murder.'

'And the pub was locked, right? So did you find the key he used to get in, and then lock himself inside?'

'No.'

'That's odd. What does your forensic pathologist say?'

'Well, the blood biochemistry has turned up features of both hypothermia, and an alcohol binge. It's a bit complicated and I knew colleagues would ask, so I wrote it down.'

He pulled a small notebook from his pocket, flicked through some pages and then read out, '*Alcoholic hypoglycaemic ketoacidosis*. That's from the alcohol. They've also found *metabolic ketones*. The pathologist said the metabolic ketones could be from his body trying to generate heat and energy in response to the cold. They're going to run more tests.'

'And that's it?'

'No; the man's stomach was empty, so either he hadn't eaten for at least six hours, or....' Clive voice drifted.

'Or he'd vomited?'

'Yes, but we didn't find any vomit in the pub.'

'What about the bin search?'

'No shoes or socks, I thought I'd said but... yes, you've got a point; I'll check with Stickley. They were probably concentrating on finding his footwear, not vomit.'

'So that really is all you have?'

'No. The pathologist found changes he said were down to hypothermia. Some brown spots on the man's stomach lining, and some reddish-brown skin discolouration over his elbows and knees.'

'But didn't I hear somewhere that the man was a thatcher? Wouldn't he have had calluses on his elbows and knees?'

'Possibly, but the discoloured patches were from the cold. Oh yes... and there were traces of blood in his knee joints; apparently that can happen in hypothermia as well.'

'So you're saying....' Chrissie was having trouble following the *is it* or *isn't it* nuancing of the post-mortem findings. She turned her focus onto things she could understand better. 'It's all very well saying it could be manslaughter or murder, or-or misadventure, but have you found any reason why anyone wanted to kill him?'

'Hmm, on first glance Jason Brookford was a perfectly ordinary thirty-five-year-old thatcher. But scratch a little deeper, and he had troubles with money and women.'

'But that doesn't sound particularly out of the ordinary for a thirty-five-year-old guy.'

'No, perhaps not.' Clive leaned forwards to reach for his mug on the low table. 'I was forgetting my coffee; it'll be getting cold.'

Chrissie waited for him to say more, but his slight frown told her there'd be no further loose talk about his case. Not this evening. However, she figured it was still worth a little nudge.

'Don't stop, Clive. You were about to say something about the dead man and scratching the surface for motives.'

'No I wasn't, Chrissie. Look, I've probably said more than enough about the case. I really don't want to get into any sensitive areas in our enquiries. Particularly when I don't know which leads will be dead ends. You know what you're like. So try to fill your mind with something else and don't get fixated on this case. Please? All right?'

'Well I was thinking of looking into the history of the Poachers Basket. You know – around the Cold War years, and maybe going back earlier to the Second World War? That couldn't possibly get in the way of your case, could it?'

He didn't answer, so she forged on, 'Also Nick has a project he wants me to look into for him.'

'Really?'

'Yes, seriously. Remember I told you about his great-grandmother's Polyphon?'

'Oh yes.'

'Well he wants me to help him work out why she took it out of its original maker's case and kept it in a homemade one instead. Both have survived from around 1910. Why do you suppose she needed two cases?'

She looked at Clive and caught his mild disbelief.

'No. I'm being serious. Nick was on about it when I saw him on Saturday afternoon. I better text him to find out when he's bringing the cases over to the Clegg workshop.'

'The case of the additional Polyphon case.' Clive said the words as if he was testing them out. 'It has a certain Holmes and Watson ring about it.'

Chrissie responded by aiming an affectionate dig at his ribs.

CHAPTER 6

'It's a bit odd them finding a dead guy in the Poacher's Basket, don't you think?' Dave said and looked at Nick.

It was the Friday afternoon tea break and the carpenters at Needham Market's Willows & Son were enjoying their mugs of tea. They sat on an assortment of plastic stacker and fabric-covered chairs arranged around a table doubling as a desk in their office-cum-restroom. The air was mildly stale and the décor was tired.

Nick felt surprised and a little put out by the question. 'Why look at me? I don't know anything about it. I don't even know the man's name.'

'It's Jason Brookford. I knew him as Jason from the Land Rover club. It was a bit of a surprise to hear it was him,' Dave said.

'Did you know him well, then?' Alfred, the elderly foreman, asked.

'No. I've only spoken to him a few times at club events. He owned a series II Land Rover. That's all I remember him talking about; that and him taking bets on our off-roading challenge days. He seems too young to have dropped dead in a pub.'

'I heard he was a thatcher. You have to be fit to be a thatcher,' Alfred said.

'Yeah, so even less likely to die in a pub.'

'Yes, Dave. But it wasn't a working pub. It's been closed a while.' Alfred sipped his tea with the air of someone who had just imparted a great wisdom and solved the mystery.

'So have you heard anything about it, Nick?' Tim, another carpenter, asked.

'No; why're you asking?' Nick's face flamed with irritation.

'See; you do know something,' Tim teased.

'No-o-oh.'

Why did they always assume he was privy to police evidence simply because his good mate Chrissie had a DI as her live-in partner? And furthermore, why presuppose he'd spill the beans on confidential information? As it happened, Chrissie hadn't said much about it. Her most recent text was purely a reminder to bring his Polyphon and its spare case to the Clegg & Jax workshop.

He avoided eye contact and concentrated on his mug of tea.

'Well I think,' Alfred said, cutting back into the conversation, 'all of you should take into consideration the fact the pub's been empty for a while. The boss is happy for us to give our own time to community projects, including coming into the workshop at weekends; he reckons it gets the firm's name out there. But if anyone is thinking of volunteering to help renovate the Poachers Basket, remember it's just claimed a life.'

'What? Are you saying we shouldn't repair the window frames because Jason Brookford dropped dead in the pub?' Dave said, his manner blustering up.

Nick tensed, ready for heated words as superstition faced logic. When no one said anything, he chipped in with, 'But Dave is like our local historian. He'd know if the place was possessed, wouldn't you Dave?'

'Thank you, Nick! At least someone in here has the sense not to believe in bad omens.'

An uncomfortable silence fell while they drank their

tea. Nick couldn't help stealing a glance at Dave, middle-aged and tubby; the inveterate chatterbox full of good hu-mour and best intentions. Dave had been his trainer when Nick first left Utterly Academy to start his apprenticeship. But working with someone who had once been his teacher could be awkward. Overwhelmingly, Nick felt loyalty and respect for him. But, as a tall, fit, twenty-four-year-old bloke, he didn't always play second fiddle to his one-time trainer.

And then he found himself saying, 'Yeah, OK; count me in. I'll help with the pub's ratty old windows, Dave.'

The rest of the afternoon flew as Nick made doors for some bespoke kitchen units. He marked out his cut lines for the doorframe mortise and tenon joints, and set the plunge depth on the mortiser. From there on, production-line effi-ciency took over.

He was surprised when Alfred shouted across the workshop, 'Come on, Nick. It's after four. Don't you have a home to go to?'

It was twelve minutes past the hour.

'Bugger!' He'd told Chrissie he'd drop by their work-shop no later than half past four. He'd have to hurry.

Like a whirlwind, he tidied away his tools, swept up, and ducked under the closing roller shutters before sprint-ing through the secure area at the rear of the workshop.

The sound of a train hurtling past on the nearby Lon-don line added to his sense of urgency. His Ford Fiesta was parked next to the chain-link fence, and he flung himself into the driver's seat, started the car and accelerated away.

Needham Market was soon behind him as he raced to Barking. He took the quiet Hascot Hill road to trace a route to the Wattisham Airfield boundary lane and the Clegg &

Jax workshop. The entrance track seemed longer and even more rutted than he remembered.

The old barn, with its rough concrete courtyard and outbuildings, was a stark contrast to the efficient but modest, single-storey warehouse that was home to Willows & Son. He couldn't understand why Chrissie chose to work in a two-hundred-year-old barn, originally made to store hay and grain. Surely it was obvious that a spacious, well-ventilated purpose-built workshop was so much better? For him it was a no-brainer. He supposed it might be something to do with her past.

He parked between Chrissie's yellow TR7 and the Clegg & Jax Citroen van, and lifted the Polyphon and its extra case out of his car.

He felt he was sneaking into a past century, as he pushed the heavy door to the workshop with his shoulder. The old familiar smell of beeswax and mahogany greeted him as he stepped inside.

'Hello, Nick.' Ron's voice carried from the far end of the barn.

'Hi! Are those Suffolk Ball Back chairs you're working on, Mr Clegg?'

'Yes, come and have a look, if you like.'

'Hey wait a minute, Nick! That top one's sliding off.' Chrissie hurried from where she'd been busy with tea bags and mugs. 'Wooah.' She put out her hand to save the Polyphon case sliding on the plain wooden box balancing in his arms.

'It's OK, Chrissie. Just tell me where to put them.'

'Right, over here would be good. Brilliant timing, by the way. I'm just making tea. Do you want a mug?' Her words came fast as she led him past a scattering of mahogany shavings to a vacant workbench.

'Mrs Jax has been telling me about your grandmother's Polyphon and its extra case,' Ron said as he limped across from his work. 'I hope you've brought some discs.'

'Well yeah, that's what this is all about; the clockwork and the old-world tunes from, well actually, it was my great-grandmother's time. It's kind of weird watching the metal discs going round.'

Ron's face lit up as he focused on the Polyphon cases, and Nick felt encouraged to add, 'The tunes sound familiar, but half the time I can't place 'em. I'm sure some of the notes are missing.'

'I expect the mechanism needs an overhaul and a good clean. Does it have a single or double comb?' Ron asked, before pulling a work stool closer and sitting at the bench.

'A single comb.' Nick hadn't expected Ron to know anything about the workings of disc musical boxes, but then as Chrissie had said, *he's full of surprises*.

'Now let me take a look.'

'Hey wait for me!' Chrissie carried over mugs of strong tea and the atmosphere turned conspiratorial as they huddled around the workbench.

'Right, first things first. Let's start with the maker's original case.' Ron moved the maker's case nearer. 'It's heavier than I expected for an empty case.'

'I put the metal discs in it. I thought they'd be safer.'

'Well that explains it.' Ron ran his finger over an in-laid name plaque in the centre of the lid. 'Hmm… this is, yes this is Ivorine.'

'Yeah, it's got the name POLYPHON written on the lid in err… Ivorine,' Nick said as he concentrated on reading the fancy lettering. He reckoned Ivorine was the term used for any material pretending to be ivory, and he nodded to lend conviction to his words. He caught Chrissie's glance. It was obvious she knew he was winging it, and he grinned at her.

'Ivorine was invented sometime around the end of the eighteen-hundreds. It was a kind of very early plastic,' she said, mildly.

'Milk was one of the ingredients, would you believe? Unfortunately it wasn't very good in water,' Ron added.

'Well we don't come across it much at Willows.'

'No I don't suppose you do,' Chrissie said and then sipped her tea.

Nick watched Ron tap the sides and lid of the case, the resonance changing as he moved his hand across it. Nick waited, riveted as Ron opened the case and lifted out the metal discs, turning each one over to view its underside.

'They're cool, yeah Mr Clegg?'

'It's clever how the metal's been punched to make the projections. If you look at the right angle, you can see they're curled at the end like a letter P.'

'I reckon that's because it's the shape which catches on the star wheels best.'

'Yes, except some 've been flattened back against the disc… or possibly broken off.'

'My missing notes!'

'Possibly. And judging by the marks on the inside of this case, you're not the first person to keep the discs in it.' He closed the lid, turned the now empty case upside down and gave it a firm tap.

'What are you doing, Mr Clegg?' Nick was puzzled.

'I'm not sure about the base and sides. Look, you can see the hole for the winding handle in the outside of this panel. But there's no trace of the hole inside. I think some-one's put a wooden liner in it. I wondered if it was loose.'

'Well a liner makes sense. It'll 've stopped the discs rattling around.'

'Quite right, Nick. But if the liner lifts out, it might be interesting to see what's underneath.'

'Hmm, if I was going to make a secret place in there, I'd choose the lid. Much easier to get at,' Chrissie said.

'Too obvious,' Nick murmured.

'Why's it too obvious? It'd be easy to hide something under the sepia picture on the inside of the lid. What do you think, Mr Clegg? Nick clearly doesn't reckon the wind-swept nymph playing a lute is concealing anything.'

'I don't know yet, Mrs Jax.'

'Yeah, but why are you looking for secret compart-ments and hidden things?'

'Mrs Jax was the one mentioning secret places, Nick. Best ask her.'

'Well,' Chrissie said, without waiting to be asked, 'be-cause if there is one, it'd be very exciting.'

'I agree, Mrs Jax, but the question remains - why are there two cases?' Ron repositioned the homemade case next to the maker's case he'd been examining and murmured, as if voicing his thoughts, 'The homemade case is marginally bigger. Now why should that be?'

'If I was going to make a new case for the Polyphon, I'd at least make an exact replica, not something slightly larger.' Chrissie shrugged.

'You're right, Mrs Jax. It's easier when you're copy-ing something if you copy it precisely.'

'It could be down to the thickness of the wood. The inside dimensions may be the same.' Nick waited while

Ron took some measurements.

'So, what've you got?' he asked.

'The homemade case is a centimetre taller on the outside, but I can't get the inside depth. The mechanism housing stops me.'

'One centimetre? Is that all?' Chrissie's face fell. 'Clive is forever telling me I'm making mysteries out of nothing. Maybe I'm wrong about the lid as well.'

'Hmm, it's time you played some discs, Nick.'

'Yes come on; play the one you played on Saturday.'

'That'll be *Love's Old Sweet Song.*'

Chrissie checked through the metal discs covering the workbench and Nick steadied the homemade case while he turned the winding handle. When she handed him the disc, he noticed she'd bitten more of her fingernails.

'Thanks,' he said, momentarily concerned for her, and set the disc on the drive post. 'Right, now for the pressure bar to hold it in place and....' He pushed the start lever.

The clockwork mechanism clicked and creaked as the disc turned. A mix of crisp and discordant notes tinkled from the homemade case. He glanced at Ron to catch his reaction. 'What do you think?' But he needn't have asked; Ron appeared transfixed.

C-lunk! The music finally stopped.

'It's kind of weird, the way the disc draws you in. I can't stop watching it turn, and I don't want it to end,' Nick said.

'It takes me back to when I was a young'un. Can we hear that one again, Nick?'

'Yeah, sure, Mr Clegg. I wish my grandparents had shown me this when I was a kid.' He wound up the mechanism and set it to play again.

They had finished their mugs of tea, and were on to seconds by the time they'd listened to most of the discs, some several times.

'So how do I find out more about its history?' Nick asked as he packed the discs into the lined Polyphon maker's case.

Chrissie answered without a pause, 'I guess you'll have to go back through your family tree and trace the various owners, starting with your great-grandmother.'

'Or it might have belonged to your great-grandfather.' Ron sounded wistful.

'Yeah, 1910 – you could be right.'

'Yes, so ask your mum,' Chrissie added, 'she's bound to remember her grandparents; they'd be your great-grandparents, the generation for 1910.'

'Shite, Chrissie; I'll have to trade information with my mum. She'll want to hear all about my girlfriends. I left home to get away from that, remember?'

'But where's the problem in telling your mum about them? It's only talk. Tell her about an ex, or the latest one-night stand. It doesn't matter; she'll still love it. And don't pull a face. You know you like all the attention from her.'

He didn't bother to dignify Chrissie's dig with a comment. 'OK, I've got it. But how do I find out why the Polyphon was mounted in the homemade case, Mr Clegg?'

'Well, why don't you leave the two cases with me for a few days? I'd like to spend more time with them. I think I'll remove the liner and have a look at what's underneath.'

'And the cleaning and servicing of the mechanism?'

'It's a dying art, and pricey, Nick. I'll ask around.'

'Thanks, Mr Clegg. That'd be cool. Hey, I nearly forgot; I've volunteered to help Dave repair the Poachers windows. So I may see you down the pub. Our old foreman thinks the place is haunted or cursed.'

'Haunted?' Chrissie sounded surprised.

'I know; I thought it was rubbish as well.'

'Saying it's haunted accounts for odd noises and keeps people away. That's all,' Ron said softly.

When Nick got back into his car, he couldn't help thinking that Chrissie and Mr Clegg weren't the only ones with a fondness for things from the past. What about him? Why else was he still driving the family's cast-off nineteen-year-old Ford Fiesta? Why else was he thinking of getting the Polyphon restored?

As always, the car representing a heap of his teenage memories started first time. He eased away from the Citroen van and the TR7, all the while conscious of the old barn looming behind him.

He reckoned his interest in the Polyphon was partly related to its musical connection. He'd often wondered about his musical streak. It hadn't come from his mother, who was tone deaf, or his father, who couldn't carry a tune in his head. So could it have stemmed from the relative who had owned the Polyphon in 1910?

His Fiesta rocked along the rutted track back to the road. He swayed with the movement while phrases like *old mistakes* and *old regrets* and *old hurt* rolled in his mind. Were they emotions associated with past girlfriends and dredged from his psyche? Could the phrases be the Polyphon's history talking to him through its music? This was the problem with thinking too hard about the past. 'It can turn you in on yourself,' he muttered. 'Good lines for a song, though.'

He slowed to a halt at the junction with the Wattisham

Airfield boundary lane. It was time for a change of mood. He turned on his radio and racked up the volume. The local newsreader's voice took hold as he headed towards Bury St Edmunds.

This is the six o'clock news brought to you by Radio Suffolk... Nick braked and indicated left, catching the end of the *Man Dies after Reed Bed Rescue* headline. He concentrated on the road but his attention was pulled back to the radio.

This is Nawal, reporting to you live, out and about in Suffolk. Today another muddy creek off the River Deben became a death trap when a man got stuck waist-deep in water, mud and reeds.

The drama in the reporter's voice was compelling; Nick slowed his speed.

An early-morning dog walker raised the alarm and the Sea King search & rescue helicopter winched the man to safety. He died in Ipswich Hospital this afternoon. I asked John, from one of the rescue teams, what lessons we can learn from this tragic accident.

Nick rather liked Nawal's voice.

Yes, thank you, Nawal John boomed against the background wind. *We must remember the dangers from cold water. We lose our body heat very quickly in it, and the cold can kill. It is vitally important to wear...* Nick's attention drifted.

It is unclear... the sound of Nawal's voice pulled Nick back... *how or why this man came to be in the reed beds alone at night, and why he was unable to raise the alarm when he got into trouble. For now we have no further information and the police haven't released the man's name. This is Nawal reporting, out and about in Suffolk.*

CHAPTER 7

Chrissie was running late after Nick's Friday afternoon visit with the Polyphon. It was already twenty past six, and she was only just leaving the barn workshop. Her thoughts were in a flurry. What was that business about the Poachers being haunted and Ron saying it kept people away? She paused, took a deep breath, told herself to relax, and increased the volume on her car radio as she turned onto the airfield boundary lane.

The presenter's voice rose above the engine noise.

Thanks, Josey, for calling Radio Suffolk and reminding us about the dangers of hypothermia. I think the message is clear: wear plenty of layers when walking along the muddy shorelines of our estuaries. And keep those waterproofs on if you get into trouble in the water. You can seriously lose temperature in a matter of minutes once you're immersed in cold water. OK, time for another song before our next caller on air rescue and dangers of hypothermia.

Chrissie concentrated on the road as the talking stopped and Ed Sheeran's vocal hook from his latest hit, *Don't*, filled her car. She didn't catch all the words but there was no mistaking the intensity of the track.

And now we have Magda on the line the radio presenter's voice oiled.

Hi, an edgy voice cut in. *I want to ask what will happen after the Search & Rescue helicopter is taken away from Suffolk next year. When you're trapped in cold water, every minute can mean life or death. I know this poor man died today, but at least he had a chance with the helicopter coming from Wattisham. What happens in 2015 when it's based down in Kent or somewhere on the South Coast? We must keep the Sea King at Wattisham.*

The passion in the caller's voice was palpable. Chrissie hadn't heard the story behind the on-air calls, but the key words, *hypothermia*, *Sea King* and *died today* spelled both drama and tragedy.

Her TR7 ate the miles and as she drove, she remembered Clive's description of fatal hypothermia. Sadness replaced her optimism for the weekend ahead. By the time she drew up outside her end-of-terrace cottage in Woolpit, all she wanted was to offload the feeling of hopelessness. When she saw Clive's Ford parked along the lane, she practically ran the last few paces to her front door and into her narrow hallway.

'I'm home,' she called.

'Hi, I'm in the kitchen.'

She flung her keys onto the hall table, its surface chaotic with postcards and a pewter-framed photo of a man with dark hair.

'Have you been back long?' she said as she hurried into the kitchen. 'What the…?'

Her words died as she stared at Clive. He stood near the porcelain butler sink, his shirt discarded on the floor, his trousers smeared up to the knees in sludge. Fine mud-spatter peppered his face. A smidgeon of green marked the smile lines close to one eye, and then swept towards his short auburn hair in a raffish arc. A faint but distinctive smell hit her.

Her brain froze and refused to make sense of it.

'What's going on, Clive?'

'I'm taking my clothes off so I don't traipse mud through the house.'

'Mud? You smell of…. What've you been doing?'

'Looking at where a man who died today was rescued from.'

'But–'

'I know; this morning it was a tragic accident. But now he's dead, it could be a murder scene.'

'What are you talking about?'

'He's Jason Brookford's partner from work. He's a thatcher as well, Chrissie. He should know those reed beds like the back of his hand. He'll have been working them for years. We have to wait for the post mortem, of course, but unless he had a heart attack or a stroke or something, how d'you explain he became trapped?'

'Right… so what are you saying?'

'First Jason dies unexpectedly in odd circumstances, and now his partner dies. It could be a coincidence or it could be foul play. I figured it needed checking out.'

'But what's happened? I didn't catch the news today.'

'Ah, right. Well, a man was found this morning in Shottisham Creek by a dog walker. Didn't you hear the Sea King take off from Wattisham?'

'No, not specifically. All the helicopters sound pretty much the same to me. Where's Shottisham Creek?'

'It's off the east bank of the Deben, not far from Ramsholt.'

'That explains the radio phone-in! Is the creek tidal?'

'There's a sluice gate; I don't know how much it controls anything. But it's pretty marshy round there, so you can imagine what the rescue teams have done to the ground. Just look at me! I visited the scene a couple of hours ago – and I got like this walking from my car.'

'But…?'

'I made the mistake of crouching to take a closer look, and bugger me, I'm nearly in. Anyway, we've cordoned off the area, and depending on what the post mortem shows, we may send in the SOC team.'

'What are you expecting to find?'

'I don't know. His mobile, if he had one.'

It was a lot to take in and Chrissie needed a moment. Action usually helped, and she scooped Clive's shirt from the floor. A whiff of estuary seaweed and sewage caught her. 'Ugh!' She brushed past him to consign it to the washing machine. 'Come on; let's get the rest of your clothes in the machine before you stink the house out.'

By the time Clive had showered, the washing machine was on its first rinse cycle and the smell of freshly brewed coffee filled the kitchen. Any plans for a subtly flavoured meal had changed when she shoved whole garlics and heavily seasoned squash into the oven to roast. She chopped fresh tomatoes, and diced half a cucumber while a medley of spicy mixed beans warmed on the hob.

'That smells good,' Clive said as he padded into the kitchen wearing a plain blue shirt and slate-coloured chinos.

'There's coffee, if you'd like it.' She cast an eye over his clothes. 'I guess you're still on duty, then.' She tried to keep the disappointment from her voice.

'Err… yes.' Clive nuzzled close and kissed her.

'Hmm.' She returned his kiss, 'But at least you smell better. What've you done with your shoes?'

'I left them outside.'

Chrissie frowned. 'I didn't notice. I'm surprised I didn't smell them. Strange how shoes…. Was the man who died today wearing shoes?'

'Wellington boots, or rather there was only one with

his possessions when he was admitted to hospital. I expect the other one will be deep in the creek still.'

'My God; it's barely a week since Jason Brookford died.' She felt drained by it all.

'I know. We're still waiting for his bank statements. But at least now there won't be anyone from his work to object. And next week we'll have the logs for both of his mobiles.'

'He had two phones? Will you need to see his thatching partner's accounts and phone records, now that he's died as well?'

'Only if there are suspicious or unexplained circumstances surrounding his death. As I said, we're waiting on the coroner's post mortem. But ye-e-s, in the meantime, it wouldn't do any harm to run the name past Matt.' Clive's last words were barely audible, like a vaguely formed thought.

'But....' She caught Clive's warning frown, and changed track, 'What is the latest man's name?'

'Caleb Coddins.'

'I've not heard it before. Did you know it's going round that the Poachers Basket is either haunted or cursed?'

'Or both, no doubt. What rubbish people talk! I expect they'll be saying Caleb Coddins was the leader of a coven, next.' He laughed.

'The trouble is, if things are said often enough, people begin to believe them.'

'Not with curses and hauntings, Chrissie. Not nowadays. And when I last checked, the occult, horoscopes and tarot readings didn't count as evidence. I'd rather put my money on Matt.'

'What?'

CHAPTER 8

Matt was surprised by the caller's ID. He let his phone ring a few more times in case it was some kind of a mistake, and then answered, 'Hi Clive.'

'Good morning, Matt.'

Matt looked up at the sky and waited. From where he was standing, all he could see were clouds. If Clive was referring to the weather, it was hardly a good Sunday morning.

'Matt? Are you still there?'

'Yeah.'

'Is it a good time to ask you something?'

'What you mean?'

'Well is anyone with you? Are you alone?'

'I'm waitin' for Maisie.' He could have added he'd scootered to a car boot sale out Stonham Aspal way and there were plenty of people milling around.

'OK, so I'm guessing you're alone. I want to ask... have you come across the name Caleb Coddins in your work?'

'Caleb Coddins? Why's that then?'

'I can't tell you; it's... off the record, a bit like Jason Brookford. So keep this to yourself.'

Matt visualised the name as if printed, but it didn't trigger anything in his photographic memory. 'No, I can't say I 'ave.'

'Are you sure?'

This time Matt added a frown and screwed his eyes tighter, as he pictured his computer screen filled with lists. He scanned down the columns for the name. There was a

Coggins, but no Coddins.

'Matt, are you still there?'

'Yeah, I'm still 'ere, and no; it aint a name I've searched. But it don't mean Damon aint. He's the one dealin' with the clients direct. He gets the names; I only see the ones he wants me to see. He don't let on about the ones he's been searchin'.'

'But you'd be able to find out, wouldn't you?'

'He turns funny if he thinks I'm nosin', but I s'pose I could ask.'

'Thanks Matt. See what you can find out, and don't let on it's me asking. Get back to me if you have anything.'

'OK. Hey Mais, over here!' A vision with crazy blonde hair, and dressed in a billowing blouse and cropped jeans, waved to him.

'Right, I can hear you're busy, and I've got a half marathon to run. Don't forget to check it out for me.'

'Yeah, yeah.' Matt barely listened as he cut the call.

'Mais!' he called again, his voice lost to a gust of wind.

The car boot sale filled a grassy area, the size of a football pitch, with wooden barns to one side and a vista of open fields beyond. Maisie hurried past a van selling old plant pots and garden tools, and gave him a hug.

'We kinda match,' she said as she stood close, 'Who you been talkin' to?'

She had come at him fast, and her perfume hinted flowers and summer. The sunny-cream of Maisie's blouse almost matched the pastel yellow of the tee-shirt he wore under his denim jacket. But the word MEGAPLEX on the front didn't match the understated *cool gear* label on Maisie's blouse.

'Yeah, s'pose we match,' he said, wondering what she meant exactly, and kissed her.

'You still aint said who you were phonin'?'

'What?' Clive had said not to say anything about Caleb Coddins. 'Half marathon,' he blurted.

'Who?'

'It were Clive callin' me; Chrissie's bloke. He said he were about to run a half marathon.'

'Ooo… so why's he callin' you about it?'

'I dunno. Chrissie said somethin' weeks ago. They'll be runnin' round Ipswich.'

He pictured the heading on the flyer. **The First Ipswich Half Marathon. Sunday 21st September 2014 Start 10:00am Ipswich Town Centre.** He checked the time on his phone. 09:54. 'It begins in six minutes.'

'You aint entered, 'ave you, Matt?'

Her question rattled him, and his Suffolk broke through, 'Nah, don't be clout 'eaded.'

'Well, I reckon you'd die if you ran thirteen miles. Will there be trouble if you don't show?'

'I aint entered, Mais, so how'd I be in trouble for not runnin'?'

'But you can still get the tee-shirt, right?'

'I tell you what, Mais; why don't we look round here quick, and then ride over to Ipswich?'

'Yeah, awesome – we'll get the tee-shirt.'

***

Monday morning was cloudy but less windy than the previous day, the day of the half marathon. Matt gazed out through the Balcon & Mora office window in Bury St Edmunds, and gently moved his shoulders and neck. The tension in his muscles eased as he studied the narrow street below. He focused on an empty plastic bottle. It lay flattened in the gutter, a casualty to a passing car. It struck him as a visual image of how he felt.

'There were hundreds of them bottles lyin' all over the place in Ipswich yesterday,' he murmured as he moved away from the window. He took care to keep the back of his tee-shirt facing Damon.

'Are you talking about the *Ipswich Half Marathon*?' Damon asked from behind a large monitor screen, and sounding out the words as if he was reading them.

'Yeah, they were handin' bottled water to the runners.' Matt let his words hang in the stale office air as he remembered yesterday. He'd held Maisie's hand and they'd cheered with the crowd. They'd even walked a shortcut to Christchurch Park to catch a glimpse of the route as it wove through hectares of lawns, open grass and woodland, close to the town centre. It had been exhausting.

Matt smoothed his tee-shirt across his chest, and hoped the words on the cotton lay flat and easy to read across his shoulders. If only he'd thought to put it on back to front, then he'd have known when people were looking at it.

'Hackin' hell!' Matt slumped onto his stacker chair.

'Yes, I have noticed you're wearing the *Ipswich Marathon 2014* tee. Did you really run yesterday?'

'Nah, but I were a supporter, an' I walked miles. That counts.'

He'd seen Chrissie and Sarah briefly; neither of them had been running, but they'd all stood together and cheered Clive on as he'd pounded past to the finish. It counted.

'Was Maisie running, then?'

'What, Maisie? Not her kinda thing.'

At least he didn't think it was. Matt knew how he felt about her; he liked the warm glow when she was close, and the way she made him feel when she kissed him, but he'd never tried to analyse what made her tick.

'So who were you supporting?'

'Errr....' He couldn't say Clive. It would sound like he was a good mate, and Damon already knew Clive was a detective. And after mentioning Clive, any question about Caleb Coddins would be a dead giveaway that Matt was scouting for a detective. Spam!

'Errr... s'pose I were supportin' everyone.'

He kept his back to Damon while his stomach lurched. What was he going to do? Matt scratched his beard and waited for inspiration.

A newsflash popped onto his screen. He knew the same newsflash would have streaked onto Damon's monitor. 'Hey, get this,' Matt said, thankful to move the talk on from the marathon.

'*Man Pulled from Deben Reed Beds Named.* It'll be the man they had the Sea King out for on Friday. He died, didn't he?' Damon said.

'Yeah.' Matt couldn't believe his eyes as he read from his screen, 'It says he were *Caleb Coddins, a sixty-year-old man rescued on Friday from Shottisham Creek.*' Matt paused and adopted his smoothest tones, 'Coddins aint a common name. Have you come across any Coddinses? I can't say I 'ave.'

'I don't know... I'd have to look.'

It was Matt's lucky break. He waited a few seconds and then shifted his chair to get a better view of Damon. 'Well?'

It was obvious from the patch of colour on Damon's

cheeks that something was wrong. His tawny eyes, usually darting with his thoughts, barely moved as he studied his screen.

'What's up?' Matt asked.

'I don't know. It was a few years ago.'

'Yeah, but what you got? If it were before 2012, it were before I were workin' for you.'

Damon didn't say anything, so Matt persisted with his thread.

'If I'd been workin' for you, then I bet you'd 've put him on me list of names to search, right?'

'Maybe.'

'So I'd 've seen what you're readin' now.'

'Only if I'd shown you. All I've got here is the client's request.'

'Aint that what I just said?'

'No. Anyway, I turned it down. I don't do physical searches and I'm not a private detective. I wasn't one then, and I'm not one now. I set my business to fit my skills.'

'Yeah, computin' and IT.'

'Right. So I wasn't interested in a client asking me to trace a pair of missing cowboy boots.'

'What? I've always fancied a pair of cowboy boots.' Matt studied his computer-geek boss. Even the denim-and-sweatshirt-clad Damon would look cool in rodeo boots.

'Do you s'pose Ed Sheeran wears cowboy boots?' Matt asked.

'How'd I know? Anyway, I didn't take the case. But now it appears the client I refused, died last week.'

'Yeah, but it were years after you turned him down. It can't be nothin' to do with his boots. So why'd they go missin'?'

'I don't know. At the time I thought it was a joke. Here, read his request, see what you make of it. And remember; what you read in the office stays in the office.'

'Yeah, yeah.'

Damon didn't say more, and Matt silently thanked the god of lucky breaks. He budged his chair back to its original position to face his computer and the wall, and waited.

True to his promise, the Caleb Coddins communiqué arrived on his screen. It took the form of an email dated September 20th 2005.

Dear Messrs Balcon & Mora,

I want to take you up on the "no find, no fee" introductory offer.

Please find my cowboy boots. I last saw them in the bar at the Poachers Basket, Wattisham, last Tuesday, the second Tuesday in September. They are genuine brown Texan leather and originally belonged to an American airman. He gave them to my mother in 1945. He called them his Justin, Fort Worth boots. I can give more information on request.

Yours faithfully

Caleb Coddins.

Matt read the email twice, the second time more slowly.

'Well?' Damon asked.

'I s'pose I'd 've started by searchin' *Justin, Fort Worth boots* and newspaper sites.' He was careful not to point out that the Poachers Basket in Wattisham was the same pub where Jason Brookford had been found dead, just over a week ago on Saturday, 13th September 2014. The loss of the boots and Jason's death were separated by nine years to the month. A rush of excitement told him it might be more than coincidence.

'You've got thirty minutes to show me you could have done it at the time – count it as your coffee break.'

'Yeah OK, Damon. You're on.'

Thank blog! Damon didn't seem to have noticed the September link. Matt glowed.

He opened his calendar app, scrolled back to 2005 and looked at September. The second Tuesday in September 2005 fell on the 13th day of the month.

'Pixels,' he breathed. It was nine years to the day; exactly the same date in September that Jason Brookford had been found dead in the Poachers Basket. It felt significant.

He knew Damon would be watching through administrator view. Pixels! He needed to distract him before he spotted the connection or decided it was a police matter. In a flash, Matt closed the calendar app and typed *Justin, Fort Worth boots* in the search box on the local news site, narrowing the year to 2005 and the month, September.

Nothing.

Poachers Basket, Wattisham he typed instead. This time he was in luck; one result for September 2005, and several for other months in 2005. He worked his way through them.

'Looks like Caleb Coddins put in a reward notice with a local paper for anyone finding a pair of cowboy boots gone missing from the Poachers Basket,' Damon said.

'Yeah, an' there's a contact number on the notice. 'Ave you got the same number for him, or were it just his email address we got here?'

'Just his email address.'

'Right, I'll try the number, then. You never know, it might still be active.' Matt reached for the office phone, tapped in the number and waited. Excitement hustled his pulse.

'Yes?' a voice answered. It was only one word, but the pitch took him by surprise.

'Yeah hi.' Matt paused to soften his tone into the silky one reserved for birds. 'I'm callin' about a pair of cowboy boots.'

'What? Who is this?' The strident quality now conjured an older female.

'I'm callin' because I 'ave a pair of unclaimed cowboy boots,' he said, pronouncing each syllable slowly.

'What?'

'I deal in unclaimed lost property. You must've heard of the annual sales of unclaimed property left on trains an' buses, and the like? It's me line of work.'

'Y-e-e-s, but I fail to see why–'

'Yeah well, we always check a few things before articles go to auction. We wouldn't want to sell somethin' that's on a stolen list. Or somethin' the owner's got proof of tryin' to find.'

'Y-e-e-s, but I don't see why you're phoning me.'

'Ah well, that's coz we did a newspaper search. Someone with this phone number placed an ad tryin' to find some lost cowboy boots.'

'What?'

'Perhaps if you could describe 'em to me, I'd know if you were the owner?'

'How do I know you're not a hoaxer? You describe them to me.'

'OK then. They're brown leather, and they're Justin, Fort Worth cowboy boots. I'd say they look kinda old; what I'd call vintage.'

Matt listened to the silence on the line. He'd made enough tracing calls in his time to know something he'd said had struck home. He reckoned the woman was weighing up how to respond. If he waited a few more seconds, would she give herself away and say, *but that was nine years ago*?

'Tell me more about them,' she said slowly.

DOS-in' codec! He'd told her all he had. 'Well,' he coasted, as he pulled up a Google image of some *Justin, Fort Worth cowboy boots*, 'they'd fit a man. So takin' that… and the style… I'd say they're men's cowboy boots.'

'So now you'll return them to me, will you?'

'Well yeah, but first I need to know you're the owner - like you tell me somethin' 'bout the boots only I'd know. Or show me the receipt for placin' the ad. And we'll need your name and address to get 'em back to you.'

'You want me to tell you something only you'd know?' Her tone changed, 'It's a few years since the ad in the paper. How come you haven't contacted me sooner?'

He sensed her attack, but rollin' codec - she'd given herself away! He punched the air; a victory sign to Damon.

'We're new,' he said without missing a beat, 'we only took on the lost-property contract a month ago. There's a whole warehouse full of stuff. We're workin' our way through it.'

'So do you deliver, or can I collect?'

'It's a locked warehouse. We prefer to deliver. If you give me a name an' address….'

'Raelynn Harris, I live out towards Wattisham Stone. Phone me when you're on Wattisham Road and I can direct you from there. You've got the number.'

'OK; we'll call you when we got a delivery date.'

The line went dead.

'I thought you were trying to find the cowboy boots; not return a pair you don't have,' Damon said quietly.

'Yeah, but who the botnet is Raelynn Harris? She must've had somethin' to do with it in 2005. S'pose now I'll have to check out Raelynn Harris.'

'Or search the net for a pair of Justin, Fort Worth cowboy boots to give her.'

'What? I aint spendin' on her.'

'And neither is Balcon & Mora. And time is money so coffee break over. It's back to contact details for the card companies.'

Ping!

'And if that's personal business, it can wait till lunch.'

Matt sneaked a look at his mobile. Why was Nick texting him mid-morning?

CHAPTER 9

Nick re-read the text message he'd sent to Matt during his coffee break. *Hi Matt. A couple of lagers for you if you trace some info about my great-grandparents. I'll get their names off Mum this week.*

Matt had answered with a curt *when?* Was he asking about a timeline for Nick getting names from his mum, or the promised couple of lagers? A simple *OK* or *I'll need more than 2 lagers, mate*, was what he'd expected.

'What's up? Girlfriend trouble?' Dave asked, before downing the rest of his coffee.

'Why d'you say that?'

'We've all finished our coffee while you've hardly touched yours. And you've been frowning at your phone.'

'No, it's just Matt. He's… he takes things so literally. There's no….'

'Wiggle room?'

'Yeah, that's it.' Nick wasn't going to mention the fleeting Pansy – the latest girl to idolise him as a singer and make him into her fantasy bloke. He would have described her more as girl trouble, than girlfriend trouble.

He watched the other carpenters rinse their mugs in the sink. The morning coffee break had ended and it was time to get back to the bespoke kitchen units in the workshop.

Monday, at Willows & Son, had turned into a haven of calm after the craziness of his weekend. Saturday afternoon had been unexpectedly spent with Pansy, a girl he'd flirted with briefly after the Frasers gig the previous Saturday. Yesterday, Sunday morning, he'd felt somewhat hung over and had a possessive Pansy in tow. By the afternoon he'd confused her name, and called her Panda by mistake.

'Who's Panda? Or is it Pandora, you cheating, superficial prick?' she'd screamed, before hammering down the flat's stairs and out into Bury.

'But how can the song Leaving Marcelle be about you?' he'd called softly after her.

He hadn't followed. Her perfume and melting brown eyes couldn't blind him; her reactions were dramas built on emptiness and her reality was disturbingly complex – too complex for him. And so, he'd picked up his guitar and strummed chords and sung phrases, as a new song took shape. Phrases like *borrowed emotion* and *words can't make it real*.

'I want to drop round the Poachers sometime this week,' Dave said, interrupting Nick's thoughts. 'I'm going to ring Steve Corewell and fix a time. Any day difficult for you?' He had paused in the workshop doorway, and stood watching Nick.

'Nah, I've nothing planned.' Nick tipped the remains of his coffee into the sink. He intended to pursue the Polyphon's history, but first he had to speak to his mum, and he was still waiting to hear back from Ron and Chrissie about the Polyphon case.

Ping!

'Sorry Dave, I need to get this.'

He opened the text message from Matt, and frowned as he read: *Have you got any cowboy boots?*

'Are you sure you haven't got girlfriend trouble?'

'What? No, I'm fine. It's Matt you should be worried about. He's asking me for cowboy boots.'

CHAPTER 10

Chrissie was pleased with her work on the early Georgian side table. Another wax polish and it would be ready for Mr Croft to collect. An unsuspecting person would have to look very closely to detect her repairs to the single, shallow drawer.

'You got a good match with the mahogany, in the end,' Ron said, from his work stool.

'Hmm, but I still think having a single handle is wrong.' She eyed the drawer stretching the length of the table. 'I know there're no marks to suggest there were ever two, but with only one, it's difficult to pull out straight – at least not without twisting it.'

'Maybe the drawer front was replaced back in Georgian times, and the original pair of handles was split up or lost.'

'But why, Mr Clegg? It's more likely this is a country piece and one brass handle costs less than two. You've been puzzling over the Polyphon case for too long.'

'Hmm, possibly, Mrs Jax.'

'So what've you worked out so far? I'll make us both a mug of tea.'

The old barn had begun to feel crowded with work still to be done. A wooden sea chest, a tallboy and a couple of Ercol breakfast chairs waited patiently at the far end of the barn, while the set of six Ball Back chairs filled space between workbenches.

Ron might have denied spending time on the Polyphon, but something was interfering with his efficiency. She suspected he might have discovered something.

'Come on then,' she said, when she carried their mugs of steaming tea over to his workbench a few minutes later.

'Thank you, Mrs Jax.' He sipped his tea, and his shoulders sagged while he frowned. 'When I listen to the discs, the music brings back memories.'

She wanted to ask *what memories* but knew to hold her tongue and wait.

'I remembered listening through the door to discs like these being played in the Poachers' guestroom.'

'Really?'

'When I say discs, I mean some of the same tunes.' He indicated the metal discs in a neat pile next to the original Polyphon case.

'These discs on the bench here?'

'I'm not saying they're the exact same discs. But the tunes sounded pretty much the same and some, like these, had notes missing.'

'So do you think you listened to *this* Polyphon when you were a kid?'

'I don't know, Mrs Jax. I didn't get to see much; I only got to hear the tunes through the door.'

'Well these discs and Polyphon belonged to Nick's great-grandmother.'

'I know; but some of the notes missing sound the same as on the discs played at the Poachers. It doesn't make sense, unless it's my memory playing tricks.' He stared into his tea.

Chrissie thought back to Ron telling her about the fight at the Poachers and the broken door panel. 'Was this before or after the door got broken and you helped to clear up and mend it?'

She watched him frown again, and waited. When he

didn't answer, she forged on, 'Come on then, Mr Clegg. Tell me about the Polyphon cases. What have you found?'

'Well,' he said slowly, 'I've been mostly looking at the original maker's case and its liner. We thought it was likely made to hold the discs securely, but... a few days ago, I noticed two small holes.' He pointed and she peered in.

'You mean these?' She squinted at two holes, one each side and the size left by a panel pin. The two identical holes were obscured by scuff marks from the rims of the metal discs, and lost amongst the peppering of genuine woodworm holes in the lining.

'I suppose they're fractionally smaller than the woodworm,' she murmured.

'Exactly; not easy to see. But when I inserted these steel panel pins, like so... and lifted, like this....'

'Wow; it's moving.' Excited, she grasped a free edge and helped ease the lining out of the maker's case. A piece of paper, the size of a luggage label, lay flat against the bottom.

'What's that? What's written on it, Mr Clegg?'

Without a word he reached in and lifted the paper with studied care.

Her impatience bubbled over. 'But what does it say?'

'Well you tell me, Mrs Jax. I'd like to hear what you make of it.'

He'd lit a fuse. Chrissie blinked and searched his face. He smiled, his manner speaking colleague rather than teacher, and passed the paper across the bench for her.

'It's got handwriting on it,' she said, turning the pale sepia paper over and then back, before laying it flat on the bench. 'It's old. The way the letters are formed is... it's a style from a past era; all swirly, and in ink. Yes; definitely penned with a nib.'

Some of the words were difficult to read, but she did her best. '*L'Elisir D'Amore*; *Waltz Rondo*; *Last Rose of Summer*; *Love's Old Sweet Song*; *Home Sweet Home*; *The Merry Widow*; *William Tell*.' She looked up and caught Ron's eye. 'Love's Old Sweet Song? Isn't that one of the discs?'

He nodded.

'But isn't this a list of the disc titles? It's numbered like an inventory of what's in the box.'

'Yes, except it doesn't include all the discs Nick brought in this box.'

'Right… so it's telling us the disc collection has changed over the years.'

'It could be, but only the ones on the list have notes missing.'

'Really? Maybe they're the oldest and have been played the most?'

He shrugged and the slackness resettled around his shoulders.

She waited, sensing he had more to say.

'When the liner came out, I realised the original lock mechanism had been removed. I guess it was harvested for the homemade case, and the oblong hole here,' he pointed, 'was patched with wood. But the hole for the key has been continued through the patch. It struck me as odd.'

'You mean, like they were going to reset the lock mechanism on the other side of the patch, but then changed their minds?'

He nodded.

She thought for a moment. 'So the liner was, in effect,

blocking off the keyhole.'

'Yes. When I brushed it through, I found this. It must have been pushed up tight against the liner because the key went in happily enough.' He passed her a small glass container, along with a sheet of paper with his handwriting on it.

At first she thought it was an empty jar, and then she spotted a little scroll of paper in the bottom. It looked like an old, lozenge-shaped, papier-mâché bead - disintegrating and slightly larger than the diameter of the keyhole.

'Is it a roll of paper, Mr Clegg? It seems too bulky to have fitted in the keyhole.'

'It fitted snug enough when it was rolled up tight. I opened it out to take a look, but the paper wouldn't stay flat and it's curled again, now it's in the jar.'

'Wow,' she breathed, 'was anything written on it?'

'Yes. Some numbers and letters. It was so fragile I–'

'You photographed it, Mr Clegg?' She raised her eyebrows.

'No, Mrs Jax; I copied what was written. See what you make of it.'

She smothered a grin, and concentrated on his sheet of paper. Ron had written a series of letters and numbers in a straight line. 'There's a 4 followed by the letters A to G, in a random order. Is this exactly how it was set out?'

He nodded. 'I wondered if it was some kind of code or puzzle. I thought with your accountant's mind, you'd be good at this kind of thing, Mrs Jax.'

'An ex-accountant's mind, Mr Clegg. I gave it up back in 2009.' She drank some of her tea, her mind a hailstorm of thoughts and ideas. 'Wasn't there a number 4 written on the inventory against Love's Old Sweet Song?'

'Yes.'

'Then perhaps that's what the 4 on this refers to.' Her rising excitement was checked by realism. It was going to take a long time to crack the code, assuming it was a code and not some combination for a safe or deposit box.

'I'll take some photos of it. And we should tell Nick. He'd want to know.' Secretly she wondered if Matt would be the obvious choice to help break a cipher.

For the rest of the afternoon Chrissie worked on the traditional old Ercol chairs. But her subconscious ran with the Polyphon, and by the time she'd packed away her tools and headed out to her TR7, she was convinced even Clive was bound to be intrigued. 'The song, the disc and the missing notes,' she murmured, 'somehow they've got to link together.'

She drove out of the courtyard, anxious to get home and concentrate on the code. She'd settle with a mug of tea, her laptop, and some paper to scribble on.

As she threaded between hedgerows and glanced across acres of ploughed-in wheat stubble, the miles drifted by. Did she need the actual disc, or would simply the title do? Well, it was too late to turn back now. She slowed as she took the lane leading to her end-of-terrace cottage. Late-flowering chrysanthemums gave a welcoming splash of burgundy outside her home. From a distance, some could have passed for blooms on the climbing rose nearby. Closer, it was obvious the climber only bore dead heads and green leaves. The shocker, however, was the blackberry bubblegum Vespa; an explosion of colour waiting at the kerb outside her cottage.

'Mother of Pearl,' she breathed, 'what is Matt doing here?'

CHAPTER 11

Matt hadn't needed to knock on Chrissie's front door – he'd barely had time to raise his hand before the latch turned and the door opened with a whoosh.

Clive stood facing him. 'Ah, good timing, Matt. I've only just got home myself. Come on in.'

He sounded friendly enough, and Matt followed Clive down the narrow hallway, past the side table with the photo of Chrissie's dead husband Bill, and into the sitting room.

'Thanks for dropping round, Matt. You confused me a bit when you rang, so it's probably best if we talk where no one can overhear or interrupt us.'

The words *no one can overhear or interrupt us* were delivered in a flat tone. Matt searched the DI's face. Was it a threat or a reassurance? But Clive was definitely smiling and Chrissie's living room exuded an air of cosiness, in spite of the old stripped floorboards.

'Take a seat and don't look so confused. Some conversations are best kept off record.' Again the monotone delivery followed by the obvious smile.

'So you aint testy? I aint done nothin' wrong?' Matt said, grasping for clarity.

'It's all good.'

'Killer app!' He felt like an operative reporting to his handler, and launched into explaining about Caleb Coddins' request to Balcon & Mora back in 2005. In Matt's mind, he'd been elevated to special agent.

'Justin Fort Worth cowboy boots, you say?'

'Yeah – genuine Texan leather.'

At some point, and Matt couldn't have said exactly

when, he relaxed sufficiently to slouch further into the sofa while Clive sat in the armchair. He even relished the frowned look of concentration on Clive's face while he recounted his phone call to Raelynn Harris and his promise to return the boots.

Finally, he felt emboldened to ask if there was a lager in the fridge.

'Before we go down that road, Matt, I need to get a few more things clear.'

'Oh yeah?'

'It's one thing pretending to be a lost property worker when you phoned Raelynn Harris, but what exactly had you planned to do next?' Clive stretched his legs out and sat back, as if settling to watch a show.

'I s'pose return them boots. 'Cept I aint got 'em.' Matt let his voice hang in the air, and focused on the geometric patterns on the rug and then the cracks between the floorboards.

'But how can any of this help? How does it tell me if Caleb Coddins has multiple phone numbers? That's what I asked you to find out, Matt.'

'Yeah, but don't you see? This Raelynn bird must've known him? I bet she had a number for him back in 2005. Maybe even more recent. You said you wanted all his numbers, right?'

'Yes, his current and recent ones, not ones nine years out of date. This isn't a game, Matt.'

'You're forgettin' about them dates.'

'What dates?'

'I already said. Caleb Coddins lost his Fort Worth's at the Poachers exactly nine years ago on the same date that Jason Brookford were found dead in the Poachers.'

'You... hadn't made it clear. Are you sure about the dates?'

'Yeah.'

Seconds passed, and Matt swallowed hard. He pulled at his scrappy beard and tried to read Clive's expression. So how would a special agent behave, he wondered. Ask for a bottle of lager and a wedge of lime, and this time sound as if he meant business?

The silence broke as a key grated in the lock and a rustle and swish sounded down the hallway.

'Hi, I'm home,' Chrissie announced.

'Hiya, we're in 'ere,' Matt called. The words had barely left his mouth before she appeared in the doorway. He grinned, pleased to see her and hoping she'd offer him a lager.

'Is everything all right?' she asked. Matt noticed how she looked at Clive.

'Yes, of course. I asked Matt to check something out for me, off the record.'

'So is it secret?' Again, her question was directed at Clive.

'It's not for wider consumption.'

'Yeah. See I were just reportin' back on stuff,' Matt said, feeling sidelined from his centre-stage, special agent position, 'but if you're talkin' consumption, I reckon I could sink a lager.' It was a line worthy of a comic-strip superhero agent, and he tried his cool, half smile.

'Right, Matt. Like your tee, by the way,' she said, as if she'd finally noticed him.

He smoothed the front of his pale khaki tee-shirt, 'Yeah, Chrissie; *Two-Factor Authentication*. I got it last weekend.' It had been a find on a stall at the car boot sale.

Matt reckoned it gave him a hint of special agent, as well as staying true to his techie IT roots.

'Right, a lager for Matt. How about you?' Chrissie directed her question at Clive. 'I can see something's going on. It's written all over your face.'

'Just a development in one of my cases. And yes, a lager would be nice, thanks.' There was something in the way he set his jaw.

Matt wished for the nth time in the last half hour that he could read faces, but at least he recognised Chrissie's frown as she turned on her heel and headed to the kitchen. He knew it meant trouble. Sounds of a fridge door opening, bottles clinking and an opener flipping tops onto a counter ran in the background while he turned his attention back to Clive.

'You know what she's like, Clive. If you don't tell her, she'll keep on at me till I do. It aint fair. You gotta say somethin'.' He searched for agreement in Clive's flicker of a smile.

'I tell you what,' Chrissie said loudly, her voice travelling ahead of her as she returned from the kitchen. 'I'll trade you some information... or rather some fascinating things I learnt today. And in return you get to drink your lagers *and you tell me* what's going on. Is it a deal?' She stood in the doorway holding a tray laden with a small glass of wine and a couple of bottles of opened lager.

Clive got up, weariness in his movement, and took the tray from her. 'OK, it's a deal. But I suppose it's not really a secret because it'll be all over the news tomorrow.'

'What?' Matt couldn't believe the cowboy boots would be splashed across the news channels by the morning. It was... well, it was spooky.

'I'm only going to give you the broadest of facts. There aren't many details, and testing takes time. So any suspicions, and they are only suspicions, stay in this room. Do you understand?'

'Yes, of course, Clive.'

Matt nodded. 'Yeah, sure,' he mumbled and focused on the opened lager. Clive set the tray on the coffee table before saying, 'We got some of the test results back today from the post mortem on Caleb Coddins. It appears his death may not have been quite as straightforward as we'd supposed.'

'But why you sayin'…?' In a flash Matt caught on. This was a Clive-style smokescreen, a handler at work deflecting attention from his operative's mission.

'I seem to remember you saying something about hypothermia and an accidental death,' Chrissie soothed as she settled next to Matt on the sofa.

'Hmm, but the pathologist has flagged up the man's symptoms before he was helicoptered out of the reed beds. He'd vomited and had diarrhoea, which isn't typical of hypothermia.'

'But what if he was blind drunk and started vomiting, and then got caught in the reed beds overnight?'

'Yeah, Clive. Or swallowed a load of reed bed water,' Matt chipped in.

'I think it was the, *and diarrhoea* which was unusual.'

Chrissie seemed to still, and Matt opted to follow her lead and stay silent. He could look up more about hypothermia later.

'The problem with the toxicology,' Clive continued, 'is that he'd been resuscitated, so all the fluids and drugs he was given may have skewed the results. The pathologist wonders if he'd been poisoned, or if it was something he ate or drank... and before you say anything, he didn't mean the estuary water.'

'Right,' Matt breathed.

'Our breakthrough may be in the hipflask he had in his pocket. It contained his favourite tipple - damson gin. It's gone for analysis.' He pulled a small notebook from his pocket and read, '*gas chromatography* or some kind of *spectrophotometry* – it'll take a while to get the results.'

'And at least no one resuscitated his hipflask.'

'Exactly, Chrissie,' Clive chuckled.

'Hmm, damson gin's sweet and strong; I guess it'll disguise bitter flavours. You know, it's starting to sound like what happened to that poor man at the Poachers.'

'Not quite, Chrissie. It was at least a litre of vodka for Jason. Poor Caleb probably only drank a couple of hundred mls, judging by the size of his hipflask.'

'Wooah,' Matt breathed. He wasn't entirely sure what was behind the reference to Jason, and he wasn't going to ask. At least not now; not while Chrissie was engrossed with Clive's smokescreen.

'So what will you tell the press?' Chrissie asked in her matter-of-fact way.

'Something on the lines of appealing for any sightings of him on the evening he got trapped in the reed beds. And we need to go through what he was doing earlier that day, as well as getting more background information about him. His death is still unexplained.'

'In other words, foul play hasn't been ruled in or out – and you've a load of work to do?'

'Exactly, Chrissie. Now what was your news? I seem to remember we were being tempted with lager and some fascinating information.'

'Yeah, Chrissie; what news you got?'

***

It was barely six thirty by the time Matt, Clive and Chrissie decamped to Woolpit's White Hart. Matt was hungry and Chrissie had made it quite clear she'd rather go on talking than cook a meal for them all.

'The fresh air'll clear our minds and help us crack the cipher,' she said as she led the way, linking her arm with Clive's, as they walked. Matt trailed behind, eyes down as he scuffed loose chippings in the lane and pictured the Polyphon cipher Chrissie had shown them.

Woolpit seemed quiet and the old narrow pavements were pretty much deserted. The stuccoed White Hart was set back from the ancient, triangular market place. A pair of half-barrels had been planted with flame-orange flowering alstroemeria. They brightened the entrance to the main bar and their blooms were visible from fifty yards, despite the fading evening light. Their colour made Matt think of baked beans; it stoked his hunger as they ordered drinks at the bar.

'Yeah a Corona with a wedge of lime in the bottle, mate,' Matt said.

'Sorry, we don't have any Mexican lager, but I can do you a wedge of lime with–'

'Nah, forget it. I'll have the lager on tap. Straight.' He figured it was best not to stand out if he was a secret operative. 'So what we eatin'?' he asked.

'Let's order a selection of bruschetta,' Chrissie said, 'just to be getting on with while we're choosing our mains. We can take the menu with us to a table, OK?'

'Bruschetta?' It sounded Italian, more likely to be a

tractor than a motorbike – but, like his Vespa, Italian was cool. 'I'll have a beef burger, chips and baked beans for me main, if they've got it,' he said without making a move to leave the bar counter.

'I'll have the....' Clive checked a menu card propped near the beer pump pull handles and said, 'Red Poll beef burger and chips.'

'In that case....' They waited at the bar while Chrissie ordered a vegetable lasagne. She led the way as they carried their drinks past a selection of salvaged treadle-based tables and through to an empty dining area in a side room.

Matt felt mildly confused by her *leader of the expedition* bossiness. Why couldn't they set up camp in the friendly main bar with its reassuring smell of beer? 'Why we sittin' in here?' he asked.

'If we're eating, we're better off with a large table. We'll all be able to see everything *and* there'll be room for our glasses and plates as well.'

She put her glass and a pad of papers on a scrubbed pine table for six.

'It would be nice to actually see the originals, Chrissie,' Clive murmured as he pulled back a chair to sit down.

'I know, but they're fragile and Ron thought they should stay with the box. The shots I took with my phone should be enough, and there's what Ron and I copied out.' She selected two sheets of paper. 'The rest is to scribble on.'

'Aint Ron got a camera on 'is mobile?'

'No Matt, he hasn't even got a mobile,' Chrissie sounded weary.

'No one would have given the disc inventory a second look if you hadn't discovered the paper in the keyhole,

Chrissie.' Clive pulled the sheets of paper closer and frowned.

'Ron and I think the 4 refers to the 4 on the list of song titles for the discs.'

'4 is... *Love's Old Sweet Song*,' Clive said, running his finger along the paper with Chrissie's handwriting on it.

'Yeah, but this is old, aint it? The 4 could be part of somethin' like a Caesar cipher.'

'It's not Roman, Matt.'

'Yeah I know, Chrissie, but it's old, like last century. It could be an old-style cipher. See, you move each alphabet letter on by 3 letters if you were Caesar. The 4 could mean you move each alphabet letter on by 4.'

'Let's try it,' Chrissie whispered and scribbled on a sheet of plain paper.

Matt leaned across to get a better view of Ron's copy of what was written on the scrap rolled into the keyhole. 'Scammin' hell, there's only 18 alphabet letters.'

'Yes, the number 4 and a mix of 18 letters from the first 7 letters of the alphabet.' Clive sipped his beer and eyed Matt.

'Well that's a right pain in the codec. See, 18 letters aint goin' to be enough letters to break the cipher. We need 22, or 23 minimum, if I'm gonna write an algorithm to break it.'

Chrissie frowned. 'I don't understand.'

'Ah! I've read something about this,' Clive said. 'I'm guessing it's something to do with the *TE* factor. If it's in English, then there are 26 letters in the alphabet and some letters appear much more frequently than others, such as T and E. Am I right, Matt?'

'Yeah. How many letters in *Love's Old Sweet Song*?'

Chrissie scribbled on another plain sheet. 'It comes to a total of 17 letters. There are 3 Ss; 3 Es; 3 Os; 2 Ls and one each of a... D; G; N; T; V and W. And if you count the apostrophe on *Love's*, then it's a total of 18.'

'18 on both the keyhole scrap and the title on the inventory,' Clive said softly.

'Then I s'pose it could be a kinda substitution cipher. Yeah, you could make a kinda grid out of it.'

'And the song title is the key? Is that what you mean, Matt?'

'Yeah, I s'pose so. Except without more letters, it's goin' to be scammin' hopeless. What did you get by movin' them *Love's-Old-Sweet-Song* letters on by 4, Chrissie?'

'PSZIW SPH WAIIX WSRK – it's pure gobbledygook.'

'Then it aint a straight modified Caesar, and it don't match them letters on the scroll of paper either.'

'But why does it have to be a coded message, Chrissie? Why couldn't it just be the combination for a lock, or... a safety deposit box, or a bank account?' Clive asked.

'Because there's only one number and then a jumble of letters. Most combination locks have numbers.'

'Yeah, I reckon Chrissie's right. Course it could be a password.'

'A password? For what, Matt? The Polyphon belonged to an era of mechanical engineering, not computing.' Clive fixed him with a straight look, a bit like his look when he'd asked what Matt planned to do after calling Raelynn Harris. It felt unnerving.

'Would it help if we knew the name of Nick's great-grandfather?' Chrissie asked.

'It might be 18 letters long,' Clive laughed.

But Chrissie was right. Hadn't Nick sent him a text asking for help tracing his great-grandparents? There'd even been the promise of a couple of pints in it. 'Yeah, I oughta get back to Nick for 'is data. He wanted me to help him do one of them on-line family searches.'

Matt sat back and relaxed. It felt cool being the expert in breaking ciphers. Who'd have thought he'd be the brains at a meeting like this? What he'd give for his mum to see, just for once, that he wasn't the waste of space she kept telling him he was – her so-called *grut lummox*.

'Are you OK, Matt? You look kind of sad?' Chrissie said.

He was saved from answering by a teenager wearing a kitchen apron and bearing a large platter of bruschetta.

CHAPTER 12

'You're quiet, Nick. Is everything OK?' Dave asked. It was Friday morning and Dave sat in the Willows van, one hand on the wheel, the other on the ignition.

'I was thinking about my ancestry,' Nick said and fastened his passenger seatbelt before adding, 'I've loaded everything. We're good for measuring up; let's go.'

'What's made you think about your ancestry?'

'My grandma died last month and it's set me wondering.'

He didn't want to mention the Polyphon. He reckoned Dave and the other carpenters would make fun of him. Mr Willows ran a forward-looking business; they even had a vacuum press and were looking to buy the latest laser engraver and cutter. And in that vein, Nick had a reputation to protect. He was a millennial, the most recent recruit to the firm. His fascination with a windup mechanism might be laughed out of the conversation.

Dave pressed the ignition, threw the van into reverse, manoeuvred and lurched forwards in low gear.

'Wooah,' Nick moaned.

Acceleration and torque launched them out of the Willows yard and the Needham Market industrial estate. Nick tried to relax.

'Sorry about your grandma. Were you close?'

'Not really. Mum was talking about her when I dropped round yesterday. Mum makes a wicked pie; killer suet crust – hey, slow down. Ughh....' He clamped his mouth shut.

Dave chuckled. 'So what did you learn?'

'That... I'm from a long line of only children on my mum's side.'

'So no cousins?'

'Only on my dad's side. My mum and her mum didn't have any brothers or sisters. In fact, I'm the first boy on her side going back at least two generations. She didn't know much about my great-grandmother.'

'So you broke the mould by being a boy?'

'Yeah, but I'm still an only child.'

He caught Dave's frown. 'It's OK; I've loads of friends.'

The journey had settled into smooth forward movement; few bends, just the straight old Stowmarket Road. They met a series of roundabouts as they entered Combs Ford. The van swayed with gyratory force as they spun off exits and headed at speed towards Great Finborough.

'So where did you get your singing voice from?' Dave asked as he steered a line through tight bends.

Nick closed his eyes and swallowed the bile. 'Mum reckons it has to have been my great-granddad, Harold.' He didn't add that his mum had told him the Polyphon had originally belonged to him.

'Why?'

It was a simple question, but not the one he'd expected to have to answer; not if he wanted to keep his fascination with the Polyphon secret.

'Yeah, well my mum doesn't know much about my great-granddad. I reckon that's why she thinks the musical streak comes from him. My mate Matt is going to look up his birth and marriage certificates, but it won't tell me what he was like.'

'You could try the National Census. When was Harold

born?'

'Mum reckons around 1900.'

'So he might just have been old enough to serve in the Great War – the 1914-18 one.'

'I hope the poor bloke didn't have to. Mum said she didn't get to see him much; I don't think she really knew him.'

Conversation died as they entered Great Finborough and Dave slowed to a less reckless speed.

'We turn off… here.' He pulled hard right and the van careered past the small green with its huge old chestnut tree. 'This is it!' he said triumphantly, and jammed on the brakes in front of a terrace of old cottages. It was obvious which cottage needed the porch repair.

Dave parked the van and Nick jumped down, relieved to be off the rollercoaster ride. A short path led to the front door and a rotting, open frame porch with a low course of bricks supporting its wooden uprights.

'It'll be the foundation and floor that's caused the rot. There'll be no damp proofing and those wood supports sit directly on the bricks,' Dave muttered.

The cottage door opened and an elderly man stepped out to greet them. 'I saw the Willows van.'

Niceties and names were quickly exchanged as they introduced themselves. It didn't take long before they were discussing his choice of wood for the open frame and the height of the brick course to support the porch.

Dave explained the importance of laying a good foundation and including a damp proof membrane. The measuring up was straightforward and Dave roughly sketched the plan while Nick took photos of the dilapidated porch.

Back in the van, Nick scrolled through the photos on

his phone. 'I don't really wanna have to lay concrete footings. I'm....'

'Not at your best laying tiles or flagstones to fit? Don't worry, we'll get Mark in to do the footings and lay the bricks and flags. Hey, and close your ruddy door. It's cold.'

Dave started the van, barely waiting for Nick to close the passenger door. 'Right, to the Poachers next!'

By the time Nick had secured his seatbelt, they were on the main road and heading towards Hitcham. Houses and bungalows hedged the road until at last they broke free of them and into the rural landscape, riding the hill crests and dipping into shallow bends. Harvested fields, some already ploughed, gently rolled as far as the eye could see.

'Wow,' Nick breathed.

'You can see why there'd be airfields out this way. If I could make this van fly....' They drove on until Dave turned sharp left at the start of a blind corner. 'This'll get us to Wattisham.'

The quiet lane twisted through tighter and tighter bends. The van swayed horribly and Nick tried to distract himself by thinking about the job ahead. He had no idea if the Poachers windows were so far gone they'd need to be replaced or if it was a case of make do and mend.

'Wooah,' he yelled as Dave misjudged his speed on a ninety-degree bend near the Baptist Chapel. They covered the last half-mile into the centre of the village in no time at all.

'Here we are; the Poachers Basket,' Dave said as he eased the van to a halt on the grass verge.

The old pub was set back a little from the sleepy road cut short by the airfield. A couple of men stood talking outside. Nick sensed Dave's excitement as they jumped down from the van and strolled over.

'I reckon that'll be Steve Corewell; he's in charge. He'll know all about the body they found.' Dave indicated a middle-aged man with a broad face and light brown hair. He was deep in conversation with a youth dressed in work clothes and trainers. A spade, shears and telescopic extending ladder lay across the wheelbarrow.

'Hi, we're from Willows. I'm Dave, and this is Nick.'

'Ah yes – the windows. Thank you; it's great to have your support. And Oakley, here, is about to clear the bramble and ivy at the back of the building. I'll walk you round the outside. You'll get an idea of the size of the job.' Steve led the way, Nick and Dave falling into line behind him. Oakley followed with the wheelbarrow.

'It looks like the standard old cottage design with a bit of an extension,' Dave said.

Nick took in the sash windows with their flaking paintwork and rotting sills. The panes of glass, some cracked, were held together by crumbling putty and whittled-thin dividers. The sliding sashes had been sealed shut by layers of paint. This was going to be a big job.

He followed round the end extension and traced along the pub's rear aspect. 'These look more recent,' he said as they passed narrow toilet windows with frosted glass.

'Yes, they smartened up the toilets when they laid this paved patio area. That'll have been about ten years ago.'

'So what was over there?' Nick pointed to a raised area covered in brambles and shrubby weeds, about thirty feet from the pub.

'I think it's where we'll find the old cesspool or septic tank.'

They walked on and gazed up at ivy-clad stucco and

cracked downpipes. Climbing tendrils had crept around sills and into crevices, and reached into the thatch overhang.

'Clearing this lot isn't a one-man job.' Nick tossed the words for anyone to hear.

Oakley grunted in agreement as he trundled the barrow behind.

'Hey, so this here'll be like a back wing. It makes the pub into a kind of L,' Dave said, a few paces ahead of Nick.

'Yes, it houses the kitchen, and there's a small room annexed to the bar. It could be used as a separate dining area. I think it was a guestroom years ago.'

'Well at least the kitchen windows are in a better state. Casements, not sashes, and they look as if they can still open.' Nick was counting windows and he'd reached double figures.

'Can we see inside, now?' Dave asked, as they left Oakley behind with his wheelbarrow and rounded the far end of the pub.

Stepping through the old front doorway and standing in the main bar felt spooky. Light filtered through the grimy sashes and cast faint shadows around the bar counter.

'It looks better in here now the boarding's down from the windows,' Steve said.

All Nick could think of was the dead man. Where had they found him? Had the body sprawled where he stood now? Maybe it had curled closer to the wood burner in the small open fireplace, or lain spread-eagled where faint footprints tracked to the centre of the dusty floor? Or....

'So where was this bloke? The dead one?' Dave asked, his voice breaking the spell.

Steve's blank expression gave nothing away.

'Look, I only want to know out of respect. If I'm

working in here, I need to know, right? I don't want to be insensitive... like dumping all our rubbish on where he was found.'

'No, it wouldn't be fitting,' Nick murmured. He nearly added it would be even less fitting to stand the radio on the exact spot and let it belt out pop and rock while they worked. But if he knew the exact spot, how would he feel? Would he skirt around it, avoid stepping on it and be unable to get it out of his mind?

'He was found in here. That's all you need to know. Let's move on.'

Dave nodded. 'Yes, I get it. This building has been standing for well over a couple of hundred years. Lots of people will have reached their natural end here.'

'Yeah, but was it supernatural?' Nick's words were out before he could stop them. He bit his tongue but he needn't have worried; Steve didn't appear to have heard him as he started the tour of the pub. It had been mostly cleared of everything, the empty rooms echoing to their footsteps. Only the small room off the bar was filled with old furnishings, stacked high like a storeroom.

Cold air, laden with the smell of mildew, surrounded them everywhere. It pervaded the emptiness and gave its signature to the Poachers. Its strength was almost tangible and it punched like a voice saying *this pub is dead. You're traipsing through past scenes from a forgotten world.*

By the time they'd finished measuring and taking photos of the worst of the windows, the morning had drifted into the afternoon and there was a danger the melancholy might seep into Nick's soul. He hummed and ran lyrics through his mind about watching where *you tread in old-timers' footsteps.*

Something caught his eye as he carried the tripod, clipboard, and laser measurer through the main bar. The natural light picked out the cast iron wood burner in the open fireplace. He paused to gaze at the fire irons and old metal bucket. Familiar shapes lurked further back in the shadows. He made out a selection of iron horseshoes resting against the soot-stained bricks in the hearth. Was there something else hiding amongst them?

'What?' he breathed, 'it can't be!' He leaned closer. It was dented and blackened, but the shape was unmistakeable. It was… Jeeeez, he was looking at the rim of a Polyphon disc.

'Come on, Nick; we've spent far too long here. Old Alfred'll think we've fallen foul to the Poacher's curse. He'll be rounding up volunteers for a search party.'

'Fat chance! No one'll volunteer to step in here. Not after what he was saying the other day.'

'Huh. Well, don't waste time looking at rusty iron in a fireplace. Leave it for now – it won't be going anywhere.'

'But–'

'That junk will be here next time; take a look then. It's time to go.' Dave led the way out through the door.

Behind him, Nick dropped to a squat, reached for the thin metal rim, grasped and pulled. Metal clanked on metal and thumped against brick. Horseshoes toppled. He stood up. It was time to stride on without a backward glance, as he held a metal Polyphon disc firmly against his clipboard.

CHAPTER 13

'At last,' Chrissie said, as she parked as close as she dared next to Ron's ancient run-around van. Saturday morning had dawned dull and overcast and the Poachers seemed to embody a broken spirit; pure sadness dressed in a cracked stuccoed coat and with rotting thatch for hair. A handful of cars and 4x4s had filled the grass verges to the sides and opposite the old pub. Clive sat next to Chrissie in the Clegg & Jax Citroen van.

'You're close, but I'm sure Ron will be able to get his van out OK.'

'There's heaps of space.'

They opened their doors, and as they got out she tried to make it seem like she had plenty of room on her side of the van. 'The thatch looks in a bad state. Jason and Caleb may have died, but it's still going to need to be done,' she said as they stood together and gazed at the pub.

'Hmm, you could be speaking motive. Now don't talk about the deaths when you're here, OK?'

'Sorry, not thinking… but if Ron or I find anything–'

'You won't. The pub's already been searched by our team.'

'Yes, but if I do….' She almost skipped away from him, excited to be getting a proper look inside. And then the memories hit, like a dense rolling fog; the horror in Steve's eyes, those pale, bare feet…. She'd expected three weeks to be long enough to blunt it all. It wasn't.

She forced a smile, conscious of her racing pulse. 'OK then, I'm heading in to find Ron and the furniture store. Good luck with clearing the brambles and ivy from round the back.' She kept her tone light, unwilling to disclose the sudden flashback and too nosey to shy away.

'Inspector! Chrissie! Good of you to come.' Steve strode out of the pub, his greeting distracting her. 'Ron's inside looking through the furniture. Just put what you think needs repairing in the main bar for me to check over. We may decide to chuck some of it out.'

'No problem; I'll leave you to give Clive his briefing.' Chrissie moved towards the pub door.

'We've an enthusiastic work party round the back to-day,' he said as she passed him.

As if on cue, a shout and clank sounded from behind the pub. A brief silence and then distant laughter followed the din. Work *party* might well be the operative word, she thought.

Chrissie stepped into the pub, leaving Clive and Steve to talk. She dreaded another flashback, and walked looking straight ahead, refusing to pause or stare at the spot where Jason Brookford had lain on the floor. 'Ron... Mr Clegg? Where are you?' she called.

She found him in a modest-sized room, off to one side where the back extension joined the main bar. Stacks of chairs and tables hemmed him into a space just inside its doorway.

'Good morning, Mrs Jax. I thought I heard you. I've made a start on what's closest.' He straightened up, one hand supporting himself on the back of a dining chair, and smiled.

She shivered. 'It's colder inside this pub than outside. So, what's the plan, Mr Clegg?' She ignored her inner voice murmuring *it was hypothermia... hypothermia.*

'I thought we'd have more space in the main bar, but I

didn't know how you'd feel about working in there.'

'We couldn't swing a cat where you are at the moment, at least not until we've got some of the chairs moved out. We use the main bar.'

She returned his smile in a business-like manner, conscious that he too must have memories, although his would stretch back further than three weeks. The thought of action steadied her mood. 'Come on then, Mr Clegg. Let's carry some of this lot into the bar.'

'Good.'

'Ah!' A thought struck. 'Is this the door you helped repair?'

'I was only about eleven at the time, but... yes; this was a guestroom back then.'

The door to the room was a simple wooden frame with four oblong panels, their bevelled edges blunted by layers of chipped paint and held by the door's rails, stiles and mullions.

'Which panel?'

'You'll need to look at both sides of the door, Mrs Jax.'

She stepped into the room and swung the door to. 'Ah,' she murmured as she spotted the extra thickness to one of the upper panels. Under the paintwork, an exactly fitting rectangle of wood had been fixed to reinforce the central unbevelled area. 'I can't see the split from the other side. I suppose the old paint covers a multitude of sins, but why did you have to reinforce this side?'

'I was told we were making the quickest repair possible, Mrs Jax. Replacing a panel takes time. There should have been a thin sheet of wood pinned to both sides, but the panel flattened and came together better than we'd expected on the saloon bar side.'

'That was lucky.'

'Yes, it was likely caused by something blunt hitting it from the guestroom side. No wood was lost, as I remember.'

'Something blunt? Like what?'

'I wouldn't know… but there was blood on the door.'

She thought for a moment. 'A head or a shoulder is blunt and… a cut on the scalp can bleed a lot.'

'And so can a nose getting broken. It was a brawl in a pub, Mrs Jax. Now let's concentrate on the task in hand.'

'Right, Mr Clegg.'

The light wasn't ideal, but at least there were bulbs in some of the sockets and the electricity was on. She counted a dozen old rickety chairs made from beech and fruitwood, and with elm seats. All of them had small wooden ball-like spindles in their backs, identifying them as Suffolk Ball Back chairs. They began by carrying chairs into the main bar.

'These ones are Mendlesham carvers,' Ron said as he ran his hand over a broken leg stretcher.

Conversation was sparse as they concentrated on assessing the chairs before examining some tables and an old settle. Nothing was beyond repair. The time flew, and Chrissie was about to suggest they stop for a break, when Steve hurried into the bar.

'Is everything all right?' She searched his face and felt dread.

His eyes spoke shock. His skin looked grey. It was a re-run of three weeks ago, except this time they both stood inside the pub.

'Do you need to sit down?' Ron asked softly.

'Yes, there're plenty of chairs. This one isn't too bad.' Chrissie moved a wooden chair closer to him 'Just sit down slowly and don't lean back… it needs some work on it.'

Steve slumped onto the proffered chair and leaned forwards, elbows on his knees and head in his hands.

'Are you all right?' she asked again.

'No, i-it's horrible. Really horrible.' He spoke into his hands without lifting his head.

'What's happened? Do we need to call an ambulance?' She glanced at Ron. It felt like déjà vu.

'No, the inspector's done all that. He's taken charge now.'

'Do you mean Clive? What's he–'

She stopped as she caught Ron's warning look.

Steve straightened up and opened his eyes. 'We took the lid off the cesspool. We had to. It was split and… we needed to see if we could make it safe; seal it off properly.'

'Is there a cesspool here?' She bit her lip and glanced at Ron.

'Yes, round the back, hidden under brambles. We couldn't just leave it once we'd found it.' Steve screwed up his eyes, as if trying to squeeze the image away.

They waited.

'We found…. There's a-a body in it.'

'What? In the cesspool? Oh my God,' Chrissie gasped.

'I thought I was going to be sick. It was awful. Clive said we were definitely looking at human remains.'

'Are you sure?' She clamped both hands to her mouth.

'Yes. You can't mistake a-a human skull.'

CHAPTER 14

Clive had been too busy to have more than a few snatched words with Chrissie, since finding the body in the cesspool on Saturday morning. It was early evening by the time a police car dropped him off in Woolpit and Chrissie, curious to the point of excitement, put her half-drunk mug of tea on the kitchen counter and hurried into the hallway.

'What a bloody awful day,' Clive murmured as they hugged each other.

'I could have come and collected you. You only had to ask.'

'I figured you and Ron'd be busy at the workshop unloading those rickety chairs.'

'We were, but it didn't take us long. Hey, tell me about your day.' She pulled away to see his face in the fast-fading daylight and caught the faintest whiff from his stale, morning work clothes.

'I'm sorry, I know it's my weekend off. But I was there; I had to get involved. Until we know more, I'm assuming the body could be connected to Jason Brookford's death, and possibly Caleb's as well. They're my cases.'

'Yes of course. It's like the place is cursed.'

She wished that sometimes he'd turn a blind eye and accept that other people could do the job until he was back on duty. She sighed and gave him a quick kiss. 'Come on, I expect you could do with a beer or a glass of wine.'

He followed her back into the kitchen. She'd been partway through preparing a meal when he'd opened the front door. Sliced and diced vegetables were heaped on a board in precooked *waiting for inspiration* mode. Pieces of free-range chicken marinated in lime and ginger, and heat radiated from the oven, ready to bake jacket potatoes.

She opened the fridge. 'I thought it wouldn't matter too much how long the chicken marinated or the potatoes baked, if you were….'

'I'm back now. A beer would be nice.'

She handed him a bottle. 'I don't think I've ever seen inside a cess…' She bit her lip. 'Will you be… are you OK to eat later?'

She watched him for a moment and recognised the controlled tightness around his jaw and mouth. It was obvious he was holding his emotions at bay and she guessed he was nowhere near ready to eat.

'It must have been horrific. I think… yes, I think I'll pour myself a small wine,' she murmured and turned the oven down. 'The food can wait.'

'Let's go and sit,' Clive said, his voice flat.

They settled next to each other on the sofa in the cosy living room. She glanced at him, concerned by his quietness and not knowing if she should stay silent or talk. He had obviously been affected by finding the body. Was it too soon to ask him about it? She waited, peaceful on the outside but on the inside, her mind almost exploding with the noise. Cesspools, cesspits and septic tanks - what was the difference? And who was this latest dead body? How had it got there? What had it looked like in the cess–

'You're frowning?' Clive's voice broke into her spaghetti maze of thought.

'What? Oh… I was just wondering….'

'I can guess. Look, I know you want to ask. And it isn't going to get any easier, so… let's get it over with.'

He swigged some beer straight from the bottle and

stood up. 'It's getting dark in here,' he murmured and switched the room lights on.

She wondered if he felt a brighter light would drive away the gloom and uninvited images from the cesspool.

'Are you sure you're OK talking about it? You don't have to; I don't want to make anything worse for you.'

'You can't make anything worse. It was disgusting, Chrissie. It stank inside that cesspool. Something like rotting cabbage and foul garlic with faeces and a bad egg mixed in for good measure.'

'Ugh – that's revolting.' She pulled a face as she imagined the filthy smelling cocktail.

'When we got the lid off, we didn't know what to expect. Obviously we looked inside. At first, all I could make out was a space about two feet deep. And dark. It seemed to have a black base. And then I realised.'

She caught her breath. 'Realised what?'

'The black base was liquid.'

'Ugh!'

'I played my torch across it to be sure, and… it was obvious from the way it reflected the light. I flashed the beam around a bit more and saw something on the surface.'

He paused, as if gathering his thoughts before sitting down next to her again.

'Go on, don't stop. Sorry. You don't have to say, not if you….' She bit her lip.

'It was brownish, the colour of sewage… but I knew. You always know. It was a human head.'

'Oh my God!'

'It was the back of a head, like a brown dome. The face was down in the liquid. I could make out some neck vertebrae… and maybe a shoulder blade. It was all coated in brown stuff - kind of shrink-wrapped and bony.'

'That's... it's horrific; really awful for you, Clive.'

She was repulsed and distressed, but like a child hiding behind a sofa from a TV, she felt compelled to catch more of the horror. 'Go on,' she whispered.

'I figure air in the lungs or gas in the bowel kept some of the body afloat when it was... dropped in. But most of it was submerged in the sewage. We've found that out,' Clive almost spat the words.

She screwed up her eyes to block out the image. 'So you think....? But doesn't the liquid in the sewage drain away over time? Doesn't it turn into something solid?'

'No you're forgetting it's in a sealed concrete tank – that's what a cesspool is. That's why they have to be emptied regularly when they're in use. They simply fill up with liquid and solid matter. Solids are referred to as sludge.'

'Sludge? It must have been nauseating.' She found his hand and squeezed it gently.

'Yes. The forensic pathologist said that because the tank is buried in the ground, the cold slows any natural breakdown by microbes. And the oxygen-loving microorganisms can't get to work on it because of the liquid and compacted solids, so it just sort of stays there. Huh, and remember the broken lid? Rainwater may have got in.'

'Which is why you looked! So what happens now?'

'You may well ask. Today was like *pass the parcel*. The police surgeon called the forensic pathologist because it wasn't a recent death. Then the forensic pathologist asked for the forensic anthropologist because all he could make out was... mainly bone.'

'Wooah... and the SOC team?'

'They'll be working with the forensic anthropologist.

They've had to get in special equipment to suck out the old sewage and whatever else is in the cesspool. They'll filter it all and we'll see what they find.'

It was sickening. Phrases like *it'll be like panning for gold* and *won't it be preserved like those ancient bodies found in peat bogs*, popped into Chrissie's mind – protective, sanitised, replacement images to distract her from the true ghastliness of it all.

'How long do you think the body's been in there?'

'I don't know. The pathologist said to think in years.'

'So when did they stop using the cesspool?'

'Good question. Someone in our work party seemed to think Wattisham got a main sewer in the sixties. But you have to pay to be connected to the main sewer, so not everyone was connected. There are still houses in the village with septic tanks.'

'So,' Chrissie sipped her wine, 'this... this body you found today. It could have been there since the sixties; that's over fifty years. How can you identify someone after all that time?'

Clive shrugged, and then swigged more beer.

'Is it even possible?' She squeezed his hand again.

'Maybe. There'll be basics like is it a male or female skeleton? We'll get a rough age range; teeth, skeletal clues like past fractures... that kind of thing. We'll look for matches against missing persons from over the years. And if we're lucky, we may find something with a name or identification on it in the sewage.'

She raised her glass. 'Well, I'll drink to striking it lucky.'

He smiled, not the humorous smile with the creases reaching his eyes, but something more distant and mechanical.

She put her glass on the coffee table and leaned closer to slip her arm around him. 'Poor you. What a truly terrible day it's been. How do you cope with all the horror?'

Her nose caught the faint smell from his old jeans - musty with a hint of foul garlic and, oh no... what had he said earlier? *Foul garlic and faeces*?

'The key is not to dwell on the images and smells. Just to stay focused on the investigation,' he said.

'But it permeates!' she squeaked.

'I know.'

'I meant it whiffs. You need to change.'

'What?'

She saw the struggle in his face as he pulled his mind from a distant place. She smiled. 'You need a shower, Clive. Clean clothes and then food.'

'Yes, sorry, Chrissie. I think my sense of smell must have curled up and died today.' He got up slowly from the sofa. 'I've been meaning to ask how you're getting on with your history of the pub. You were going to look into it.' His tone was casual, but she couldn't miss his real meaning.

'I haven't got far with it at all. I've been side-tracked by Nick's Polyphon and the coded message.'

'Yes, but you will tell me anything you think might be relevant, won't you?'

'Of course, but relevance may depend on how long that body's been in the cesspool.'

He looked at her for a moment, frowned, nodded and then headed into the hallway and up the narrow stairs to take a shower.

CHAPTER 15

Where had Maisie disappeared to? Matt propped himself up in bed against his pillow and opened his laptop. His mouth felt stale and dry while a steel band tightened around his forehead. He blinked and checked the time readout on his laptop. Pixels! Sunday morning had leached into midday. That would explain it; she must have left earlier.

But he didn't recall her saying goodbye. Questions fought with memories of cans of lager - a six-pack and countless rum 'n colas drunk between them.

Without really thinking, he logged on to a favourite news network.

The page loaded. A headline leapt from his screen and grabbed his attention. *Body Found in Cesspool. Yesterday morning, volunteers clearing the grounds of a disused Wattisham pub had the shock of their lives when....*

His bedroom door opened.

'Hi!' Maisie's whisper filled his world.

'Mais?' The news headline was forgotten as he focused on Maisie and felt a rush of confused desire. 'I thought you'd gone.'

'Shush.' She put a finger to her lips and raised her eyebrows as she closed the door behind her. 'Your mum aint up. We don't want to wake her, right?'

'Dead right. But you're... all dressed, Mais?'

'Yeah. Showered and dressed. I got to get back for Gran's sixtieth by one. You're givin' me a lift. Remember?'

Maisie's bleached hair seemed wilder and spikier than the previous evening. 'What you starin' at?'

'Nothin', Mais.'

His head throbbed. He closed his laptop, resigned himself to her leaving and swung his legs out from under the duvet. The threadbare carpet felt harsh to his bare feet. Unwashed clothes lay discarded in heaps. They separated him from Maisie standing near the door. His comic-strip imagination saw the carpet as a sea awash with perilous icebergs. Daylight filtered through the curtains, casting red and blue tints where the faded Spiderman design played on the sea. Why the spam had he drunk all six cans of lager?

He staggered and swayed as he pulled on his pants, jeans and sweatshirt, shoved his feet into trainers, and grabbed the memory stick from his backpack.

'What you want that stick for?' she whispered.

'The Academy library, if I can get in.'

'But it's Sunday.'

'Yeah. Spammin' hell, I nearly forgot this!' He swept up his Utterly Academy *Computing & IT Assistant Demonstrator* ID pass.

They crept into the stale hallway corridor and out through the kitchen, barely glancing at the sink choked with plates. His Vespa stood padlocked against the bungalow's side wall, the blackberry bubblegum bodywork in vibrant contrast to the brickwork stained from past cistern overflows. Without a word he unlocked the Vespa, slipped his helmet on and waited while Maisie climbed onto the saddle behind him. Seconds later, he pushed the start button and sped out of Tumble Weed drive; away from his mum's modest semi-detached bungalow, the Flower Estate and Stowmarket.

The Vespa's engineering gave him the freedom and elegance to weave his way out of the warren of cul-de-sacs. Speed gave him balance and with it came confidence and exhilaration. His hangover was literally blown away, his tubby body forgotten as his mood shot into the stratosphere.

He rode the best part of a circuit; out to Stowupland to drop Maisie home, then back under the A14 and along country lanes before slowing to turn into the Academy car park. He realised, as he locked the scooter and stowed his helmet, that his Vespa had pushed his comic-strip fantasies into soft focus.

Chrissie had once said that having an absent dad and a sadistic bully for an older brother were bound to have created a vacuum in his early life; something to fill with comic-strip fantasies. But times had changed and Matt had read up about vacuums, and he was pretty scammin' sure the Flower Estate would have needed to be in outer space for such a vacuum.

Chrissie had laughed and said something about *emotional vacuums* and then corrected it to *deserts... emotional deserts* and *not to take things so literally.*

'Yeah, well, me Vespa aint no camel,' he murmured as he cut towards a side entrance in the sprawl of Academy buildings. He paused to stare up at the main block, an Edwardian country residence built by the long dead Sir Raymond Utterly.

A feeling akin to peace washed over him. He really did belong - one session a week supervising students in the computer lab. More importantly, Damon couldn't watch him here. Currently, Matt had a military records and ancestry site he wanted to use. Damon would never have paid their subscription, but the Academy library had recently joined.

He took a deep breath and slid his ID pass through the door lock reader. *Click*, he pushed the scuffed door and stepped into a passage. Grey, heavy-duty carpet led him and his memories to a wide corridor with a wooden-boarded floor. Soon it gave way to pale marble tiles; he had reached the old mansion building. Information boards were busy with notices but the space felt deserted. His trainers squeaked in the silence as he climbed the main stairs to the library on the first floor.

It only took him a moment to key in the lock sequence and slip into the library. He glanced around. Thank blog! He had the place to himself. Weak afternoon sunlight flooded in through tall windows. Instinctively he chose a computer station near one of them. It meant he didn't have to switch on the library lights and inadvertently announce his presence to the outside world. Being secretive was his default position. How else could he have survived his childhood?

The computer booted up slowly while the dusty smell of old books, wooden floorboards and gothic-styled ceiling beams went a little way to sooth his impatience.

'At last!' He signed in, inserted the memory stick and located a file he'd previously created named *Nick's old fam*.

Nick had told him that according to his mother, the Polyphon had originally belonged to his great-grandfather and had passed down through the female side of the family. This nugget of information, along with the few family names that Nick's mum could remember, was the sum total Matt had to work with. He already pictured the file's contents in his photographic memory but he opened it anyway. It was somewhere to store his findings in an orderly system. He scanned through his bullet points:

1. Nick Cowley, born 1990
2. Nick's mum – Phyllis, born 1962

3. Nick's dad - John Cowley.

3. Nick's mum's mum (his grandmother) was Louisa.

4. Louisa died in 2014 and left the Polyphon to Nick.

5. Louisa's mum (Nick's great-grandmother) was Alice.

6. Alice married Harold in the 1930s.

7. Harold - probably the first owner of the Polyphon.

8. Alice and Harold now dead.

'Hmm,' Matt sighed, 'but it's really 'bout the Polyphon.'

He supposed he should start with either the first or last owner and work forwards or backwards. He could discount Nick so it was either the long-dead great-granddad Harold, or Harold's daughter, the recently dead Louisa.

'But bloggin' hell, I aint got no last names for Louisa or Harold.' He rubbed his head and pulled at his short sandy beard. The long lines and joins of the floorboards drew his eyes while the family tree turned into an algorithm in his head.

'Yeah, I got it now; Louisa's maiden name'll tell me her dad's last name.' He reckoned if the gods of blog were looking down kindly, then it should be one and the same name.

'Yeah an' Nick said his mum thought it sounded somethin' like *Rome*.'

But he needed a way in, as well as the algorithm. The words *died recently* spun in his head. 'Spammin' pixels. Death announcements!'

Fired with his plan, he logged into the Eastern Anglian Daily Tribune site and clicked the deaths announcements tab. He keyed in the year *2014*, and then selected the months *August* and *September*, narrowing the search to

Louisa. It didn't take him long to find the announcement for a Louisa who was a *loving mother of Phyllis and grand-mother of Nicholas....* The announcement gave him the date of her death along with her full name and age. Some simple maths told him the year she was born. He was ready to search for her birth record and birth name. He was on a roll.

So, should he use the freebmd.org.uk site or chance his luck on an ancestry site - the one he'd managed to fa-miliarise himself with the library's membership login and password? He'd asked Rosie, his favourite library assistant, about old Sir Raymond Utterly. It had been more of a chat-up line than genuine curiosity, but it had resulted in her logging in to the site and showing it off to him. And of course, he'd watched, automatically memorising the pass-word in the neat, precise movement of her fingers across her keyboard.

'It's great, isn't it? See how easy it is to get his mili-tary records as well,' she'd said.

He logged in now and using a combination of search-es, matching the names and dates, he found Louisa's maid-en name through the marriages and births records.

'Roan!' he said in triumph, 'Yeah, s'pose it could sound like Rome.' And great-granddad Harold? Well, his full moniker was Harold Bertram Roan.

The military war records he accessed via the site gave Matt his next break. Harold would have been just about old enough to catch the tail end of WW1, and he reckoned a Suffolk lad would have signed up to The Suffolk Regiment. It turned out he was right; there'd been two Roans – an HB Roan and a BS Roan.

'Brothers?' Matt breathed.

But a few more clicks told him they weren't. Their

WW1 records showed that the HB (Harold Bertram) Roan had joined up in Ipswich aged eighteen. BS Roan was already a brigadier.

'So Nick's great-granddad joined in May 1918.' The war records showed he'd gone for basic training, then communications training, and joined the battalion headquarters as a Morse code operator. He'd ended the war in France in Haudricourt, November 11th 1918.

'An' he were a hero – he were awarded two medals: a Victory medal and the British War medal.' A bit more research and Matt realised the medals were awarded for serving in the war zone, in Harold's case, France. There were no specific superhero accounts. No comic-strip material. Matt felt disappointed.

The other Roan, the BS Roan, turned out to have been an uncle. Matt supposed the uncle's rank must have been key to Harold surviving. It was probably why the raw Harold had been posted to the relative safety of battalion headquarters; that, along with his Morse coding skills.

'Yeah, but there aint nothin' 'bout him bein' a musician. So what were he doin' after the war?'

The National Census records weren't available online beyond 1911 so Matt couldn't find out from them what Harold did for a living post war. 'S'pose I'll have to see what's written on the births and marriage records.'

It took him a while, but eventually he was confident he was looking at the records for Nick's Harold Bertram Roan. His marriage record of 1931 to Alice had his *Rank or Profession* recorded as *Teacher*. 'Well that aint obviously musical… and Harold's dad weren't no musician either. He were also a *Teacher; mathematics* accordin' to the record.'

But there was more. Alice and Harold's daughter

Phyllis was born in 1933 and her birth record documented Harold as the father and once again, his *Rank or Profession* as *Teacher*.

It took Matt another hour, but by the time he sat back and stretched his arms in the air, he'd learnt that Harold had died at the ripe old age of 81 and Alice, although ten years his junior, had died the following year after no mention of music, musicians or musical instruments.

'Blog, I need a lager.' He groaned and eased the stiffness in his neck and shoulders with some stretching and twisting movements. 'Yeah… an' Nick owes me a couple a' pints.' It was time to save his changes and additions to the *Nick's old fam* file, eject the stick and contact Nick.

CHAPTER 16

It was Monday morning, and Nick cupped his coffee mug in his hands as he stood studying Dave's drawings for the new porch. It was certainly going to make the terraced cottage in Great Finborough look more cared for.

Dave, who was sitting at the table in the office-cum-restroom, glanced up from the computer screen. 'I'll ask Mark to use the old bricks. The mortar's crumbling, so I reckon they'll clean up easy enough. Hmm, let me have another look at the photos.'

While Dave concentrated on the photos, Nick's attention was focused on the plans for the wooden frame supporting the porch roof. He was more interested in the base beams and simple crossbeams, than details about waterproof membranes and concrete footings.

'Did you hear they found a body in the Poachers cesspool at the weekend?' Dave's words were delivered in a studiedly casual tone. Nick sensed he was fishing for information.

'No,' he lied. He wasn't going to let on he'd learnt it from Matt's phone call, late Sunday afternoon.

'It were on the local news site,' Matt had said, 'but I aint callin' 'bout that. Your great-granddad got a couple a WW1 medals. Aint that cool? Yeah, an' listen coz I got some more facts an' dates for you.'

Nick had found it difficult to concentrate on the details from Matt's search, mainly because all the while in the background, Jake had been playing a new riff, and visions of cesspools swirled in his mind.

'But were there any musicians?' he'd cut into Matt's

preamble.

'Nah, mate.'

'Look – sorry but you've caught me at a bad moment. How about we meet up down the Nags Head? Monday at six, OK? Tell me everything then.'

Dave's voice now interrupted any further memories of the call.

'Just as well we took the window measurements on Friday. It could be weeks before they let anyone near the place again,' Dave said, dragging Nick back to the workshop and the subject of the Poachers.

'What? Yeah, right. But… how does a body get in a cesspool?' He tried to sound cool.

'How'd I know? Just don't say jinxed. If anyone else says the place is jinxed or spooked, old Alfred'll put a veto on us repairing the windows. Have you drawn up the plans yet?'

'Give me a chance, Dave. You've been on that thing for ages.' He eyed the computer.

'You could've drawn them by hand. We always used to.'

'Hmm, well not today. Anyway, I thought we were supposed to do the community stuff in our own time.' He rinsed his mug in the sink and went back through to the workshop and Tim, leaving Dave to the porch plans.

Nick had been working with Tim on some bespoke wooden stable doors, and as he pictured the black iron bolts and T hinges complimenting the oak boards, he remembered the Polyphon disc.

His face flamed. Shite - the blackened disc in the Poachers fireplace! He'd slipped it into his driver's door pocket, the obvious place for safe keeping on Friday when

114

he'd driven back to Bury. No point in letting it slide around on the passenger seat or into the footwell. But being out of sight had pushed it out of his mind. Hell, what had he been thinking? He'd as good as stolen it. Or had he?

Wasn't it an unwanted, tarnished piece of metal, barely recognisable as a Polyphon disc? Surely it was more of a rescue than a theft?

'Hmm, don't answer that,' he muttered.

'Don't answer what?' Tim asked as he handed Nick more lengths of oak, cut ready to tongue and groove on the router table.

'I... I was wondering about the horses. I mean the oak doors. It must be one hell of a smart set up.'

'Mrs Lamanby likes her horses. I s'pect they get more fussing than her husband.'

'Well, this is one stable I definitely have to see.'

'She wants the doors fitted by the end of the week,' Tim said by way of an answer.

If it had been Dave, Nick guessed he'd have been told all about Mrs Lamanby by now, but it wasn't Tim's way.

For the next forty minutes, Nick worked at the router table, changing the cutting head between running all the boards through for the tongues and then the grooves. Across the workshop, Tim cut oak braces on the table saw to strengthen and hold the boards when slotted together.

'So why're we only lining the bottom doors with heavy duty beech ply?' Nick asked in an effort to stop his mind from wandering back to the disc.

'It's what the lady ordered. They're what the horse is more likely to back into or kick.'

'Right. And also chew, yeah?' Nick said, referring to the anti-chew strip on the drawings.

By mid-afternoon they had joined the oak boards into stable door widths, slotting the tongue and groove joints together before holding them tight with cramps. It felt like a production line as they worked together nailing on the wooden braces and removing the cramps.

He was thankful to escape when they broke for tea. 'Got to make a call,' he said, and slipped outside to his Fiesta, parked next to the security link fence. He reached into the door's pocket, his excitement laced with guilt. The disc felt cold against his fingertips. He held it by the rim, balancing it between his hands, turning and tilting it this way and that. Was it the same size as his other discs? Would it play on his Polyphon?

He squinted as the light played across the surface; he tried to convince himself that he could just about make out the faint outlines of yellow painted lettering on one side under the dirt and grime. He guessed it would be the title of the tune. Dimples of dirt filled the holes where the metal had been punched through to make the P-shaped prongs. He turned the disc over – no P shapes; just flattened, bent and broken projections, blunted by time. 'What a mess. And it's buckled,' he whispered.

But his Polyphon was still with Ron at the Clegg & Jax workshop. Without it, he couldn't tell if the disc would even fit. He checked the time – three o'clock. He finished work at four, so he'd have two hours after work before he was due to meet Matt in the Nags Head. It should be long enough to hurry over and catch Ron and Chrissie.

He slid the disc back into the door pocket. He could always return it to the fireplace if it wasn't the right size or too damaged for repair. It felt like a plan, and he texted Chrissie before heading back to work on the stable doors.

It was just after four-thirty by the time Nick's Fiesta rocked along the ruts in the Clegg & Jax entrance track. This time he wasn't burdened with the Polyphon boxes when he pushed the heavy door and stepped into their old barn.

'Hi!' he called and closed the door behind him, holding the disc close to his chest.

'The kettle's on. Tea OK for you?' Chrissie called from across the barn.

'That'd be great. More Ball Backs, I see, Mr Clegg.' Nick indicated the rickety chairs stacked two or three high just inside the door.

'Yes, Nick. They're the ones we're repairing for the Poachers.'

'Ah – yes, I heard about Saturday; the er… cesspool.'

'Hmm, the body. Best not….' Ron's words drifted like a thought. 'You know,' he said in a brighter tone, 'I'm pleased you've come round. I've some things to show you.' He smiled from his work stool and laid an arthritic hand on the original maker's case, open on the workbench in front of him.

'I see you've got the liner out.' Nick hurried past the pillar drill and the shelves of oils and polishes, stains and varnishes. 'You know I've got something to show you as well?'

'Mrs Jax said you were dropping round.'

Nick placed the blackened disc next to the liner on the workbench.

'Tea's up,' Chrissie said, carrying brimming mugs.

'I want to know if it's the right size. If it'll play on my Polyphon.'

No one spoke for a moment.

'What is it?' Chrissie asked.

'Isn't it obvious? It's a music disc for a Polyphon.'

'Really? It doesn't look much like these ones.' Chrissie lifted a clean metal disc from the top of a neat pile in the centre of the workbench.

'That's because I found it in a fireplace.'

'A fireplace? What fireplace?' Ron asked softly.

He felt his face flame. 'At the Poachers, behind the wood burner. It was last Friday when Dave and I dropped by and measured up the windows for repair or replacing.'

He didn't like the way Chrissie frowned. It made him feel light-fingered; a thief.

'It looks as if it's been in the fireplace a long time,' Ron murmured.

'It's very sooty and tarnished and bent, and... oh my God, Nick!'

'What?'

'It could have been there for years! Don't you see? It could be....'

'It could be what, Chrissie?' Nick prompted, impatient and confused.

'I was going to say evidence but that sounds stupid.'

'Evidence for what, Mrs Jax? If you're talking about the dead man on the floor, I thought the police went through everything with their SOC team.' Ron's words were calm and deliberate.

'Yes, they will have, Mr Clegg. But Jason Brookford died from... alcohol and the cold; not from being beaten to death with a fire iron from the wood burner, or falling on a dirty old metal disc. His death was clean; recent. The SOC team may not have thought this old disc relevant enough to dust or swab it.'

Nick frowned. 'I don't get what you're trying to say, Chrissie.'

'The body in the cesspool has been there for a while. Maybe years. The whole pub could have been a crime scene back then. I think we should ask Clive if… if he needs to see the disc first. He may want it checked over by the SOC team.'

'You think it could be connected to the body in the cesspool?' Nick couldn't conceal his disbelief.

'No, but if you want to keep it, I think you should OK it with Clive first.'

'Chrissie may be right, Nick. Let Clive decide. There's plenty else to keep you occupied with your Polyphon. Let me show you.'

'But this is amazing,' Nick whispered as Ron showed him the roll of paper found in the keyhole, the two holes in the sides of the liner for the panel pins to lift it out, and the old piece of paper, the size of a luggage label found under the liner.

'Wow!' he breathed.

'Yes, and some of the song titles on the discs are listed on that old piece of paper,' Chrissie said, before sipping her tea.

'It could be a coincidence, but they seem to be the discs with notes missing. Isn't that right, Mrs Jax?'

'Yes, and the rolled-up scrap from the keyhole has the number 4 and then a mix of 18 letters from the first 7 letters of the alphabet.'

'You mean A B C D E F G, Chrissie?'

She nodded.

'But….' It seemed obvious, 'but won't they be musical notes?' Nick said.

He caught Ron's frown.

'They're the major notes, the white ones on a piano, Mr Clegg. They're the building blocks in a scale. Could it be a tune written in letters?'

'Of course!' Chrissie as good as shouted her delight.

'But what does it mean?' Nick didn't get any of it.

'We haven't a clue. We thought the number 4 referred to the song title against the number 4 on the list. *Love's Old Sweet Song*. That's basically as far as we got.'

'Yes, well summed up, Mrs Jax.'

'But why write a load of musical notes and stuff it in the keyhole? It's weird,' Nick reasoned, mentally humming the 18 notes in the order written and getting a tuneless sequence.

'How do we find out the names of the notes missing on the discs?' Ron asked.

'By ear; I'll play them and work out what's missing.'

'I expect you'll want to take the Polyphon home to do that.'

'Yes, Mr Clegg. It could take a while.'

'You know, I'll be sorry to see it go....'

'No, it'll free up a workbench. And if you're taking the Polyphon with you, I don't think you'll miss this old disc from the Poachers,' Chrissie said with efficient briskness. 'If it's OK with you I'll put it in a plastic bag and take it for Clive?'

Nick nodded. He felt mentally exhausted, and he still had Matt to meet up with in the Nags Head. WW1 medals, family histories and lager for Matt; he'd definitely need a pint of beer, himself.

CHAPTER 17

Chrissie bagged up the grimy metal disc after Nick said his goodbyes and carried the Polyphon cases out to his car. She felt like a member of the SOC team, except her bag wasn't an evidence bag and there was no label to fill in. But what would she have written?

'Is something troubling you, Mrs Jax?'

'I was wondering how to make it clear why Nick's prints will be all over this disc.'

'And yours too. Don't forget you picked it up.'

She laughed. 'Well, thanks for reminding me. At least I can tell Clive before he tells me.'

She caught the faint sounds from outside as Nick started the Fiesta and drove away. He had said something about meeting up with Matt in the Nags Head for some family history updates. She was curious, and part of her wanted to tag along. She'd even been on the point of asking, except the disc felt more urgent. Even now it made her feel uneasy beyond reason.

'Isn't it time you got off home as well?' Ron said.

Ten minutes later she was in her TR7 and heading home to Woolpit, the disc safe on the rubber mat in the passenger footwell. Would Clive think she was crazy for bringing it back for him? The Crazy Bag Lady? She smiled as she imagined Matt using the title for her.

Once inside, she put the disc on her busy hall table, nudging along keys and post to make space for it. As it was, the plastic bag pushed Bill's photo frame towards the edge. She paused to look at his face smiling at her, the wind lifting his dark hair.

She stood lost in thought, wondering what Bill would make of her now. If he came back to this world, would he recognise in his widow the accountant he'd fallen in love with and married? She figured that if he'd been asked to predict any change in her career, he'd never have said carpentry.

The sound of a latch turning cut short her speculation. The front door opened.

'Clive, you're home.' She smiled warmly at him.

'Hi. Is everything all right?'

'Yes, of course. Why?'

'Well, you're just standing in the hall.'

'I'm fine. Stop being such a detective.' She felt stupid. Wasn't that part of his attraction? 'Actually, if you must know, I brought this back for you and… it set me thinking.'

She indicated the plastic bag sitting awkwardly on the end of the narrow hall table.

He reached to pick it up.

'Don't touch what's inside until I've explained about it.'

She led the way into the kitchen.

'Whatever have you got in here?' Clive said, peering into the bag.

'It's from the fireplace in the Poachers saloon bar.'

'What?'

'I didn't take it. Nick was there on Friday with Dave. As you know, Willows & Son are donating their time and repairing the windows. Nick recognised it as he walked past the fireplace.'

'So Nick didn't just *recognise* it, he *took* it?'

'Well ye-e-e-s. He realised it was a Polyphon disc, so he picked it up and brought it home. He said he *rescued* it.'

'OK, so why have you got it?'

'He brought it along to the workshop today. He wanted to see if it was the right size to play on his Polyphon.'

'And is it?'

'Yes, it's pretty much the same size as his discs, but we didn't try it. You'll understand why. Take a look.'

She watched as Clive slid it partially out of the plastic bag. She couldn't help noticing how he held it by the plastic, balancing and turning it this way and that, automatically avoiding any contact with his hands.

'It looks as if it's been used to clear the ash out of the wood burner,' he said.

'That's probably why it's bent.'

'Hmm, I haven't seen Nick's Polyphon or discs, but I can't imagine this making music. He must be mad to think he could get this to play. Why'd you think I'd want it, Chrissie?'

'It's....' She took a deep breath, 'it's just that it's old. No... listen. The body in the cesspool has been there a while. You said maybe fifty years. So, what might have been in the Poachers at the time could be part of... the old crime scene?'

He sighed and slipped the disc back into its plastic bag. 'I think I need a beer. How about you?'

She watched him open the fridge door, its inner light gently catching the weariness in his face. His striped beige shirt looked tired, creased on the back from his car seat. She guessed she was irritating him, but surely it was just a case of finding the right words; she'd started at the end when she should have kicked off with the beginning. She ignored his offer of a beer and tried again.

'Ron remembers hearing a musical box, maybe a

Polyphon, being played in the pub when he was a kid. It would have been back in the early 60s.'

She knew she'd got his attention by the way he frowned.

'Ron also remembers some fights in the pub, or rather he mentioned a particular fight. He only said about it because he helped repair a door afterwards. It's what got him interested in carpentry.'

'OK… so?'

'The man in the fight was never seen again. Ron was only a kid at the time, but according to him the police weren't involved and it wasn't spoken about afterwards.'

'Are you suggesting the man's our body in the cesspool?'

'No, but if he is, anything dating from the incident wasn't looked at back then as part of a crime scene. I wondered if you'd want the opportunity of looking at this before Nick tries to clean it up and straighten out its prongs. That's all.'

Clive nodded slowly.

'Oh, and it'll have Nick's fingerprints, and probably some of mine on it as well.' She shrugged and pulled a face – a sort of *I rest my case* and *I'm sorry* kind of gesture.

She left Clive to mull through what she'd said while she checked inside the fridge and decided what to cook for super. 'Do you fancy the leftover chicken? It could be quite tasty in a one-pan rice, veg and chorizo dish. Or we could stroll up to the White Hart?'

'What? Oh, not now I'm home. I think I'd rather eat here.'

He smiled. She saw it reach his eyes. So he wasn't annoyed about the disc. She relaxed.

'Perhaps I will have that drink while I cook,' she murmured. 'How was your day? Any progress on your cases?'

'Yes, we've finally got all Jason Brookford's bank statements, mobile calls and text logs; that's from both of his phones. But the real surprise is the contents of Caleb Coddins' hipflask. Remember the pathologist thought he might have been poisoned? Well, the labs have prioritised it.'

'And so they should. His getting caught in the reed beds has turned political, what with the plans to relocate the Search & Rescue helicopter.'

Clive nodded. 'Well, some won't like the result then. It seems he was poisoned. The damson gin in his hipflask contained cytisine.'

'Cytisine? What's cytisine?'

'A poison. It's found in laburnum trees and it's used in some meds as an aid to stop smoking.'

'But…. So do you think he was murdered?'

'Judging by the concentration in his hipflask, yes, unless he was trying to kill himself. So now we have to search for his phone in the reed beds, and request his bank statements and mobile call and text logs.'

'The modern process of investigating death,' she sighed before adding, 'So how does cytisine kill you?'

'The pathologist said in high doses it makes you sleepy, possibly even inducing coma and convulsions. And it can upset your stomach – vomiting and diarrhoea – which is exactly what you wouldn't want if you were stuck in cold water and becoming hypothermic.'

'The poor man. Some comforting swigs from his hipflask, then after a nice warming glow from the damson gin, the laburnum gets to work. But his phone – won't the water have destroyed it?'

'The phone, yes, but the SIM card... I don't know. They can be quite resilient. We might be lucky.'

Something occurred to Chrissie as questions bubbled from her subconscious. She spoke as ideas took shape in her mind.

'It must be difficult not knowing right from the start if you're dealing with a murder. How do you decide how much crime scene forensics you need?'

'If it's an unexpected or unexplained death then it'll be basic forensics from the scene. You know... like bagging the empty bottle of pills on the bedside table, or photos of the body where it's been found. But there'll be a coroner's post mortem with toxicology studies from blood and maybe stomach. I suppose it depends on how suspicious the officer or doctor at the scene is... of foul play.'

'So with limited police resources, how much in-depth inspection will Jason Brookford's accounts and phone records get? I assume his was an unexpected death?'

'Yes, he died of hypothermia and alcohol but there are still questions surrounding it, such as how he came to be inside the locked pub and what happened to his shoes. So – I guess it'll be a cursory look at his accounts and a closer look at phone and text records over the twenty-four hours before he died. If there's nothing suspicious then we report back to the coroner and move on to our next case. Why?'

'Who takes the cursory look at his accounts?'

'It'll be me or one of the team. If I want a more in-depth analysis, we can use forensic accountant consultants or the fraud team.'

The idea taking shape in her mind felt more concrete.

Thinking about Bill earlier had planted a seed. He wouldn't have predicted carpentry, but what about forensic accountancy? But she had to approach this the right way - from the beginning. She made her decision as she chopped and then sweated an onion in a frying pan before adding a cup of dried rice.

'So someone like Matt is unofficial. He's not on a list of computing specialist consultants or part of the Cyber Crime police staff investigators. Not on the payroll.'

'Whatever's made you bring Matt into this?'

She heard the slight surprise in his voice and stirred the rice harder. Where was she going, indeed?

'I suppose I'm asking if you use trusted experts *off the record* and is Matt a case in point? He doesn't say and you don't say… but…?'

'Hold on, Chrissie.'

'No, let me finish. What I want to ask is… would it help if I cast an eye over some accounts for you? Anything suspicious and you'd know to refer it to your police forensic accountant staff or consultants or fraud squad… or whoever you use. It strikes me that half your work is constrained by cost and the other half by resources and police numbers, right?'

Had she overstepped a line? Now that she'd blurted out her offer there was no way back. She bit her lip and hid her unease by pouring water onto the rice and stirring it madly while she waited for Clive's response.

His chair scraped back on the tiles. She heard his beer bottle go down on the scrubbed pine table.

'There are diplomas in forensic accounting – online ones,' he said standing behind her and sliding his arms around her waist. 'I've often wondered if a side line in forensic accounting could supplement your carpentry business.'

'Really?'

'Well, no. I've wondered if it would satisfy your nosey gene, realised you'd be good at it and *then* wondered if it would supplement your carpentry business.'

'Right,' she laughed, 'but you mean it wouldn't bother you if I was snooping around the accounts of suspects in police cases?' She turned in his arms to face him.

'Not if you've got the diploma. You're already an accountant – you can get your forensic certification after three years' forensic experience.'

'Have you been looking this up?'

'Yes, Chrissie.'

'Oh.'

She'd never in a million years expected the conversation to take a turn like this.

'But I don't want to stop being a carpenter. It's changed my life.' She felt her face flush. Bill dying was what had changed her life. Why else would she have entered an emotional wasteland, a life crisis, and only found her way through by taking up carpentry?

'Don't you see? Carpentry has made my life unpredictable, more creative. For a start, I would never have met you.'

'No, but you don't have to stop being a carpenter.'

'Didn't you just say something about needing three years' experience in forensic accounting before I'm certified?'

And then her brain geared up a level; she didn't need him to answer, not when she remembered there was such a thing as working part-time and job sharing. It might take her years longer than the three he'd mentioned, but it would be possible. She frowned and pulled a face.

'I tell you what… and this is….' He paused as if hesitating to finish what he was about to say.

'Highly irregular?' she suggested.

'You don't know what I'm going to say.'

'You're going to say that I can take a peep at Jason Brookford's accounts if I sign up for a distance learning diploma in forensic accounting.'

'Am I?'

'Yes.'

CHAPTER 18

Matt felt good about himself. He'd wowed Nick with his ancestry search findings, down the Nags Head on Monday. There hadn't been much meat on the bone in terms of detail but Nick had been impressed, and Matt had enjoyed the promised pint as a reward. He reckoned if Nick could come up with more family details, then more searching was in order and more reward pints would follow. That had been two days ago. He pulled his thoughts back to the here and now, and Balcon & Mora.

'They're sayin' the skeleton they found were male and aged between twenty-five and fifty,' Matt said, before leaning back in his plastic stacker chair and putting his hands behind his head. It was the closest he'd get to stretching expansively in the cramped office. He knew he didn't need to explain what he was referring to. Damon would be keeping half an eye on his screen through administrator access.

'They haven't said how long it's been in the cesspool,' Damon murmured.

'Nah, an' what I don't get is why the sewage dint preserve 'im like them bog people?' He turned his attention back to the Wednesday lunchtime October 1st, *Breaking News* splashed across his screen.

Behind him, Damon's keyboard pattered quietly.

'Right, Matt; I've looked it up. It says bog bodies get naturally mummified by being submerged in peat bogs that have sphagnum moss. And also, the water's acidic.'

'So how's it work then?'

'The bacteria don't like it. According to this, the pickling effect of the acid and a kind of tanning effect to the skin from the sphagnum moss preserves the body and turns it a peat colour. Ye-e-s, and calcium is leached from the bones and makes them soft.'

'Tannin'? You mean like in sunbathin'?'

'No, as in leather. Which reminds me; a woman phoned – you told her you were from a lost property disposal service. Remember?'

How could he forget? Clive had said he hadn't thought his plan through.

'Yeah, but that were more than a week back.'

'Well, she's left a message on the answerphone.'

'What? When?'

'Yesterday.'

'Tuesday? But what she say?'

'Basically *where are my cowboy boots?* And *why's no one got back to me with a delivery date yet*?'

'Malware! But I aint got no boots.' Matt tried to keep the note of panic from his voice. He twisted in his stacker chair in an appeal to Damon. The pasty face was difficult for Matt to read at the best of times. Today it seemed expressionless behind the trestle desk, but the tawny eyes were sharply alive. The hard drive fans whirred in the background.

'Well... you told her you had the boots; you even described them to her,' Damon said slowly.

'Oh, blog!'

'And you used the office phone, so she rang back on the number.'

'Yeah, an' she's only gotta use reverse directory enquiry and it'll give her the Balcon & Mora name. Then she'll know where to get me.'

'I don't want to risk her leaving bad reviews all over

Twitter and Instagram. Sort this out, Matt.'

'But then I'll have to get her a pair of cowboy boots.'

'Dead right - unless you come up with something better.'

'So you'll pay for 'em?'

'No, Matt. You made this problem, so you make it go away. You pay for the boots; it's either that or more overtime.'

'Scammin' malware,' Matt muttered. He hadn't expected to be spending his lunch hour scouring the internet for a pair of vintage Justin Fort Worth cowboy boots. It was one thing to find a picture of what they looked like, or rather what this particular pair might have looked like, but quite another to find some for sale in the UK.

Autumn sunshine broke through a gap in the clouds and shafted through the dusty sash window. Matt's shoulder and back warmed and he glanced down at his tee. It might say MEGAPLEX on the front, but the image it conjured was of Maisie. Inspiration struck.

'I'm gonna have to make calls if I wanna find boots, Damon. And some of me contacts are kinda personal. I'm,' he searched for a word, 'I'm savin' the firm, right?'

'Just get on with it and make the calls. And use your own phone, not the office one. OK?'

'Right.' He pressed Maisie's automatic dial number and waited.

'Hi, Matt. What's up? Why you callin' lunchtime? It aint like you.' She spoke in a hushed tone, and to Matt's ears her voice held promise.

'Yeah, well....' He pictured the vintage clothes shop.

'Hmm, lucky you've caught me while it's quiet. So…?'

'So 'ave you got any vintage cowboy boots in the shop? Texan leather?'

'Nah, doubt it, but I can look. Why you askin'?'

'It's kinda complicated.'

'Complicated? Who want's 'em?' Her voice sharpened.

'Me.'

'Well that's alright then. Wait a sec.'

He caught rustling sounds and hung on.

'Sorry, Matt. There aint none,' she said eventually.

'Spammin' hell! Well… can you order some for me?'

'I don't know. I'll ask the boss. Hey, I gotta go. There's a customer. Bye.'

The line went dead. He'd lost his *get out of jail free* card, and his world spun.

'I've found a pair of Justin Fort Worth's for sale on an American site,' Damon said between sips of coffee, 'They might take a while to reach the UK though.'

'Argh, DOS-in' flamewar. That aint goin' to save me.' Matt pushed his keyboard out of the way and rested his head in his hands.

'Or there're some Justin Roper vintage men's cowboy boots… they're from the 1970s. They'd also need to be shipped from the States. Shipping time is two-plus weeks.'

'Bloggin' hell, what am I gonna do?' Matt moaned. What would his comic-strip heroes do? Fly halfway round the world to the States? But how about his computer geek superheroes?

'*Two-Factor Authentication,*' he murmured, as he remembered his techie tee discarded in the dirty laundry heap that morning.

'Are you OK, Matt?'

'Yeah… I think, yeah I think I got an idea.'

'Do you want to run it past me?'

'Nah. I-I'll do it… live; build it as I go. I'll put the phone on speaker for you.' He didn't pause to ask which phone to use. This had to come from the office number.

'Her name were Raelynn Harris, right?' Matt said, more for his own benefit than Damon's, and visualising her contact number in his mind. His pulse thumped in his ears, masking the key pad beeps as he pressed the numbers and waited, now deaf to the whirring from the hard drives.

'Hello?' It was the same female voice as before; elderly, sharp and suspicious.

'Hello Ms Harris. I'm ringin' about the Fort Worth cowboy boots.'

'Oh good. Are you close by? I would have liked more warning before you made the delivery.'

'No, no, Ms Harris. I'm not callin' to make a delivery. I'm callin' to tell you someone else is claimin' the boots. I won't know if you get 'em until I've processed and evaluated the other claim.'

'What? Who? Who wants to take my boots?'

'I'm not at liberty to say, but no one will take 'em without proof they own 'em.'

'But this is outrageous. You approached me. You described them to me. You thought they might be mine and I told you they were.'

'I'm simply keepin' you informed, madam.'

'So what happens now?'

'I'll need more specific proof of ownership… like a receipted bill for the boots or photos of them bein' worn by the owner.'

'And what if this… this other person hasn't got a re-

134

ceipted bill or photos?'

'Well....' He groped for an answer.

'How will you decide then?'

'It's usually clear... an' if not, then the boots go into the auction of unclaimed items.'

'So now you want me to look through all my old photos?'

'I didn't quite say–'

'But they're men's cowboy boots. It'll be a photo of my brother... or father. I'm not going to have a photo of me wearing them.'

'I wouldn't like to say,' Matt coasted.

'Really this is ridiculous. They're size ten, a US size ten!'

Matt had run out of inspiration, but before he could mumble something like *thank you for your time* or *goodbye*, the line went dead.

'Wooah – that went well,' Damon said softly.

'Yeah, well she aint expectin' me to deliver them boots now. So I reckon I'm in the clear.'

'And if you're not, at least you know the size to buy.'

'What?'

'And don't bother wasting time searching her on the net – I've already had a quick look and there's nothing popping up yet. Right, it's time to earn your money. There are more contact details to trace for the names on your list.'

When Matt finally logged out of his computer, stood up and with a last glug, drained his bottle of cola, he felt shattered. It was 17:12 according to his mobile, but before slipping his arms into his denim jacket, he checked the new weather app he'd downloaded.

'You could just look out of the window,' Damon said.

'Yeah but this way I get to know if there's a wind chill factor before I get on me scooter.' He didn't add that the phone app information was patchy for East Anglia.

'Bye, Matt. See you tomorrow?'

'Yeah, I might ride over after me computer demonstratin' mornin'. Depends if I get what I want from their library newspaper sites. Otherwise it's Friday. Bye.'

A few lumbering strides and Matt was out of the office and into the pint-sized waiting room. He thumped down the narrow stairs, thinking about Maisie and how much to tell her. Scam! She knew his shoe size was a UK 8.5 in a wide fitting, and that's the size she'd have asked her boss to find. But Matt needed a US size 10 for worst-case scenario insurance. Scammin' hell! How did a US size 10 boot translate into its UK equivalent size when it was at home in Suffolk?

Outside in the back alley behind the Buttermarket, he slipped on his helmet, unlocked and rocked his Vespa off its stand, and accelerated away.

Twenty-five minutes later he was in the centre of Stowmarket and waiting for Maisie to hurry through the old walkway from the market place and into the church green. It was a quiet oasis, a hidden leafy square tucked away from the traffic and main roads. He sat astride his scooter, bum on the saddle and feet on the tarmac in the drop-off bay outside the John Peel Centre for Creative Arts, once the old Corn Exchange. He straightened one leg and contemplated his grubby trainer.

'What you doin'?' she asked, startling him as she gave him a brief hug.

'What?' He pushed up his visor, 'Hi Mais.' He was met by a vision of crazy bleached hair with pink yarn braids dangling from one side. 'Like them braids.' He handed her the key and she opened the top box for her helmet.

He waited while she slipped onto the seat behind him.

She wore cropped linen trousers tight on her trim thighs, and her ankles were bare between her pink thick-soled trainers and trouser hem. 'Can we ride straight there?'

'Yeah sure, Mais.' He racked his brain, trying to re-member where he was meant to be riding straight to.

'You'll like 'em. It'll be fun.'

'Yeah sure, Mais.' What would be fun and who would he like? And then he had it, ten-pin bowling! She'd told him last week about her mates' bowling team.

'You still want to come, right?'

'Yeah sure, Mais.' This time he put some conviction into his voice.

'Come on, smile. I had a bit of luck with me boss.'

'What you mean?'

'She reckons cowboy boots will be trendin' this win-ter. So she's biddin' for a box of mixed vintage ones from the States. She'll know if she's got 'em by Friday.' Maisie ended with an excited squeal.

'You aint kiddin' me? She done that for me?'

'No, she were already doin' it. But it's a mixed lot. I don't know if there'll be some in your size.'

'That don't matter. I need a US size 10.'

'Is that why you was lookin' at your foot?'

'Yeah, Mais.'

'Come on then. Woohoo! Ipswich, here we come.'

Matt flipped down his visor and smiled. It looked like the evening was going to turn out all right, after all. And his weather app had said Ipswich would be dry.

CHAPTER 19

Brr brr, brr brr! Nick pulled his mobile from his pocket, and with a cursory glance at Tim in the driver's seat, murmured, 'Now what can Matt want?'

The van swayed as they rounded a corner.

'Hi?' Matt's voice sounded distant against the sound of the van's diesel engine.

'Are you OK, mate?'

'Yeah, yeah; just wonderin' if you got any updates on your great-granddad?'

'But I'm at work. Couldn't it have waited?'

'Yeah, 'cept I aint demonstratin' all day. I'll be in the 'cademy library later. Figured I'd use their newspaper sites. Sniff round a bit more.'

'I'm in the van with Tim. We're on our way to fit some stable doors.' Nick took another look at Tim, but he didn't seem to be listening.

'Got anythin' new for me, then?'

'Well Mum's been remembering more stuff. She said great-granddad used to go away a lot.'

'How'd you mean? Workin'? Travellin'? Takin' trips in school holidays? What kinda thing? He were down as a teacher, remember?'

'Yeah, but Mum doesn't even know what he taught. She said my great-grandma Alice often came to stay with her and Grandma... that's Mum's mum.'

'Louisa?'

'Yeah. Mum said Alice used to come by herself to stay. She reckons it's because great-granddad Harold went travelling without her.'

The van slowed as they turned into a short section of leafy driveway blocked by closed gates.

'Look, we're here now. Sorry, I've got to go. Cheers, mate.' He ended the call and glanced at Tim.

'Hop out and work the intercom, will you?' Tim said, his voice testy as he added, 'You'd 've thought they could 've left the gates open for us.'

Nick jumped down from the Willows van and hurried round its front, his work trainers crunching the gravel. He spoke into an intercom above the keypad on the gatepost. 'Willows here - to fit the stable doors.'

He waited.

'*Hiss... crackle*! Hello. I'll open the gates. Follow the right fork in the drive... *crackle*. It'll take you straight to the stables... *hiss*.' The voice sounded distorted, metallic, barely human, but male. Somehow he'd expected a female voice. Hadn't Tim said it was Mrs Lamanby who was horse-mad?

The gates swung open without a sound. Nick stepped up into the van and Tim drove forward slowly. Nick smiled as he pictured how the van's tyres would have spat gravel if Dave had been at the wheel, impatient and accelerating wildly.

Hawthorn hedged the drive. Occasional field maple and hazel pushed through, breaking the uniformity and tickling the eye. It was like a play in controlled nature, an orchestrated wildness. Grass meadow stretched into the distance. Dave would have said something about horse-friendly planting and to notice there wasn't a laurel bush in sight. But Dave was a natural informer and teacher; Tim wasn't. Chalk and cheese, Nick thought; chalk and cheese.

The stable block, when they reached it, was built of

old Suffolk brick and faced a modest yard. The doors were central, with the building extending on either side. It suggested a pair of generous sized stables. A low wooden barn stood close by. It was part open-fronted and the blackened weatherboarding looked neat and well-maintained. A dark green horsebox trailer was parked next to it. The overall impression was of order, but Nick's main focus was on the existing stable doors. He half expected to see damaged wood hanging from loose hinges and split posts. But from his vantage point in the van, they didn't look too bad; weathered but functional. The top doors were hooked open, the bottom ones were bolted shut.

'Ah, I guess this'll be Mr Lamanby.' Tim said, directing his words at the windscreen, as if he was pointing with his chin at a thickset man wearing a khaki baseball cap and driving a ride-on mower towards the van. The grass cutter wasn't engaged and the ride-on crossed the courtyard at a fair pace before halting next to them as they got out of the van.

Mr Lamanby's voice sounded rich and affable as he raised it above the noise of the ride-on motor chortling in idle mode.

'Hello. I'm George Lamanby. One of you must be Tim? My wife will be here shortly. She's taken the horses to the field but she'll join us soon.' He indicated somewhere beyond the stables.

Nick smiled, instinctively drawn to Mr Lamanby's easy manner. 'Hi, I'm Nick Cowley. I'm working with Tim today.'

'Nick Cowley? I know that name from somewhere.' The frown quickly changed to a smile. 'Ah, I've placed you now. You're repairing windows at the Poachers Basket, along with a Dave Townsend, also from Willows.' He smiled more broadly, a kind of satisfied, winner-of-a-quiz type of smile and switched off the ride-on motor.

Nick nodded, sensing the invitation to ask how he knew, but instead left it to Tim to ask.

'I'm the chairman, or should I say the chairperson of the Friends of the Poachers Basket Community Project. Steve is the one on the ground managing and coordinating the repairs, but he keeps me informed.'

'I'm impressed you can remember Dave and my names,' Nick said.

'Ah, well with this latest body, the one in the cesspool, the police wanted a list of everyone who's been working there. And as I said, Steve keeps me informed.'

Tim dropped his gaze. 'They're saying the place is cursed.'

'Nonsense. The pub's got a rich history, but curses? No.'

'A rich history? Would that include a musical history?' Nick said, picturing the Polyphon disc in the fireplace and imagining fifties live jazz in the bar.

'I don't know, but this latest business makes me wonder if it's a lot richer than we thought.'

'Do you know the names of any of the pub's past landlords?' Nick asked, and then added, 'Dave Townsend is like a kind of local historian. He'd be interested to know more.'

'Well there was plenty of interest when we formed the Friends of the Poachers. Enough to raise funds by selling community shares in the pub. People started donating all kinds of pub mementoes and old photos, once they knew we'd won the day.' He chuckled at his own joke.

'So I've some stacker boxes filled with newspaper cuttings and black and white photos. You and Dave are welcome to take a look... anyone is,' he added.

'Really?'

'Yes of course, Nick. It's a community project. My wife is the archivist for the Friends. Now don't let me hold you up any longer.' Mr Lamanby smiled and flapped his hand towards the stable block. 'Those are the stable doors – I'll leave you to get on with your work. And as I said, my wife will be with you shortly.'

They set up their work station in the courtyard, the collapsible workbench near the van, its doors open like a mobile tool shop. Once they had knocked the pins out of the hinges and removed the old stable doors, they concentrated on the doorframes.

'We're in luck; the doorjambs aren't as bad as I was expecting,' Nick said, running his fingers along the wooden frame uprights that held the brick walls at the side of the doorways.

'Hmm, the horses have damaged some of these stopping strips and...,' Tim indicated where screws holding the bolt slide casing had pulled away from the brickwork and trim, 'let's have a closer look at where the hinges are fixed.'

'Better check the doorjambs are standing dead straight.' Nick held the long spirit level against each upright in turn.

'Hello, Tim. And this is...?' A woman's voice startled Nick and broke his concentration.

'Hi, Mrs Lamanby. I didn't hear you coming,' Tim said as Nick changed his focus from the air bubble in the spirit level, to a woman wearing tight-fitting riding jodhpurs and short leather boots. She must have walked from behind the stables without them realising.

'Hi, I'm Nick.' Still surprised, he flashed a smile, his brain now processing the mixed messages from a shapely pair of legs and trim body, and a face showing its age with a lined forehead and sun-damaged skin. He couldn't decide if she was the same age or a little older than her husband.

She nodded a greeting. 'Hello, Nick. So, Tim, what's the verdict? Will the doorjambs need replacing?'

'This hinge one will,' Tim said slowly, 'We're still deciding about the other one.'

'Do them both. Just get on with it. I want the horses back in their stables by this evening.' She strode away.

'Yes, Mrs Lamanby,' Tim murmured.

Nick didn't say anything. He hadn't heard her foot-steps approaching before she spoke and he wasn't going to risk her overhearing any loose comments when she was supposed to have disappeared. His thoughts were running more on what her age was and how easy she might be to approach. Not with chat up lines, but to ask if he and Dave could look at the collection of old pub photos and newspaper articles. And as far as the doorjambs were concerned, if she wanted new ones, she could have new ones. After all, she was paying.

It turned out to be a longer and harder job than he'd expected. Tim removed the door jams while Nick cut the replacement ones to length. Nick, being taller than Tim, stood in the doorway and widened the notch in the doorframe head plate, and together they eased the new jamb into place, repeating the whole process for the second stable. It was fiddly work and it fell to Nick to hold the long spirit level against the doorjamb and direct Tim as he gently hammered slim wedges, between the brickwork and jamb.

'Yeah, we're dead straight vertical now.'

By the time Mrs Lamanby next appeared, the stable doors had been hung, the door stopping-strips had been replaced and they were in the process of repairing and strengthening the wall fixings for the slide bolt casings. Nick spotted her approaching and smiled a greeting.

'Will you be finished soon?' The words sounded more like a command than a question.

'Oh hello,' Tim said mildly. 'Yes, we're nearly done. How d'you think they look?'

'From here I like what I see. Yes… this is very nice.' She ran her hand over the outer surface of the nearest top half door, and then the half door below it. She opened and closed them, a look of pleasure softening the lines on her forehead. 'Good work.'

Without thinking too deeply about it, Nick grabbed the moment to make his request.

'I hope you don't mind me asking, but Mr Lamanby said you were the archivist for the Poachers Basket.' He paused and smiled while he gauged her reaction.

Her face spoke relaxed contentment, her hand still lingering on the door. 'Yes?' she murmured, as if her thoughts were miles away.

'Would it be OK if some of us from Willows could see the old photos… some time when it suits you?'

'Yes, of course. You've got my number… or rather Tim has. Ring me and we can arrange a time.'

'Thanks, that'd be great.'

It had been easier than he'd expected and Dave's favourite adage of *if you don't ask you don't get* had paid off.

CHAPTER 20

Hi, Chrissie? Is it OK to speak?'

'Hi! Yes, of course. Go ahead, Nick. I'm on my lunch break.' She smiled at the weak October sunshine filtering through the open barn door. It was a little windy and a light gust caught some wood shavings, edging and nudging them along the concrete floor ahead of her as she walked. It was Friday and she had just retrieved the brochure for the Diploma in Forensic Accounting from her car. She wanted to show it to Ron, a slight mix of excitement and apprehension colouring her mood.

'Is Clive keeping the Polyphon disc I found in the Poachers?' Nick's question dragged her thoughts back from the brochure.

'Ah....' She had forgotten about it. She'd been so occupied with researching the best forensic accounting course that she hadn't thought to ask Clive. He hadn't raised the subject, but that didn't mean there wasn't anything to say.

'So, is he, or can I have it back?'

'I-I'll ask him this evening... sorry Nick, I should have chased him down about it, but I've been a bit taken up with looking into forensic accounting courses.' She pulled a contrite face, as if he was next to her and could see it.

'Did you just say forensic accounting? Does that mean–'

'No, not at all. It's just a side interest... like you have your music.'

'So you're not going to–'

'No. Of course I'm not going to throw-in the carpentry. It's my life. It's what keeps me sane. And don't make any jokes about my sanity – you know what I'm try-ing to say.'

'Yeah, I s'pose I do. Will you be at the Nags Head this evening?'

'If you're wanting to know if I'll have asked Clive by then, the answer is no. It would mean phoning him this af-ternoon and I don't like to when he's working... I mean I try not to. He's more likely to clam up. Just leave it with me. I'll get back to you when I've got an answer. OK?'

'Yeah, sure. Thanks, Chrissie. So, was that a "no" for the Nags Head as well?'

'I don't know yet.'

'OK, maybe see you there. Bye.'

She frowned. It wasn't like her to forget something like the disc, after all, she'd been the one to whisk it into a plastic bag and take it to Clive in the first place.

'I wasn't meaning to listen, Mrs Jax; but I couldn't help hearing you just now. Is everything all right?'

Ron's words broke her chain of thought.

'What? Oh yes… everything's fine, Mr Clegg. Nick wanted to know if Clive had finished with that battered old disc from the Poachers.'

'And has he?'

'I don't know. I'll ask him.'

One look at Ron told her that he might've picked up the bit about a forensic accounting course. Damn and hell, she'd planned to tell him in her own way while they ate their lunch. Instinctively she wanted to drop her gaze, but she knew it would only make her look guilty.

'Y-you've probably noticed I've been a bit distracted this week,' she said, willing her face not to flush.

Ron didn't answer. He sat at a workbench, eating his

rough-cut cheese and tomato sandwiches, his manner radiating a sorrowful calmness as she crossed the barn to him.

'Look, I know you're still eating, but I wanted to show you this.' Her cheeks were on fire as she put the brochure close to his mug of tea on the bench 'I want to run it past you. It was Clive's suggestion,' she added, hating herself for shifting some of the blame onto Clive.

'A Diploma in Forensic Accounting, Mrs Jax?' He spoke slowly, as if reading the bold words on the cover, 'How's that going to work then?'

'Online. It'll be distance learning. I'm already a qualified accountant, so it should be easy for me. Remember, I'd had over fifteen years' experience working full-time before... before Bill died.'

'I know.' His voice was barely audible.

'An online course is just that... I can access the modules in the evenings and weekends using my laptop, in fact anytime.'

'But there's bound to be more to it than an online course, Mrs Jax.' He emphasized the word *online*.

'Well yes. To be accredited to work as a forensic accountant, first I do the course to get the diploma, and then I work as a trainee in the specialty for a year or so. But because I'm already a qualified accountant, it'll be faster for me. In this day and age, I can train part-time... say, one day a week or weekends. Something flexible.'

He nodded slowly.

'You haven't asked me why, Mr Clegg.'

'I think I can guess, but it's best if you tell me.'

'Well, you know what I'm like, and Clive thought this would be safer for me than some of the things I'm tempted to get tangled up in.'

'Does Clive say forensic accounting will be safe?'

'Yes. And it's not just Clive; I'd been thinking about it as well. He kind of put it into words for me. But looking at the course modules reminds me of how I felt when I worked in Ipswich. I don't want to do it full-time. Carpentry is my anchor, my life.'

'But Mrs Jax, isn't forensic accountancy mainly office work? Won't it be a little tame for you?'

'No, Mr Clegg. I think taking this course and getting the diploma and accreditation, will channel that side of me and my nosey streak. It'll only entail a few hours a week spent on paper trails… chasing numbers, linking accounts and cross-referencing sums of money.'

'So how will carpentry fit in, Mrs Jax?' He looked pointedly around the barn.

'I think the question should be how does forensic accounting fit into my carpentry? And the answer will be infrequently and only as an occasional consultant to the police. I plan to do it as a weekend hobby interest while Clive is busy on duty.'

They both fell silent and she waited while he opened the brochure. It was a watershed moment.

'Will this give you the best of both worlds, Mrs Jax?'

'I hope so.'

'Well, if you're happy with it, then I don't doubt you'll make a success of both worlds.'

'Thank you, Mr Clegg.' She glowed. 'So… you don't mind?'

'No, I can't say that I do. It'll give you something else to chew over, and that can't be a bad thing.'

'When you put it like that….' She smiled, not sure if it was a compliment or his acceptance of fate.

'The *Psychology of the Fraudster* – now that looks interesting,' he said, his eyes on the brochure.

'Yes, I've had a quick look at some of the material about that. It seems when large sums of money are taken, it's likely to be by a high-earning, well-educated male aged over sixty. Apparently he'll often have been a long-term employee of the company he's defrauding. It doesn't mean women don't or can't. It's just if you're talking big sums, there'll be fewer women in high positions, so less opportunity for them to defraud.'

He smiled and she guessed he'd caught her cynical humour, but before she could launch into the typical profile of fraudsters of smaller sums, he began to stand up, leaning on the bench top as he eased himself off the work stool.

'I'm afraid my knee is playing up today.'

She knew it was his way of saying *enough chatter; time to get on with some work*. His knee was just one of his many joints made arthritic after years of wear and tear, and it struck her for the first time that maybe he relied on her, as well as she on him. She wanted to say more but she'd learned from experience, getting on with some work was the best salve.

'I'll just eat my egg roll, Mr Clegg. Then I'm back to the toilet mirror,' she said, indicating an antique mirror designed to stand on a dressing table; its name originally coined in the seventeenth century from the French *toile* or *toilette*, and nothing to do with the modern concept of bathrooms and plumbed-in fixtures.

The flame mahogany, confusingly-named, *toilet* mirror was a circa 1860 piece for the bedroom, and in a sorry state. The old mirror glass had brownish discolouration along with black spots near the edges. Its frame had split and the two upright poles holding it had come loose from the two-drawer serpentine base unit, also in need of repair.

It was four o'clock by the time she'd dismantled the mirror supports and tilt mechanism, and carefully removed the mirror glass from its frame. It was a good moment to call a halt for the rest of the day. Further work on it could wait until Monday morning came round.

'Have you decided if you're re-silvering the mirror?' Ron asked mildly as they sipped their mugs of tea on the final tea break of the day.

It was a contentious subject; the restoration versus conservation debate.

'It's hardly a valuable example of a Victorian free-standing mirror for a dressing table, and the owner wants to use it, so the glass is to be re-silvered. If it was down to me, I'd live with the mirror as it is.' She hoped her words had come across as considered rather than defensive.

'It could be a Biedermeier. It's in the style. That would push the value up.'

She bit her lip. She'd heard of the German furniture, and knew of the emphasis on restrained practical designs to showcase the grain in paler toned wood or fruitwood. But she hadn't seen many examples of the continental pieces, not in rural Suffolk. 'Do you really think it could be a Biedermeier?'

'No, I think it's more in the *style of*. It just crossed my mind, that's all.'

It was so like him to approach the restoration versus conservation issue obtusely. She guessed it was his way of looking out for her; gently warning her that a spanking new silvered mirror might look out of place in an antique piece, particularly if it was a valuable original Biedermeier from the continent. She smiled and caught his return smile. All was well. She could relax; they understood each other. She'd read his underlying message, and the fact that he'd voiced it at all, told her that he was going to be OK about her taking a forensic accounting course.

***

'I don't know why we're going all the way to Lavenham on a Saturday morning to pick wild mushrooms,' Clive said, a vein of resignation running through his words. He looked heavy-eyed, frown lines settling on his forehead as he lingered distractedly over his breakfast.

Chrissie knew he spent time mulling over his escalating cases, Jason Brookford, Caleb Coddins and human remains no 27092014, but this morning he seemed particularly locked-in to his own deliberations. He was supposedly off-duty, but she feared he'd find a last-minute excuse to return to the investigation centre near Ipswich.

He'd got home late the previous evening and seemed genuinely pleased when she'd told him that Ron was comfortable about her part-time forensic accountancy aspirations, and that she'd emailed her application to take the course for the diploma.

'That's really great, Chrissie. I'll print out those account statements for you next week,' he'd said through an exhausted yawn, before falling asleep. She didn't get to ask him about Nick's disc.

She glanced at him now. He could muse on for a little longer before she loaded her TR7 with walking boots and anoraks. But one thing was certain. If they went collecting wild mushrooms, he'd have to stop thinking about his cases and concentrate on the mushrooms instead. And a break from thinking about his cases might refresh his thought processes. She'd always found it worked for her if she had a troublesome brainteaser. Wasn't off-duty time about recharging the brain's batteries as well as physically resting?

'Why can't we just wander over to Woolpit Wood instead?' he asked.

'We can… but the Lavenham walk is part of a guided forage for wild food. And there's a cooking demonstration afterwards which I've booked us on. I thought you'd enjoy it. It'll be over by lunchtime. I can cancel it if you'd like me to.'

She hid her disappointment and gave him a hug. 'I don't know if I've even got the right kind of basket to put the foraging in.'

A sudden thought crossed her mind.

'It isn't because it's Lavenham, is it? We don't have to drive past your house and check it looks OK - like the tenants haven't burnt it down or anything?'

She smiled at him and wondered if Lavenham brought back uncomfortable memories of his failed marriage. It was all past history and before Chrissie had met and fallen for the tall DI with the smiley eyes, but it was still a subject she trod around with care.

'I'll drive, if you like. Then you can tell me about your Friday. You didn't say much yesterday after you got in,' she coaxed.

'Hmm – I'm sorry. I didn't mean to fall asleep but I was knackered.' He pulled a face. 'So what am I looking for? Chanterelles?'

'Yes, and lots of other mushrooms like those oyster ones. Are you sure you want to do this?'

'Sure. I need to get moving.' He yawned, stacked a couple of dirty plates and carried them to the sink, 'Are we likely to get to eat the cookery demonstration, or will you be treating me to a wild lunch?'

Already his shoulders looked less tense and she guessed from the way he'd said *wild lunch* that a smile had returned to his eyes, even if it was directed at buttery knives and a marmalade spoon.

Ten minutes later Chrissie started her TR7 while Clive locked the front door. He was still settling into his seat and buckling his safety belt when she drew away, easing through the gears as she accelerated. She sensed that Clive was genuinely starting to relax. He stretched his legs into the footwell as she followed the narrow twisting lanes. It was a scenic route. The field maple and hawthorn in the hedgerows still held green foliage, while the ploughed and seeded fields already showed the first hints of sprouting winter wheat and barley. The landscape stretched as far as the eye could see, the horizon slipping out of view from time to time as they dipped in and out of shallow valleys cut by the Rivers Rattlesden and Brett.

'So why was Friday knackering?' she asked, as she slowed to follow a right-angled bend close to a road junction.

'Because there've been some developments. The forensic anthropologist has been working on the bones from the cesspool for the best part of a week now. We know he was a male and aged between twenty-five and fifty-years-old. We released that to the press earlier in the week. But here's the surprise – there's a two-millimetre-deep cut in the body of the fourth cervical vertebra. And there's no sign of healing. So it has to have occurred perimortem.'

'A cut? Perimortem? What's perimortem?'

'It means around the time of death. So either the cut

killed him, or it was inflicted soon after he died.'

'So… what are you saying?'

'I'm saying that our cesspool friend was sliced across his neck with something sharp. It must have cut through muscle and blood vessels until it stopped when it couldn't pass through solid bone.'

'Ye gods!'

'But what we don't know is if it was a crass attempt to decapitate him after he was dead.'

'What? But why would anyone want to cut off his head?'

'To make it easier to dispose of the body, perhaps.'

'Ugh, that's horrible. So you're suggesting someone tried to hack his head off with… with a sword or a meat cleaver?' She slowed to take a left fork in the road.

'There was no hacking, Chrissie. Just the one cut. And the cutting edge wasn't straight.'

'What? You mean not straight like it was serrated – like a bread knife or a saw?'

'No, I mean curved like a sabre. Smooth as opposed to serrated, but deeper in the centre of the cut.'

She was too stunned to speak. The picture he'd conjured was nauseating and made it difficult to concentrate on the road ahead. She needed a few miles to assimilate what he'd just said and move beyond the images to the implications. No wonder he'd been distracted. Engine noise filled the silence of her shock as her logical brain tried to find comfort in logic.

'But we already knew there had to be something dodgy about his death from the very fact that he was in the cesspool,' she said slowly, and accelerated to change up a gear.

'Except dodgy isn't quite the term I'd use in a report.'

'But you know what I mean. And the cut in his fourth vertebra simply confirms it.'

'Yes.'

'So now you want to find the weapon.'

'Along with identifying him; in fact, finding out anything about him would be good.'

'But what else was in the cesspool with him?'

'His clothes had rotted away but there were some old buttons; a watch but no strap, only the metal parts; a belt buckle, and the remains of a single shoe. Sifting through a tonne of old sewage takes time, they're not finished yet.'

'Ugh, it sounds like the job from hell. Everything about what happened to that man is horrific.'

Her imagination propelled her to the night he was killed. But why did she assume it was at night? *Because* her inner voice answered, *wouldn't you want darkness to cloak the gruesomeness of a gaping wound in the neck and manhandling a body into a cesspool*? She shivered. This direction of thought had to stop. *Focus on driving* her inner voice barked.

'Are you OK, Chrissie?' Clive's voice sounded sharp.

'Yes... yes. Of course I am.'

'Are you sure?''

'Yes. I was just concentrating on the road. Relax.'

The last thing she wanted was Clive thinking she couldn't cope with gory details. She daren't risk him clamming up and not telling her stuff, simply to save her feelings. But if Clive was to believe she was OK, she knew it wouldn't be enough to say it, she had to act it as well. She grasped for something she'd typically say, and a question lurking since Friday popped uninvited into her mouth.

'I've been meaning to ask you about that old Polyphon disc. Nick was wondering if he could have it back soon.' She hoped her tone sounded easy and natural.

Clive didn't answer and she glanced across at him. His eyes were closed. A frown creased his forehead. Now what? Was it his old trick of simply ignoring a question he didn't want to answer? She tried again, this time a little impatient.

'Clive, did you hear me? Do you know when you'll have finished with that old disc Nick found?'

'Yes, I heard you. I'm just wondering…. Stop the car Chrissie.'

'What?'

'Stop the car. I need to….' He pulled his mobile from his pocket. 'No, don't stop here; drive on until I get a stronger signal.'

'What? What's going on? Are you OK?'

'Yes, just keep driving.' His eyes were on his mobile. 'OK, here's better. Pull off the road here, please.'

She bit her lip, slowed and pulled into a short, rutted track close to a field entrance. She waited while he tapped an automatic dial number.

'Hello?' he said into his mobile, 'Stickley? It's Clive. Can you do something for me … yes, now … OK, I don't know if you saw that blackened metal disc from the Poachers Basket … yes, it's in an evidence bag but it hasn't been sent to forensics yet … yes, well can you show it to our forensic anthropologist? I'll phone her now and warn her. Ask if our friend from the cesspool could have been cut in the neck by the disc … yes, and if it's a possibility, get the disc sent off ASAP for full forensics before it's out of its bag … Thanks.'

'What?' Chrissie breathed 'You think that old disc could have cut the man's neck?'

'I don't know but it's got a curved metal edge. With enough force it might have....'

'What? It might have been the murder weapon? And it's bent! Something must have bent it. This is nasty, Clive.'

'Hmm. I'll give Jo a call now.'

'Jo?'

'Yes, the forensic anthropologist. She'll be at the investigation centre today, working on her report.'

One look at Clive told Chrissie that he wasn't going to settle for a foraging and cookery demonstration. A chasm of disappointment opened at her feet but a little spark of pride in bringing up the subject of the disc stopped her falling.

She bit the bullet. 'Do you want me to drive you to the investigation centre or back to Woolpit so you can pick up your own car and drive there?'

CHAPTER 21

Matt sat at a table, his backpack perched on his lap.

'So what've you got for me?' Nick asked. He held a full glass in each hand.

'I were goin' to ask what you got for me, an' I'm hopin' it's a pint of me favourite.' Matt eyed the proffered glass of amber liquid. It looked dangerously close to spilling over the rim.

'Sorry, mate,' Nick said as he set it on the table and a frothy slop ran down the side of the glass. Fine bubbles of lager settled around its base in a crescent moon and darkened the scrubbed wood surface.

'Cheers, mate.' Matt sipped his lager, leaned back and drank in the scene. The bar in the Nags Head felt pretty much as usual for an early Monday evening; the October daylight was fading and the décor looked tired. A sprinkling of men stood at the bar in their working clothes, quenching their thirst with quick pints after a busy day. The jukebox was silent.

'So what've you brought to show me?' Nick asked again, but eyeing the backpack.

Matt studied Nick's face. Was his friend impatient or irritated? He wasn't smiling and his short-cropped hair looked darker and his face thinner in the dreary saloon lighting. He considered Nick's eyes, mouth and eyebrows separately and then syphoned them into a cartoon-like emoji, but it didn't help.

'I've printed out some stuff; it aint a lot, Nick.'

'Come on then, don't hide it in your backpack. Whatever it is, I'm sure I can cope.'

'Cope?'

'Yeah, with any skeletons in the cupboard; like if my great-granddad had a second family, or if he'd been banged up in prison or something.'

'What? I aint found nothin' like that.' Matt felt confused as he opened his backpack, wiped the table with his sleeve and extracted a few sheets of paper.

Nick shifted his chair closer.

'I already told you 'bout your great-granddad an' his Morse code back in the First World War. An' his occupation were a teacher on his marriage certificate an' your grandma's birth certificate. Beyond that he's a spammin' ghost. Anyway, I did more searchin' when I were in Utterly library last week. I phoned, remember?'

'Yeah, I remember. Did he fight in the Second World War?'

'I looked it up, but he were too old. They conscripted men aged eighteen to forty-one.'

'But he'd have been thirty-nine at the start of the war. So he'd have been eligible.'

'Yeah, but I read they enlisted'em in age order, startin' with the eighteen-year-olds. They got to 1941 before they were draftin' in the forty-year-olds – so by the next year he were forty-two an' too old to be called up. And he weren't in the Forces Records for WW2.'

Nick nodded.

'So I tried lookin' for where he might've taught.'

'And?'

'Sorry, mate; spammin' nothin'. There weren't no lists of schools, kids' names and past teachers for back then in, like, one national register. I need more info to narrow me field. So, workin' down me list of search themes, like we do at B & M, I skipped to hobbies an' interests.'

'Like music and concerts?'

'Yeah, but I were thinkin' more 'bout his Morse code and… like them word an' number puzzles we found in 'is Polyphon. So I reckoned brain-teaser stuff from the 1930s might've been 'is kinda thing.'

'You're kidding me? Brain teasers? What kind were they playing back then?'

'It weren't like computer games. It were mostly chess, crosswords an' card games.'

'Card games?'

'Yeah, bridge. I read some stuff about bridge tournaments in the 1930s. See, winners get announced in newspapers and specialty mags. That's what I were thinkin'.'

Nick's breath escaped in a low whistle, '… that's deep, Matt.'

'Yeah, s'pose it were.' He sipped his lager and basked in the moment.

'See I found Harold's name in the British Bridge League and English Bridge Union archives. Lucky some of it's been scanned and digitalised. Seems 'e were a member. Here, I printed this for you from the website. There's loads more like it.'

He pushed a sheet of paper closer to Nick. It was a printout of a page scanned from an old ledger. Names had been handwritten in ink; neat columns with dates and other information filled the page: *Harold Bertram Roan; 1935; ranked player. European Championship reserve.*

'Wow. What does it mean?'

'I reckon he were goin' to Europe to play or follow them European Bridge Championships. And the records show 'e were doin' it from the mid-1930s until the start of the war. And then after the war.'

'So it explains his trips away?'

'Yeah, but his name aint there after the mid-50s.'

'Do you know why?'

Matt shrugged. 'You said your great-grandma stayed with your mum's family a lot. It got me thinkin'. See your mum weren't born till 1960. So for her to remember, he must've still gone on travellin' after 1960 while she were a kid.'

'So do you think he was still following the European Championships?'

'I dunno.' He watched Nick frown obvious furrows. 'What, Nick?'

'If he was such a star at bridge, how come he never taught his daughter and granddaughter? Mum hasn't mentioned it at all, and Grandma – I remember her playing patience, except she called it solitaire, but never bridge.'

'Weird DOS; maybe they dint approve. When me mum don't approve, she kinda blanks it, like it don't exist.'

They lapsed into silence. More drinkers were beginning to fill the bar and Matt let the ripple of their background talk wash over him while he gathered his thoughts.

'Course there's more themes on me search list,' he said, aware he was halfway through his lager and, if wanted a second, he'd have to earn it.

'Yeah, I can see there's a picture in the pile.' Nick shifted the page copied from the Bridge League ledger and stared at the sheet with a grainy picture and newsprint. 'Wow, is my great-granddad the bloke wearing glasses?'

'That one's mega cool,' Matt said. 'See I found it by checkin' out your great-grandma; like if she were doin' good works. Stuff like that gets reported.'

'You mean charity stuff?'

'An' judgin' flower an' veg shows, or singin' in a choir.'

'Wow.'

'Yeah, killer app, mate. It's from the Weekly Colchester Browser. Look, it says *Alice Roan*. An' I reckon *Mrs Roan's husband* is your great-granddad Harold standin' next to her.' Matt pointed at the figures before downing the rest of his lager. He was rather pleased with the effect he was having.

Nick leaned closer and read out the short entry, '*Fourteen-Year-Old Boy Wins the Tendring Summer Fete Crossword Competition. Mrs Alice Roan presented the winner's prize to J L Smith, aged 14. The crossword was set by Mrs Roan's husband and the prize was a handsomely bound English dictionary.* She's smiling but he looks... my great-granddad looks quite serious doesn't he? When was this?'

'July 1962.'

'So he set a crossword competition? At a fete in Essex? But that's kind of awesome. Why didn't my mum and grandma tell me?'

'Don't know, mate.'

'I thought you'd find he'd played in a jazz band or an orchestra... something musical; something relating to me.' Nick stood up, the sudden movement grating his chair over the floorboards.

Matt winced and stared into his empty glass. What had he said to upset his friend?

'D'you want another?' Nick asked, and drained the rest of his own in one gulp where he stood.

'Yeah, cheers mate.'

While Nick went to the bar, Matt considered his own

ancestry; *dreffle dawzey rum uns,* according to his mum. She had almost spat the words and Matt had never thought to question her assessment. His dad was barely mentioned, so as Matt saw it, not talking about someone was for a reason. It meant something bad; the equivalent to being "cancelled" on a social media site.

'Here,' Nick said, interrupting Matt's thoughts.

'Trojan.' Matt grinned, and took the proffered glass.

'So what next?'

'You mean 'bout Harold?'

'Yeah, Matt.'

'Right, well, music and teachin'. Ask your mum again where Harold and Alice lived. See I were thinkin' Suffolk, but this fete were in Essex. So it don't have to 've been round 'ere. Yeah an' any old photos – they'd 'elp.' He didn't add he hadn't found an obituary notice for Harold. It struck him as sad, and at the same time, intriguing.

The jukebox leapt into life, transforming the atmosphere in the bar. Raw strumming guitar and rap-like verse coursed across the room. 'Ed Sheeran,' Matt mouthed, as the catchy falsetto chorus of *Sing* filled his ears.

'To his biggest fan.' Nick raised his glass to Matt and grinned.

'Ed is like me twin,' Matt shouted across the music and scratched his sparse sandy beard to emphasise the likeness.

'I reckon Ed would have guessed what the letters A through to G stood for.'

'What you sayin', Nick?'

'The paper in the Polyphon's keyhole. A to G. I figure they're the musical notes in a scale.'

Matt frowned and Ed's voice blanked out, as for a

moment Matt was transported back to the pub table in the White Hart where he'd pored over sheets of paper with Chrissie and Clive. The list of disc titles was clear in his mind's eye. But Nick was talking again, dragging him back from his memories.

'I told Chrissie and Ron when I picked up my Polyphon and discs last week. Didn't anyone say?'

'No.'

'Sorry, mate. Anyway, I haven't had a chance to listen to the discs and see which notes are missing yet.'

'You mean where them disc prongs've been flattened?'

'It's a long shot, but I'm hoping there's a connection.'

'Hmm…,' Matt sighed as Ed Sheeran's catchy riff repeated. He let his mind visualise all seventeen letters and one apostrophe on the Polyphon disc title *Love's Old Sweet Song*. He juggled the letters, arranged them in order, sorted them in frequency, added and subtracted the apostrophe. Harold had set crosswords, so was this an anagram, a cryptic clue, or what?

He glanced at Nick who sat with his eyes closed.

'What? What you thinkin', Nick?'

'I'm starting to think this whole secret message thing seems… well, a bit farfetched. How many people have perfect pitch? You'd need to have it to know which notes were missing, just by listening.'

'So how about the number of prongs flattened? That'd be easier, right?'

'Or the number of different notes flattened… you could tell by where the prongs are flattened, working from the centre to the edge of the disc.'

'Blog almighty!'

They lapsed into silence as the jukebox belted out the opening phrases of a Tina Turner classic *What's Love got to do with it*. While Tina's strong, sometimes throaty tones chafed the drinkers in the bar, Matt sorted and shifted letters in his mind from the title *Love's Old Sweet Song*.

'There's three Ss, three Es and three Os,' he said, 'two Ls and the rest of 'em are all single letters.'

'What?'

'In them words *Love's Old Sweet Song*. An' if you take the roll of paper with its letters A through to G… I'm guessin' you'll find A is the note missin' on the disc.'

'But how do you come up with A?'

'Coz there's only one. It's the third letter on the paper roll with them musical notes. And by importin' the single A from the paper roll, and makin' it the third letter in me anagram…..'

'What anagram?'

'I'm guessin' Harold wrote anagrams. Scammin' DOS – he were into settin' crosswords, so I'm guessin' he'd 've been mega cool with anagrams. I reckon you've got… LEAVE NOW.'

'What? But LEAVE NOW is only,' Nick counted out the letters on his fingers, 'yeah, it's only eight letters!'

'Hmm, but it's a multiple of four.'

'You mean four – like the 4 written on the roll of paper and the 4 on the listing of the disc title?'

'Yeah, two 4s!' Matt had surprised even himself. He blinked and then gulped the rest of his lager. 'Course I'll 'ave to check it through on paper… but it'll be somethin' like that.'

'Well either you're a bloody genius, mate, or you're wrong. Shite! How'd you work it out? And anyway, what does it mean?'

'I dunno.'

'*Leave now*? It doesn't make any sense. I don't buy it, Matt.'

'I said I were goin' to check it.' Matt felt Nick's disbelief and feared the offer of another pint of lager might vanish. 'Look at your disc, mate. If the missin' note's an A, then I'm scammin' right and you owe me another couple 'a pints, right?'

'You're on!' Nick grinned and Matt knew it meant he was OK with him.

He sipped his lager and savoured the success of his flash of mental sequencing. If only his mum could see that he could do this kind of stuff. But she couldn't and she didn't. Was that why she blanked it out and ignored that side of him?

For a moment Matt sensed he was getting closer to the real Harold.

CHAPTER 22

Nick leaned back in his pub chair. Monday evening in the Nags Head had turned into a series of surprising reveals. He studied his friend for a few moments. Matt was truly extraordinary; half the time he didn't know if the people around him were being serious or joking, and then the next moment he was demonstrating his awesome mental maths skills in the equivalent of a mind game. 'That's cool,' Nick said. He didn't know if he completely bought the *LEAVE NOW*, but it was still a remarkable feat of mental digital shuffling.

'Thanks mate.' Matt sighed and opened a text message, 'Botnet! Maisie wants to go bowlin' again.' He didn't look up; his attention was obviously fixed on his mobile's screen.

'That should be fun.'

'Yeah, but she wants to meet now... so I gotta go. Sorry mate. Those are for you.' He indicated the sheets of paper on the table.

'Thanks. Mum'll be interested to see the printouts.'

Matt downed the last dregs of his lager before standing with ungainly effort. He slipped his arm through one strap of his backpack, and with something between a jerk and a push, slung it from his shoulder. 'Text me if your mum remembers anythin' new. See you here Friday.' And without a backward glance, Matt lumbered out of the bar.

Adele's soulful lyrics surged from the jukebox and filled the space left by Matt at the pine table.

Nick decided to linger a while longer; he wanted to think. So why hadn't he attempted to name the missing notes on his Polyphon discs? Chrissie would have smacked out the question without a second's thought, that's if she'd been sitting at the table with Matt and him. So what was his reason? He supposed, if he was honest, he feared failure.

His friends knew him as the musical one; he sang, he played the guitar, he composed. Music was part of his life. But the Polyphon was a musical box. Its sound had a tinkling chiming quality. Different notes played together making jingling harmonies with depth; some out of tune and all with confusing melodies he didn't fully know. The overall effect might be charming and almost mesmerising but it was going to be a tough call to isolate each musical note.

He shook his head slowly and ran through Matt's take on it. Hadn't there been something about counting the flattened prongs?

'Yes. Of course, just name the notes along the Polyphon's metal comb, then line it up against the disc's radius,' he breathed.

He expanded the thought as he visualised the black and white notes on a piano keyboard, the so-called sharps, flats and whole notes. If each was represented by a tooth on the metal comb and the sequence was linear and repeated with each octave... then all he had to do was identify a couple of notes and he'd know the rest. It'd be a breeze – as long as the teeth on a musical box comb progressed in an orderly fashion from the lowest frequency note at one end, to the highest frequency note at the other end.

'I'll sound some teeth, one at a time. And if I use my electronic guitar tuner it'll tell me the frequencies. Yeah, and if mine isn't good enough, I can borrow Jake's!'

Hell, some of Matt's genius must have rubbed off onto him! He gulped down the rest of his beer, before muttering,

'So now when I look at a disc, I can measure the distance along the radius to a flattened prong. It'll give me the note when I match the distance to a tooth along the comb. Simple.'

A wave of triumph hit Nick mid chest. The power of ingenuity! This deserved another half of beer.

He stood as the jukebox boomed the piano intro to an Emeli Sandé hit. More keyboards, he thought as he walked to the bar counter, his steps automatically keeping time with the catchy beat. He'd expected a musical link with Harold, something he could relate to, but this coded Polyphon message was almost better. It felt like a mind game he was playing with his great-grandfather; it felt personal.

His mobile vibrated in his pocket. Now what?

'Hi Chrissie,' he said, answering the call while he waited with other drinkers for the barman to serve them.

'Hey sorry I didn't get back to you on Friday. Clive says he'll be keeping the disc for a bit longer.'

'Really? But why?'

'I don't know. It's with forensics. Clive says the lab has two speeds; slow and stop.'

'OK… but it'd be cool to know the song title on the disc.'

The barman's voice interrupted as he took Nick's glass, 'Paying now or on the tab?'

'A half of the same and I'll pay now… and the tab. Sorry, Chrissie, I'm in the Nags Head.'

'I thought I was catching strains of Emeli Sandé.'

'Yeah, bloody jukebox.' He knew Chrissie would hold the line while he paid with his card. 'Right, you have my full attention,' he said and sipped his beer on the way back to the table.

'Are you drinking alone?'

'Matt's just left. I'm getting in an extra half before heading home. I want to test my theory for identifying the notes on the Polyphon. How about you? What are you up to?'

'I'm reading about techniques for detecting fraud. It's a module for my course.'

'It sounds riveting.'

'Don't mock, it's… fascinating.'

'If you're an accountant.'

He heard her laugh and then in a more solemn tone, 'I thought I'd put in an hour before Clive got home. I'm taking this seriously, you know.'

'Good on you. See you here, Friday? It's an open mic night.' He didn't bother to add that Jake and he were planning to take the stand for a couple of numbers. He guessed she'd work it out.

'Of course, it'll be fun. See you.'

CHAPTER 23

Chrissie breathed a sigh of relief as she ended her call, the one she'd been putting off. She checked the time; it was just after six o'clock. She'd got off lightly. Nick could have asked more questions about why the disc was still with Clive. Instead, he'd seemed accepting and laidback about the slow forensics. Had the beer blunted his reaction? She guessed he would have freaked out if she'd mentioned the sabre-shaped cut in the cesspool man's fourth neck vertebra. Or rather, the hunt for what could have inflicted it; something with a curved cutting edge... like the rim of the disc.

Hmm, well back to the Forensic Accounting Diploma. An email had arrived from the open learning college late that afternoon. It confirmed her registration and gave a code to access the online course material. She was pleased, but couldn't help wondering if the response had been overly fast; she'd only sent her application and card details late on Friday, so by the time the email arrived on Monday, it was barely one complete working day. Was she being rushed before she had second thoughts? But since she had no intention of changing her mind, did it matter?

She sat at her cramped kitchen table with a mug of tea, her attention now fixed once again on her laptop. She burrowed further into the course material like a hungry woodworm. Hadn't she told Nick she wanted to delve deeper into *fraud detection techniques*? But it was module four and it would mean skipping ahead from the earlier ones.

'Be methodical. Start with module one and work through to twelve,' she told herself, but was quickly distracted by *audit procedures to detect fraud*, starting with the *team brainstorming sessions*. 'So the team thinks up ways that a firm being audited might commit fraud and then looks for it?' she said, incredulous.

Time flew. She was so focused on her reading, that she didn't hear Clive open the front door. The first she realised he'd arrived home was when he planted a kiss on the top of her head.

'Hi,' he said affectionately. 'You look busy.'

'What? Oh hi, I didn't hear you come in.' She smiled; it was nice to have him home. 'I'm making a start on some of the course reading. Did you know I have to think like a financial fraudster if I'm to catch one? It's unbelievable.' She turned her attention from her screen and watched him.

'Yes, I can believe it, Chrissie.'

'Hey, what's up?' It was a bad sign when his smile didn't reach his eyes.

'It's the cesspool man. The wristwatch they found in the sewage is a Hamilton.'

'A Hamilton? I don't' think I know those.'

'They're made in Switzerland now, but up until the 60s they were made in America. This one is a 1957 Hamilton Electric 500. They were early battery watches.'

'Wow! So it was cutting edge technology and made in America. Does it mean he could be American?'

'It's on the cards.'

'But the pub was next door to an American airbase. The watch didn't have to have belonged to the cesspool man.'

'No, but the Americans left in 1945, and then the airbase was returned to the RAF. Remember, this watch was made in 1957. If the cesspool man turns out to be an American, this investigation becomes international. As if I haven't got enough on my hands!'

'I thought you said any information about him would be helpful.'

'Yes, but careful what you wish for and all that. Stickley told us Elvis Presley was supposed to have worn a Hamilton Electric 500. Actually, I think his model was the same year but the shield-shaped one called a Ventura. Anyway, it was an excuse for Stickley to do some terrible Elvis renditions.'

Chrissie winced. Clive's detective sergeant had a cheese-grater of a speaking voice. She didn't dare imagine what his singing was like.

'So it's been a bad day,' she said and got up to give him a hug. 'I don't suppose the wristwatch stopped when it went into the sewage? You know, telling you the date and time?'

'It stopped, all right. The glass was cracked so sewage got in. The battery's done horrible things to its workings. It's lucky anyone recognised it as a Hamilton.'

A thought took hold. 'Do the police have wristwatch experts? Horologists you can call on?' Chrissie asked, careful to keep her tone even.

'Hmm, we have access to lots of different kinds of experts. But I think I know where this is leading.' He kissed her and smiled. This time it reached his eyes.

Her voice morphed into an excited squeal, 'Does that mean you've brought Jason Brookford's accounts for me to look at?'

'Yes.'

'Really? But where are they? Come on, don't tease. Are they still in your car?'

'No'

'So have you printed them out for me?'

'I was going to but it's the digital age, Chrissie. They're on an encrypted stick. I'll give you the access code, but you're not to download anything onto your computer. You keep everything encrypted and on the stick. OK?'

'Yes sir, OK sir,' she said in a mock American accent and saluted with her hand cupped and a sloppy wrist.

He laughed and her face flushed.

'This calls for a celebration,' she said.

'I don't know about celebrating but I could do with a beer. Do you fancy going down the White Hart?'

'Yes, let's walk.'

***

The Biedermeier-style toilet mirror was proving quite a challenge. It was Tuesday morning, and Chrissie turned her attention to the mirror glass she'd previously freed from its damaged mahogany frame. It rested on a dustsheet. From its position on the workbench, Chrissie saw the reflection of beams high above in the barn workshop roof. The very sight increased her sense of history.

'It's been repaired before, Mr Clegg.'

'Yes, I had a quick look yesterday after you'd gone. It seems the backing wood was attached to the frame before putting the mirror glass in from the front.'

'And then I guess they glued the beading to the frame's front rim so as to overlap the edge and hold in the glass. I'm not entirely surprised it's split away. Is it a continental style of fixing the glass?'

'I think it's a way of saving on the flame mahogany.'

'Except the beading isn't veneered, it's solid wood. You know, I thought I'd get on with sending the glass away

174

for re-silvering, otherwise it'll hold up the whole project.'

She watched Ron nod; a kind of weary, resigned movement. He could say so much without uttering a word.

'If you're determined to, Mrs Jax, then you won't go far wrong with the glass works out Sudbury way.'

'It's not me; it's what the customer wants, Mr Clegg.'

By lunchtime, Chrissie had made a few phone calls and arranged to make a detour via Sudbury to drop off the glass on her way home from work.

'Do you know much about thatching, Mr Clegg?'

'Now whatever makes you ask a question like that, Mrs Jax?'

'I was wondering how a thatcher could cheat the system. That's if he wanted to, of course.'

She hadn't had a chance to look at Jason Brookford's accounts yet. It had been too late by the time she and Clive had got back from the White Hart the previous evening, but she'd been thinking about them ever since. According to the forensic accounting approach, she should start with some forensic brainstorming, and she guessed Ron would know more about thatching than Clive. Her problem was that she couldn't tell Ron he was part of her brainstorming team.

'So *cheat the system*. Do you mean something dishonest, Mrs Jax?' Ron asked.

'Well yes, I suppose I do.'

'Hmm. With thatching, it's all about the straw or reed you use.'

'So the thatcher could use one type and charge for something more expensive?'

'Yes, if he had a mind to.'

'Or cut costs using sub-standard straw?' She pictured

a spreadsheet with columns of money coming in and going out.

'Thatching's a small world, Mrs Jax. Word 'd soon get about. Bad straw; it'd kill a small thatching business round these parts.'

'Hmm....'

She developed her thought. 'So if a thatcher played dirty, he could spread rumours about a rival; steal or spoil the rival's straw? Or like sheep rustling, just harvest someone else's reed beds?'

'I've never heard of that kind of carryon. It'd be like the Wild West, not East Anglia. What's brought all these questions, Mrs Jax?'

'It's my forensic accounting course. It's just a case-study exercise.' She couldn't tell him she'd be looking through Jason Brookford's accounts; Clive had sworn her to secrecy.

Ron didn't comment but raised his eyebrows a fraction.

Chrissie soldiered on, 'I'm supposed to work out how a small business could defraud the system, and then look to see if I can find evidence of it in their accounts. I'm thinking of a hypothetical situation with a thatcher.' She hoped her face hadn't pinked up.

'So they suggested a thatcher, did they?'

'No. But I wanted a small local business doing a limited number of jobs in a year. And of course they'd have to have a reason to be claiming for expenses.'

'And this wouldn't have anything to do with the two thatchers who died recently, would it, Mrs Jax?'

'Of course not, Mr Clegg. Whatever gave you that idea? Would you like a mug of tea?' she said, keeping her back to him as she headed for the kettle.

By the time Chrissie was ready to pack up for the afternoon, she'd hand cut a gently curved surface on lengths of replacement mahogany beading for the mirror frame. She'd had to use an old-fashioned beading plane to get an exact match with the old broken beading, but at least she could use the modern router to cut the required angular shape on the underside. It would make that part of the job effortless, like cutting butter. And she'd have precision right-angled cuts in no time at all.

She swept up the shavings and tidied her tools. 'Right, it's Sudbury next. I better get on the road before the glass place closes, Mr Clegg.'

She wrapped the old mirror glass in dustsheets and carried it outside. It looked safer once she had laid it flat in the boot of her TR7.

The route to Sudbury was relatively direct. The map had appeared to iron out the smaller twists and turns on the B1115, but on the ground the road could have been laid by a sidewinder, snaking up short inclines, and following the cuts made by tributaries feeding the River Brett. It was a driver's drive, with a need to change up and down through the gears. When Chrissie reached the higher flattened ground beyond Little Waldingfield, she felt on top of her world and soothed by the endless views of earthy seeded fields and tentative shoots of winter wheat and barley. She relaxed as straighter road stretched ahead. She even allowed herself to imagine what she might find in Jason Brookford's accounts.

A flashback to him lying barefoot and dead on the Poachers saloon bar floor didn't give her much confidence that he'd have tiptop bookkeeping skills.

Her gut feeling was that he'd have preferred to deal in cash. But she knew it cost tens of thousands of pounds to pay for a roof to be thatched. It was far too much money for the average house owner to cough up in cash. But what if the payment was split; part cash and the rest through bank transfers, cheques and card payments? The cash component, if undeclared, would avoid payment of value added tax, the dreaded VAT. It could save Jason pots of money in VAT avoidance.

And paying for the reeds or straw? A complicit farmer or supplier might be very happy to accept cash and keep the deal under the table and away from the taxman.

Hmm... so what should she look for in Jason's accounts, or more to the point, what might be missing? 'Evidence of money leaving his bank account to pay for straw or reeds - that's what could be missing!' she breathed.

An obvious question popped into her head. Wouldn't Jason want to claim the cost of his straw against his fee for the job? But if he falsely inflated how much he said he'd paid for the straw, then he could tell the taxman his profits were modest and so reduce his annual tax bill.

So how might that look in Jason's accounts?

'He'll have claimed inflated expenses on his end-of-year returns, but his bank account won't show evidence of him paying those amounts,' she murmured. Yes, she liked this brainstorming approach to forensic accounting.

'So did Jason keep his business and personal finances separate? His partnership with Caleb Coddins meant they must have shared an account or had an arrangement.'

The B1115 joined a roundabout and new straight road whisked her round the north-east outskirts of Sudbury. It was time to concentrate on the mirror glass.

CHAPTER 24

Matt stood in a back alley behind the old Buttermarket shopping area in Bury St Edmunds. He winced as he rocked his scooter onto its parking stand. He was only a few yards from the entrance to the Balcon & Mora office but he sensed the weight of the old stuccoed buildings leaning in on him.

'Agh!' Pain stabbed in his sacroiliac joint as he straightened up. He twisted to stow his helmet. 'Botnet!' His joint caught him again. 'Spammin' bowlin',' he breathed.

Maisie had said more bowling would be good for him. 'A bit a fun an' exercise,' is how she'd described it a couple of days earlier. In his experience, things meant to be good for him generally ended in misery.

'Me shape's all wrong for bowlin',' he'd whined. He hadn't bothered to focus on minor details like his middle resembling a spare tyre or his flexible core being a distant memory.

'Yeah, but once you've planted them feet an' stopped movin', you got a steady bowlin' eye,' she'd said.

A gust of wind carried fine rain. Cloud advanced overhead, softening shadows and smoothing contours below. Wednesday greyed and the narrow pavement darkened, turning slippery and wet.

'Spammin' October,' he muttered and lumbered up the creaky staircase to the office on the first floor.

He knew something was wrong when Damon didn't answer with a cheery 'Hi Matt' to his usual greeting. He tried again, 'Mornin', Damon.'

'Hmm, well it's not a good morning.' His voice held a steely edge.

'Yeah, it's spittin' outside.'

'I don't mean the weather. It's that woman you caused trouble with. I knew we should've left well alone.'

'What trouble?'

'Cowboy boot trouble.'

'You found 'em?'

'No. It's the woman. She left another message.'

'Yeah?'

'She's after your blood.'

'What?' Matt slumped onto his plastic stacker chair, not even bothering to take off his damp shell jacket. 'She found a receipt or somethin'?'

'She didn't say. Listen to her message. I'll play it for you.'

Matt waited, uneasy. *You have one new message* an automated voice announced in metallic tones before the recording launched into crackly life.

He recognised her immediately; the strident, elderly pitch was unmistakeable. *I've waited a long time and you still haven't returned my cowboy boots. Your answerphone says Balcon & Mora. So I looked you up. You aren't lost property; you're a tracing agency. If this is a scam, I'm taking it further. I'm reporting you and making an official complaint.*

'Botnet!' Matt's stomach cramped. His throat felt dry. 'Can she? I mean, who'd she report me to? All I done is follow up an advert she placed nine years ago, right?'

He watched Damon; his jaw was clenched and his mouth a straight line.

Silence filled the office. Even the fans, constantly

whirring in the background, seemed to slow as they cooled the hard drives. Matt breathed fast. What would his comic-strip heroes do? *Biff! Pow! Bam!* wasn't going to fix this. But what if he could stop the planet Earth turning, reverse its rotation and turn back time?

'Are you OK, Matt?' Daman's voice cut him with the unexpected sharpness of paper.

'What? No. I aint OK. What we gonna do?' he wailed.

'We can ignore it.'

'Can we?'

'We didn't obtain or trick sensitive information from her. The phone number was already in the public domain on a newspaper advert. And more importantly, we haven't asked for or demanded any money, fees, or bank and card details. If we ignore her, what'll she do? I don't think a complaint would get far. We have a clear instruction to trace the boots.'

'Yeah, nine years ago. So you aint cross?'

'Cross? I'm furious. You've brought us this close.' Damon lifted a hand, his thumb and first finger almost touching, 'This close to getting us fined and shut down. Our card clients want current contact addresses; that's what we trace. That's our line of business. And that's what you stick to. Got it? Understand?'

'Sorry, Damon.'

'Right, just remember.'

'Yeah, addresses. 'Cept I dint get her address.'

Damon frowned before saying, 'That's right, she was cagey about it, wasn't she? Well she'll have to give contact details for a complaint to be taken seriously. I wonder if... maybe we've got an angle on her? Maybe she isn't the only one who can report things.'

'How'd you mean?'

'We can report her.'

'What? How's that work then?'

'I'll contact the police. Everyone knows Caleb Coddins has been in the news recently; the man who died in the reeds. I'll tell them we recognised the name and looked up his file. But it's turned out a bit odd because this woman started threatening us. I'll say I don't know if it's important but I'm covering my back in case they're interested.'

'You're sayin' you'll inform the police?'

Matt swallowed hard. What if Damon discovered he'd gone behind his back? It would be as clear as day he'd told Clive about Caleb Coddins and the email request to find his cowboy boots. Bloggin' blog, he'd even met Clive at Chrissie's and cemented his status as special agent by requesting a bottle of lager with a wedge of lime slipped in the neck.

'The police?' he repeated.

Malware! He'd pointed out Jason died on the ninth anniversary of Caleb losing his boots in the Poachers Basket. He'd even mentioned Raelynn Harris. But Clive hadn't seemed too bothered at the time.

'Are you listening, Matt?'

'What? Yeah, 'cept what if the police aint interested? What if reportin' her only winds her up and she comes lookin' for me? What then?'

'If you poke a snake, it'll hiss and back off.'

'But it don't back off when it's cornered,' Matt muttered, remembering his comic-strip books. Another fear grabbed him, 'But Damon, I asked her to prove them boots were hers. Do it give her a case against me?'

'She didn't offer any proof; no personal information was given.'

'Yeah, right.'

'But you'd still better get hold of an old pair of cowboy boots, just in case.'

'Dint you just say we were ignorin' her, Damon?'

'We are. But this way you weren't lying when you told her you'd got a pair... if you get a pair.'

'Yeah, an' what'll I do with them?'

'That's your problem. But if she visits us, I want a pair of boots for her to look at. And if they aren't cowboy or vintage enough for her, it's hardly our fault. We were simply contacting her in case they were hers. We are, after all, a tracing agency.'

'Phishin' flamewar,' Matt breathed.

'I'll call my contact at Suffolk Police. You start on today's names from the card companies. OK?'

'But....'

Damon was obviously preoccupied with searching for the number for his police contact. Matt faced the wall. His hands were sweaty and his innards churning. If Damon discovered Matt had already informed the police it'd be a sacking offence. Spammin' hack, Matt needed to do something fast. He pulled his mobile from his pocket, hunched over and fired off a text to Clive.

About the ad - CC's lost boots. Don't let on it were me told u.

He'd wanted to sign off as *L & WOL*, short for *lager & wedge of lime*, but figured Clive could already identify him from the text sender number. The CC for Caleb Coddins should also be enough to remind Clive of his special agent status. So when had Maisie said the box of old boots would be arriving from America?

CHAPTER 25

Chrissie was assessing the Davenport writing desk more quickly than she had anticipated.

One of her customers had asked her to look out for a good quality Victorian Davenport, and she'd spotted this one in the online catalogue for an upcoming auction at the Briddle & Smith auction rooms, Stowmarket. Ron had taught her to follow a checklist when assessing an item. Her apprentice days seemed distant but his teaching was still well ingrained – first she should spend time getting an overall impression of style and design. Only then should she home in on the details. These included all surfaces inside and out; specifics of wood, veneer, handles, legs and feet. Finally she needed to look for signs of genuine aging and wear, past alterations and repairs. The checklist included not only what her hands and trained eye told her, but brought all her knowledge and past experience into play as well.

'The veneer looks top quality burr walnut,' she murmured to herself, as she ran her hand over the wood. 'The leather on the writing surface will need replacing.' She tried to adjust the writing slope. 'The ratchet could do with some attention... and the piano-rise top is... oops, kind of reluctant. Drawers...? Yes, nice; they're lined with mahogany.'

And so she worked efficiently through her checklist, establishing that this was a quality piece made in the 1850s. Some renovation and repairs were needed, and with luck the auction price would be low to reflect this. After all, it was the epitome of brown furniture, and very off-trend in current fashion terms, but exactly what Mrs Peregrine had said she wanted. Oh yes; and a profit for Clegg & Jax.

She glanced at her watch. Was it only half past three? She could be home in about twelve minutes.

Blustery wind caught her as she stepped outside. Fine rain drove into her face, wetting her skin and whisking her blonde hair into short rat tails. She shivered and hurried to her car. The brick-faced industrial unit had turned into the colour of a damp beige raincoat. October had taken hold. The week seemed to be slipping by.

'Where's Wednesday gone?' she sighed as she eased the TR7 out of the parking space, 'and if Matt still wants to talk to Clive....' She thought back to Matt's brief and unexpected text message a couple of hours earlier.

I may call in to see Clive on my way home from B&M.

Great. Is everything OK? she'd texted back. He hadn't replied and she'd sensed it was best not to ask again.

'So if Matt drops in on his way back from Bury....' She pictured his wet scooter jacket and damp clothes, his inevitable need for food. It would be great to see him but once he'd arrived, she could say goodbye to any further work on her forensic accounting module. Hell, she wanted to squeeze in some time at her laptop before then. She floored the accelerator.

Barely seven miles and thirteen minutes later she stood in her kitchen and waited for the kettle to boil. A mug of tea would aid her transition from scouting carpenter to student of forensic accounting. Rain misted her view through the window as she gazed at the late-flowering asters, their lavender-blue heads bobbing in the gusts of wind. She felt as if her head too was buffeted by forces beyond her control; caught between the conflicting demands of work and her curious mind.

A few minutes later she'd settled at the small kitchen table with a mug of tea and her laptop booted and at the ready. It was time to get back to her online course and the *Variety of Financial Crime* module.

She stifled a yawn; fraud, money laundering and bribery seemed a bit old hat. But hey, there was electronic crime, market abuse, insider trading, identity theft, and - something she hadn't even considered in the past - financing terrorists. The scope felt huge; way beyond county lines. It was international and potentially global. But surely for someone like the unfortunate Jason Brookford, she'd be looking for financial crimes in the yawn category?

Gingerly, she sipped the hot tea as her thoughts raced on. And wasn't that exactly what she should be doing at this very moment – looking at Jason's accounts?

'Yes!' she muttered, and put the mug down. Without getting up, she swept her hand along the shelf on the wall behind her. Her fingers searched blindly. And then she had it in her grasp; Clive's memory stick, the encrypted USB.

Her previous and only attempt to open the USB had failed.

'But you should have *BitLocker* on your laptop,' Clive had said, his face reflecting his surprise.

'Should I?'

'Yes, it should come automatically installed on your computer. It's a Microsoft programme; it encrypts things.'

'Oh,' she'd said. Until that moment the name had been unfamiliar, in her view sinister and implying crypto currency, so she'd shied away from it.

'Hmm, but maybe you need to use the PIN as well as the password I gave you?'

She had nodded in agreement and felt stupid.

But she didn't feel stupid now; she felt emboldened. She knew the name of the encryption programme. Hell, the encrypted stick was supposed to be secure. It was supposed to be read only by Clive, and short of using his laptop, of course she might need the PIN as well as the stick's password.

She slipped the memory stick into her laptop's USB port and followed the prompts for PIN and password.

'At last!' This time the stick opened and a menu of file names appeared on her screen.

'Jason's bank statements for his personal and business accounts,' she breathed, 'so... starting with this year, except this year only runs to mid-September when he died.'

The files went back to April 2006. 'Hmm, seven complete financial years, plus this current one which he didn't survive.' She knew from her accounting days that it was standard practice for banks to keep their customers' computerised statements for only seven years. Any longer and the files would be stored in outdated solid state backup systems, and cost a fortune to locate and access.

But where to begin? The scouting carpenter in her wanted to take a generalised look before homing in on the details. The student of forensic accounting in her wanted to team-brainstorm the types of fraud Jason might have committed, and only then look for specifics as proof. Well, she'd brainstormed enough; initially with Ron yesterday, and then on her journey with the mirror glass to Sudbury.

She scrolled through each financial year and let her eyes travel across the months, absorbing the feel of incomings and outgoings, and then hovering over the statement totals. The end-of-month balances for the personal account felt consistent, barely in credit but nothing remarkable, nothing to stand out of the ordinary. However, there were large fluctuations in the business account. Of course, there were two people drawing from it – Caleb Coddins as well as Jason, but their monthly salary payments were consistent, and for Jason, matched the payment into his personal account. Now she needed to drill down on specifics; the kind of specifics suggesting fraud. Time stood still as she worked.

'Hi!'

'Oh! I didn't hear you come in!' She stood up to give Clive a hug and almost upset her forgotten mug of tea on the table.

'Something on your computer must be pretty riveting. Either that, or the carpentry is turning you deaf,' he laughed.

'What?' She glanced across at the kitchen clock. 'Is it ten-to-six already? And before you say I'm deaf, come on, detective; what about my mug of tea? Have you checked to see if it's still warm?'

He reached for her mug. 'Cold.'

'Right; because I've been totally absorbed in these files.'

'Ah.' He frowned and focussed on her laptop, 'Jason Brookford's accounts. Have you found something?'

'Yes, I think so, but....' A memory surfaced in Chrissie's mind. 'Matt? Is Matt with you?' she asked, doing a double take of the kitchen.

'Matt? No, were we expecting him?'

'He sent a text saying he might drop in on his way back from Bury. I think he wants to talk to you.'

'Well he's already contacted me and I've dealt with it now.' She caught the dismissive tone and recognised the subtle warning not to push for more specifics.

'Come on, tell me what you've found,' he said, as he pulled a stool round from the other side of the table and positioned himself to get a good view of her screen.

'So, it took me a while but on the Jason and Caleb business account, there are no cash payments into the account. I guess that way they've avoided some VAT and reduced their tax liability.'

'Sounds like a small trader working the cash economy to defraud the Inland Revenue.'

'Exactly, very common and some might say, fair game and not even dishonest. But there are big payments in and out of the business account, and I'm guessing they reflect the larger costs of the thatching jobs.'

'And they're cheques and card payments?'

'Yes. There are regular direct debits from the account for their salaries, two lease cars, insurance, and the utilities from two different suppliers.'

'So Jason and Caleb ran their cars on the business and claimed gas, electricity and water expenses for… using their homes as an office?'

'Yes, something like that. I'd have to see their tax returns to know for sure. But it's more difficult to follow what's going on in Jason's personal account. Obviously there are no cash payments into it.'

'The cash economy again.'

'Exactly, but there are loads of payments out; mainly card payments for groceries, clothes, Amazon, PayPal, TV channels, online betting… monthly Visa repayments - the usual consumer things.'

'So nothing unusual there?'

'No, but the large number of outgoings make the few

payments into the account all the more noticeable.'

'And they are?'

'His monthly salary and another regular payment of two hundred pounds at the end of every month. I've got a bank reference code for both, but the one for the monthly two hundred pounds doesn't help me. I've no idea who or what is making the payment.'

'When did it start?'

'A couple of years ago. Interestingly, there are two other payments with the same reference code, but into the business account. May and July 2012. Look.' Chrissie split her screen so that Clive could see the two accounts at the same time.

'Six thousand and seven thousand pounds,' Clive said and sucked air between his teeth, 'Payment for a thatching job, do you suppose?'

'Yes, I guess so, although slightly lower amounts than from their other thatching jobs. And then in September 2012 the two hundred pounds start appearing in Jason's personal account. They have to be linked in some way.'

'Hmm, I need to find out who's behind the payments.'

'And,' Chrissie added, 'where they were thatching in early summer 2012? It could be the same people. So what will you do? Ask the bank for more details about the reference codes?'

'Yes; and if it looks like something dodgy, then I can request the firm's business account and Jason and Caleb's personal accounts to go for forensic investigation. Good job, Chrissie.'

She smiled, for once totally happy and relaxed. 'Glad to help. And it's been fun. Really. So if you want me to take a cursory look at Caleb's accounts, just put them on a stick for me.'

It was obvious Clive was deep in his own thoughts when he said, 'And you only took a few hours. Normally I'd have had to wait for weeks to get to this point.'

'Then I'd say a glass of wine is in order.'

She watched him stand slowly, his frown telling her that his mind was still on his cases rather than wine from the fridge.

'How's the cesspool investigation coming on? Any closer to giving the skeleton a name?' she asked, surprising herself with the sudden sympathy she felt for his having to lead such a grim case.

'What? The cesspool case?' He gave his head the tiniest of shakes.

'Yes, on Monday you were worried he might be an American.'

'Ah yes; the American wristwatch.'

'So?'

'Hmm, the Hamilton 500 electric. Our expert reckons it was more likely to have been bought in America than the UK, but he can't be certain. He couldn't find the serial numbers specifically identifying exports around that time. And apparently sales were disappointing because of early teething problems with the battery connections. So the 500 electric wasn't sold in huge numbers in the USA or abroad. If he bought it new, it would have been between 1957 and 1961 because the next model, the Hamilton 505 electric, was launched in 1961.'

'And the one in the cesspool was definitely a 500?'

'Yes, but it had had some battery-holding modifications.'

'So that makes him an American?'

'It tells me the wristwatch was likely bought in the USA. It can't prove he's an American, but it's definitely on the cards. I also figure it helps narrow the timeframe when he was put in the cesspool.'

'Really? When was that then?'

'Before he could replace his watch with the next Hamilton model; the 505 electric.'

Chrissie couldn't help laughing. 'What? You're saying he's the 50s equivalent of our modern *I must have the latest mobile phone* techie?'

'Yes, except I'd call it victim profiling. Any man who bought or was given the first ever electric watch has to have been into technology and gadgets. I figure he'd have upgraded to the latest version as soon as it hit the market.'

'Sometime in 1961, you said.'

'Yes, so allowing for a bit of a margin, we're concentrating on all adult males reported long-term missing in the UK between 1957 and 1963, and aged between twenty-five and fifty. If we don't get anywhere with that, then he goes to the UK Missing Persons Unit. He'll join the other one thousand-or-so unidentified bodies and body parts they've been collecting on their files since the 1950s.'

'Wow. I suppose a good number of those cases predate routine DNA testing.'

'Yes, but Jo—'

He must have caught her frown because he stopped and added, 'The forensic anthropologist. She says we should be able to get some DNA from what's left of his teeth.'

'But if he died fifty years ago, there'll be nothing to match it against, unless…. Could his DNA be matched against his living relatives?'

'Maybe, but if they're in America it could be tricky.'

While Clive opened the fridge, Chrissie's thoughts took another turn. 'And his neck; any updates from Jo on the cut in the bone?'

'Ah, she says the width and shape of the disc's rim matches whatever cut into the fourth vertebra of his neck. So we've requested more tests. If we're to say the disc is the murder weapon, then we need to find minute markings on the bone that could only have been etched by the prongs on the disc. They have to be an exact match.'

'But Nick found it in the fireplace. It's probably been used to scoop ash from the wood burner.'

'I know. It's had at least fifty years since the killing to be damaged and bent. Half the prongs could be missing.'

'Well there's nothing else for it,' she said, feeling for once like a player in the team.

'Nothing else for what?' he frowned.

'A glass of wine and a toast to forensic accounting! Financial evidence doesn't change with time or have metal prongs that can be bent.'

CHAPTER 26

It was early Wednesday evening and Nick lounged back on the futon. It was folded like a chair, with the back upright and a double depth of mattress for the seat. Dried beer had marked its natural linen cover; the amber, hoppy stains a testament to past free-flowing musical sessions.

Ping! His phone's text alert sent a quiver of wavelengths through his electronic guitar tuner. What the…?

The sender ID told him it was Matt, 17:54. He opened the message.

R U in St Andrews St?

He smiled and texted, *Yes- decoding the discs!*

This wasn't entirely true. Yes, he was in his flat above the bakery but *decoding* was, as yet, an optimistic dream. He was still naming the musical notes along the Polyphon's metal comb. He hadn't got as far as identifying the ones missing on the discs. *Drop in if U R passing*, he added before pressing send. He leaned forwards and bent over the Polyphon on the threadbare carpet near his feet.

He'd begun by laying a strip of paper over the Polyphon's metal comb, and in the same way that he'd once taken brass rubbings when he was a kid on holiday in Norfolk, he'd used a soft-leaded pencil to rub over the paper and make an imprint of the comb's form. His plan was to write the notes on the paper rubbing, now beside him on the futon. He'd shied away from marking the comb's metal teeth; he didn't want to risk damaging them.

Ding! The sound rang out as he pinged a metal tooth with a guitar pick. Was it a B note? He pinged more teeth along the comb until his ear picked out the B of his guitar string.

He selected B, one of the 6 open-string options on his basic electronic guitar tuner and pinged the tooth again. 'Yes!' His screen told him the note was only 10 cents from the open B string, and in Nick's view, not bad for a metal comb tuned over one hundred years ago. He wrote B next to the equivalent tooth on the paper rubbing.

If he followed a chromatic note progression, the next B note on the comb would be an octave higher – and twelve teeth away (allowing for the sharps and flats, or half tones, as Matt would probably call them). He counted along the comb and twanged a tooth.

'Damn, that's not an octave.' Hell, this was going to be more difficult than he'd imagined. He could either randomly twang teeth until his ear told him he'd found the octave B, or he could borrow Jake's electronic chromatic tuner. It was able take the sound and name the note, in a range far greater than his six open guitar strings.

He had hoped to work quietly and alone, but it was obvious he'd have to ask for Jake's help, or rather his deluxe-range tuner.

'Jake!' he shouted, cupping his hands, 'Can I borrow your tuner, mate?'

'What?' Jake's muffled voice carried from a bedroom on the floor above.

'Your tuner; can I borrow it?' Nick yelled.

A few moments passed before footsteps thudded across the ceiling. A bedroom door opened and feet hammered down the steep attic staircase.

'Hi!' Jake appeared in the living room doorway holding his tuner, something the size of a chunky mobile phone. 'I wondered how long it would take before you asked for help.' He waved the tuner and grinned before nodding towards the Polyphon.

'Yeah, well the teeth on the comb aren't arranged as I'd expected.'

'But it's a musical box, right?'

'Yeah.'

'So it's not a regular musical instrument. It can't play the full range of notes; only the ones for the tunes on those discs you've got.'

'Doh!' Nick tapped his forehead with the palm of his hand. He felt stupid - the comb had to be short enough to fit in the box! 'Yeah, of course. So what note does your tuner say this is?' He bent and pinged the tooth again.

Nick caught the distinct smell of a spliff as Jake crouched next to the Polyphon and pulled his long hair back into a ponytail.

'OK – again, Nick.'

Ding Dong! Synthetic tones rent the air. The tuner's screen filled with a frenzy of wavelength oscillations.

'Jeeeez,' Jake groaned, 'bloody doorbell!'

'It'll be Matt.'

'Yeah? Hey but it could be for me.' Jake tossed the words over his shoulder as he hurried to answer the door.

Ding Dong! the doorbell repeated, upping the ante as Jake thundered down the narrow stairs to the ground floor entrance.

So who was Jake expecting, Nick wondered. He hoped it wasn't the girl who'd bared her shoulder after their last gig and then handed Jake her eyeliner pencil. She'd asked him to sign her skin and said, glancing at the pencil, *keep it for now but I'll collect later*. 'Craay-zeeee,' Nick had breathed.

His thoughts refocused as Jake's voice drifted up the stairwell; 'Oh, it's you, Matt; come in. We're working on the Polyphon.'

'Killer app! This beats callin' in to see Clive.'

'Hi, Matt,' Nick called from the futon. Thank the gods it wasn't the eyeliner fan. But Clive? Nick was curious. He smiled a welcome.

'Can we save the talking 'til we've finished this, Matt?' he said.

It didn't take them long to get into a routine; Nick tweaked a tooth on the comb, Jake stared at the tuner and named the musical note, Nick wrote it against the tooth on the paper rubbing, and then they repeated the process with the next tooth on the comb. Matt sat quietly, seeming to drink it all in as they worked their way along the comb.

'So what you got?' Matt asked when they took a pause to get cans of lager from the kitchen.

'It's not like a piano keyboard with all the black and white notes,' Nick explained.

'Yeah; it's only got the notes for the scales of C and G major,' Jake added.

Nick caught Matt's puzzled look. 'Loads of songs are played in C and G major. I'm guessing they'll be the keys those discs are written in.'

'A key? Like for unlockin' stuff?'

'No, it's a musical scale. *Do, re, mi. The-Sound-of-Music* kind of thing,' Jake chipped in.

Past experience had taught Nick that when dealing with Matt and music, demonstration worked best. So he chose *Sing*, an Ed Sheeran hit and Matt's current favourite, and broke into the falsetto chorus.

Matt tapped his foot and swayed with the beat.

'And if I change to a different key….' Nick altered the pitch of his voice and sang the chorus again, 'Got what a key is now?'

'Yeah, that's mega cool, mate.' Matt swigged his lager and hummed more of the chorus in discordant tones.

'So what'll you do now you've worked out the notes?' Jake asked.

'Name the ones missing on the discs.'

Jake frowned. 'Are you planning on mending them?'

Nick hadn't told him about the hidden message; he didn't even know whether to believe it himself.

'Them ones with bent prongs are,' Matt closed his eyes, '*Love's Old Sweet Song*, *Waltz Rondo*, *Rock of Ages*, *Home Sweet Home*, *The Merry Widow*, *Last Rose of Summer* and *William Tell*.'

'How'd you know that?' Jake asked.

'It were the ones on the list under the box liner,' Matt said, his eyes still closed.

'What box liner?'

'He's talking about some scraps of paper we found with the Polyphon.' Nick tried to sound dismissive. 'OK, so now it's time to measure distances.' He swigged the last of his lager and hoped Matt would keep the secret message to himself.

He was in luck. Matt burst into a sudden vocal rendition of Ed Sheeran's *Sing*, complete with his own take on the rap-like verse and falsetto chorus. Any questions Jake might have asked as to why they were measuring the distance from the central pole of the Polyphon to the end of the metal comb, were drowned.

'Ah, I get it,' Jake said when Nick placed the paper rubbing against the underside of the *Love's Old Sweet Song* disc, and made sure it was in the same position as the comb.

'See the flattened prongs? Now I can tell you which notes, or rather which teeth they would have plucked on the comb.'

Matt broke from his Ed Sheeran rendition to add, 'Yeah, an' if them names of them missin' notes match the scrap of paper, then me decodin' were bang on!'

'What d'you mean, your decoding was bang on?'

Nick shot Matt a frown before he could say more, and chipped in with, 'Matt thinks it could be a code. Don't ask; just run with it, OK? Now let's see which notes are missing?'

He worked his way along the disc, naming the notes represented by flattened prongs. And with each note he named, his spine tingled. Every damn one was an A note; just as Matt had predicted from the single A, the third note in the line of musical notes on the roll of paper in the keyhole. So did it make it the A in Matt's eight-letter anagram LEAVE NOW? Goddammit, did this prove Matt was right?

Matt nodded. 'Yeah, I said it'd be an A note missin'.'

'I don't get it; I don't get what you're on about,' Jake said.

'Matt's been watching too much World War II stuff, like that Alan Turing code-breaking bloke and the Enigma machine.'

'But you gotta agree them star wheels in the Polyphon are like them cogs in the Enigma machine,' Matt whined, a pained look filling his eyes.

Nick scowled a warning to Jake and winked at Matt. But his mind whirled as an unsettling thought asked, *has the tiny roll of paper lain hidden in the keyhole since 1918, or was it slipped in later*? The cipher message saying

LEAVE NOW had to imply something about his great-granddad. His stomach churned. Until he knew what to believe, he wasn't ready to bare his ancestry soul to Jake or the world.

'It's only a musical box but it's kinda neat,' Jake said before singing, '*I broke the code....*'

'*And... you stole my heart with Love's Old Sweet Song,*' Nick improvised.

Jake grinned and inverted the musical phrase, repeating, '*I broke the code....*'

'*Why did it take you so long, yeah so long?*' Nick sang, winging it again before adding, 'Hey get your guitar, Jake.'

'Yeah right, it sounds kinda sweet. There's a riff in there.'

'Killer App! It's open mic on Friday,' Matt whooped, 'You gotta sing it down the Nags Head.'

'Give us a chance, we need more than a riff.' Nick smiled, happy the awkward moment had passed.

'Yeah, we need more lager. Get some cans, Matt, while I get my guitar.'

CHAPTER 27

Matt yawned as he settled at a computer station in the Utterly Academy library.

He might not have felt so tired if he'd slept in his own bed the previous night. But he'd whooped and clapped late into the evening while Nick and Jake strummed their guitars, jamming and composing. And so he'd ended up spending the night on the futon in their living room. Spammin' malware! How his back ached.

But he'd been proved right; his anagram worked. He'd decoded the Polyphon's hidden message and it felt good.

'Yeah. It's about knowin' your players, an' gettin' their *intel*,' he muttered. He'd never have figured it was an anagram if he hadn't discovered Harold set crosswords.

Without thinking, he touched the *Assistant Demonstrator* ID card on the lanyard round his neck. He'd coasted through his duties that morning, helping IT & Computing students write HTML programming language. He felt whacked and it was only Thursday afternoon.

Aimlessly, he opened a local news site and tried to blink away his tiredness as he focused on his screen. The headline, at first glance, didn't appear very exciting.

Keep Search & Rescue Helicopter at Wattisham.

It looked more like a discussion forum than an article but the angry posts drew him in. He read on.

Shottisham Warbler: *The authorities have forgotten Caleb Coddins already. He died a few weeks ago after getting trapped in reed beds off the River Deben. Our creeks and estuaries are dangerous, tidal and muddy; often with strong currents. We must keep the Sea King helicopter at*

Wattisham, not somewhere in Kent.

'Caleb Coddins? Well I aint forgotten 'im - an' his scammin' cowboy boots,' Matt muttered, surprised by his strength of feeling just at the mention of Caleb's name. He scrolled through more posts:

A1152: I've heard Caleb Coddins died from an overdose. Has anyone else heard the same?

Political 999: An overdose? It's a political lie to save money. They try to distract us from the helicopter rescue.

ETD: There's word out he took too much of a smoking cure. If it did for him then that stuff should come with a warning. There are more people trying to stop smoking than need rescuing by a Sea King helicopter.

A1152: What smoking cure?

ETD: Heard it was cytisine.

A1152: I've just looked it up. You can make it from laburnum seeds.

ETD: Laburnum seeds are poisonous.

Ann: I didn't know he was a smoker. I never saw him smoke.

Matt scrolled on, but there was no more to read; just a final entry saying: *forum topic closed.*

'So what the blog is cytisine?' He keyed *cytisine* into the browser search box. 'Right,' he mumbled as he clicked to open the results, 'it's a poisonous alkaloid found in laburnum seeds an' it can be used as a *smokin' cessation treatment*. Trojan scam! The toxicology info on rats and mice says *rigidity* an' *convulsions*. Humans; it's *nausea, vomiting, weakness, convulsions* an' then you *can't breathe*. No wonder the bloke died.'

He scratched his beard. Why did online forums always move sideways? He'd read plenty in the past, analysing each contribution as if it was a conversational exchange. He'd hoped to see an algorithmic progression, something to guide him if he joined in. At least this forum hadn't turned into a dogfight with aggressive insults hurled at fellow contributors. But how could a post outlining the danger of moving the rescue helicopter to Kent, end with Ann saying she'd never seen Caleb smoke?

He clicked back to the forum and rubbed his head. 'It don't make no sense.'

'What doesn't make sense?'

'Oh hi, Rosie.' He smiled at his favourite library assistant, 'How long you been standin' there?'

'No time at all. Are you all right?'

'Yeah.' He liked Rosie. She wasn't as glamorous as Maisie, no braids or streaks of brightly dyed hair, yet when she fixed him with her serious eyes, he always felt flustered. He supposed she was a year or two older than him but he reckoned he could handle it if she was interested. It didn't mean he thought anything less of Maisie; he simply liked birds.

'I see you're following the Sea King relocation debate,' she said, looking at his screen. Wisps of auburn hair had escaped her loose ponytail.

'What? Oh yeah, and this thing about cytisine.'

She frowned.

'It stops you smokin' but take too much an', accordin' to this, you could die.'

'Really? Do you smoke?'

'Nah.'

'That's all right, then.' Rosie grinned and turned on her heel.

His skin felt hot under his beard. So had Caleb been a

smoker, he wondered, and who was Ann? It struck him that if she knew Caleb wasn't a smoker, Clive Merry probably knew as well.

It was time to find out more about Caleb, the bloke who'd lost the cowboy boots. He keyed *Caleb Coddins* into the search box.

Matt was in luck. He found an entry in an online parish council magazine dated 2010. It appeared Caleb had been one of a handful of local craft people featured for their traditional skills, such as blacksmiths, farriers, and of course, thatchers. The article had quotes, and Matt concentrated on the piece from Caleb's interview.

"I was a child of the fifties and thatching was the family business; it was expected of me – it's how you got into it in those days, unless you were a girl of course. Girls didn't thatch when I were a lad."

'So Caleb came from a long line of thatchers,' Matt said, as if clarifying his reading, 'I don't see Chrissie bein' fobbed off just coz she's a bird.'

He read on. It seemed the family ran out of sons, and as Caleb's sister wasn't considered suitable, they took on an apprentice around the time Caleb's father retired.

Caleb's words were again in quotes, *"The apprentice brought skills with him. My dad were old school; he'd say 'fear God and any work of the devil'. But he'd retired so I let Jason get us onto the internet. We hadn't used emails before we took Jason on. That was back in 1998. I'd say apprenticeships are good for a business."*

'I bet the apprentice were Jason Brookford,' Matt breathed.

He scanned the article again, but there was nothing new to learn on a second reading, and certainly no reference to the cowboy boots, or anything to indicate their importance. There wasn't a hint of America or Caleb being hooked on line dancing, rodeo riding or cowboy re-enactments. And there was nothing to suggest he was a fan of country and western music. Matt had drawn a blank.

'Frag,' he yawned and logged in to the Ancestry site with the library membership. It was time to find out if there was anything there on Caleb. Matt recalled a news article he'd read, repeating the words as he lifted them from his memory, 'Yeah Caleb were *a sixty-year-old man rescued on Friday from Shottisham Creek.* S'pose that makes 'im born in… 1954.'

And it was a reasonable bet that the family business would have been based near the reed beds. 'So, Shottisham Creek…? Yeah, he could've been born in Woodbridge or Ipswich, somewhere in South East Suffolk.'

Matt filled in the information in the birth records section and clicked search.

'Scammin' Trojan! His dad were called Amos Coddins. Amos? Now that's a God-fearin' name… an' Caleb were born in a maternity home in Melton. That's Woodbridge, aint it? Neat,' he whispered.

He returned to the news site, used the dropdown options and clicked on obituaries. He keyed *Amos Coddins* in the search box, and the year the family firm had taken on an apprentice, *1998.* He waited. No results – frag! He tried again, month by month through 1999 and onwards.

'Result!' The year was 2005, the month, September. *Amos Coddins, born 1928, a beloved husband, father of Caleb and dutiful stepfather, passed peacefully in his sleep after a long illness bravely borne. Died September 1st, 2005.*

'Are you still here?' Rosie said as she walked past his computer station.

'Course I'm still 'ere.'

She stopped. 'Can't find what you're looking for? What's up?'

He was tempted to say toothache and play the sympathy card, but she'd taken a step closer and was already gazing at his screen.

'That's odd,' she said.

'Yeah, I reckoned it were odd.' He waited, expecting her say something about the month and year, September and 2005. But why should the date mean anything to her? How could she know it was the same year and month Caleb had lost his cowboy boots?

'It's what's *not* written that's so telling. Why doesn't it say his wife and stepchild's names?' she said.

'What? I were taken by the month an' year.'

'How do you mean?'

'See I already know 'is wife's name were Marylou.' He could have added that he knew it from Caleb's birth record. 'I weren't thinkin' 'bout names,' he added.

Scammin' hell, he couldn't tell her he'd purloined the library login to the Ancestry site to look up birth records.

'Oh sorry, am I'm being insensitive?'

'Well....' His face flamed with his duplicity.

'It's OK. I should have guessed it must be one of your relatives. Sorry.' She hurried away.

'No,' he called to her retreating back, 'no they aint nothin' to do with me,' he added. But he needn't have bothered; she'd already disappeared into the librarian's office.

CHAPTER 28

'Penny for your thoughts, Mrs Jax,' Ron said.

'I was thinking about Matt.'

It was Thursday and they had stopped for their afternoon tea break. Her attention had drifted from the dozen or so pub chairs for repair, and centred on Matt.

'Has he made any sense of the Polyphon message yet, Mrs Jax?'

'I don't know, Mr Clegg. I haven't spoken to him all week. He sent one of his brief texts yesterday. I think he wanted to drop in on his way home and talk to Clive, but he never did. And I haven't heard from him since.'

'So have you tried to contact him?'

She frowned into her mug of tea by way of an answer.

'But it's not like you to hold back, Mrs Jax. You usually want to know the how and why about everything.'

She nodded. Ron was right; her curiosity knew no bounds.

'Clive said he'd dealt with it, so I….' She let her voice drift. The truth was she'd been too engrossed with Jason Brookford's accounts to find space to fret over Matt, at least not until now.

'I'll text him.' She rummaged for her mobile, somewhere near the bottom of her tote bag on the workbench.

Are you OK? she keyed, then scowled at the words *Are you* and reduced them to a single capital *R* and capital *U.* Did it make her message more current and on trend, or simply reminiscent of the Polyphon cipher? Either way, nuances would likely be lost on Matt. For clarity, she added, *You didn't drop in yesterday* and pressed send.

His answer pinged back as she sipped her tea.

I know I didn't. In library now - demo-ing day. Is Clive at open mic tomorrow? Got more for him... might be on phone records he got.

'Is Matt all right, Mrs Jax?'

'He doesn't say but he's at the Academy, which probably means he's OK. It sounds like he's got more for Clive. I guess he's been trawling the internet for him. I....' She stopped as her curiosity spiralled, 'I don't think I'm supposed to know or ask. You see....' Frustration caught her tongue.

'You see what, Mrs Jax?'

'I've got to stop myself asking Matt. It's this forensic accounting course. It's made me realise I'll have to sign a nondisclosure or secrecy agreement if I take on forensic accounting.'

'Ahh... and you think Matt's been sworn to secrecy?'

'I don't know. I'd have to ask him.' She almost laughed at her lapse in logical progression. Was she losing her edge?

'So,' she added, casting a glance around the barn and changing the subject, 'isn't it time we returned the pub chairs we've already repaired? They're cluttering here and the store room. There's barely room for the ones we're still working on.' Action usually restored her status quo, and with any luck it would stop her obsessing about what exactly Matt had discovered for Clive.

'A good idea, Mrs Jax. Yes, give Steve a call. He'll need to unlock the pub for us.'

She had Steve's number on her phone under *man in charge of pub repairs* and pressed automatic dial.

He answered after the second ring, and it took only a

few moments to establish he was in the Poachers and would be there for another couple of hours.

'Good. I'll bring over the ones we've repaired. I'll be with you in the next hour. OK, Steve?'

She smiled and slipped her phone back into her tote bag. 'Well that's worked out nicely,' she murmured.

'I doubt he was expecting them back for a while yet.'

'Exactly; but with pair of us…. You know, I thought I'd make a start on the two with arms next.'

'You mean the Mendlesham carvers, Mrs Jax?'

'Yes, but strictly speaking, they're Mendlesham-style Windsors.'

'We're in Suffolk, Mrs Jax; I think we can drop the reference to Windsor. They're Mendleshams,' he said slowly, before adding, 'they've twin cross rails in their backs and three single ball-turnings spacing them.'

'And the back spindles stop short of the seat.'

'Yes, to make more space for a bottom or a cushion.'

'I wonder if back in the 1800s, they had particularly big bottoms in Mendlesham.' She didn't try to stop the whimsical tone lilting her voice.

'Tailoring for the well-off clients, Mrs Jax.'

'Yes, that'll be it, Mr Clegg.' She smoothed her smile and gathered their empty mugs to wash.

The damaged chairs had been easy to pack into the Clegg & Jax van when they'd brought them from the pub, close on two weeks ago. But now repaired and more precious, Chrissie knew she couldn't just shoehorn and stack them in. She had to take extra care, positioning old threadbare blankets and dustsheets to protect their backs and legs on the journey. It took longer than she had expected and, as she drove along the airfield perimeter lane and into Wattisham village, she pictured how good they'd look in the bar. She couldn't wait for Steve's surprise when he saw how well they'd turned out.

'What the…?'

A black Ford Mondeo was parked next to a pickup truck outside the Poachers. The front door into the main bar stood partly open.

She guessed the pickup belonged to Steve. But the Mondeo? Why was Clive's car outside the Poachers? Had Steve found another dead body? The thought caught her breath.

She pulled onto the grass verge, grabbed her tote bag and hurried to the pub's front door. A surge of anxiety fired her pulse. Her first-ever glimpse into the bar flashed back – the darkness, the body on the floor, the musty smell, the sinking feeling in her stomach.

She forced herself to stop, take a deep breath, and step across the threshold.

The air still carried the damp, mildewed smell. She blinked and focused. Daylight filtered through the dirty glass. Buttery light streamed from a single bulb. It dangled on a flex from the centre of the ceiling and cast dull shadows. She let her eyes sweep the floor; no dead bodies. The tiled area looked clean where Jason Brookford had lain.

'Chrissie? Hi. This is a surprise. What are you doing here?' Clive's voice resonated from somewhere near the fireplace.

She dragged her eyes from the old tiles.

'Are you OK, Chrissie?'

She stepped further into the pub and ignored his question as she took in his latex gloves and wad of evidence bags. 'What's happened, Clive?'

'I want to take another look at the fireplace.'

'But I thought the SOC team went over everything in here?'

'Yes, but that was before....'

He didn't need to say more. She knew he meant the disc. The likely match with Cesspool Man's neck had changed things. She relaxed a fraction. It was rather flattering to be spoken to in code and even nicer to be one of the ones in the know.

'You startled me, that's all,' she said covering for her flashback.

'Oh hello, Chrissie.' Steve strode into the bar from the washroom toilet extension. He looked distracted, his hazel eyes seemingly darker in the soft electric light. 'We really need to fix the roof. We should have made a start on it by now, but who could have guessed we'd lose both our thatchers? I mean, how much bad luck is that?' His words seemed to be addressed to the room, the world... anyone who would listen.

Chrissie found herself biting back the *it's too much to believe it was just down to bad luck*, while Clive asked calmly, 'When were they due to start? I assume we're talking about the Coddins & Brookford thatchers?'

'Yes,' he shook his head in weary disbelief, 'I believe they wanted to get on with it ASAP. Before the winter. You'll have to check with George, but theirs'll have been one of the first payments from the Friends of the Poachers.'

'So they were paid up front to buy straw?' Chrissie might have been stating the obvious, but there'd been no reference to the Poachers Basket in their business account. 'Well I hope the Friends of the Poachers get their money back,' she added, the accountant in her refusing to be suppressed and the forensic module making her guess it was a cash payment.

'Too right, Chrissie. Now, I think you've got some chairs for me.'

'Absolutely. I'll bring them in. Do you want them left here or in the room where they were stacked before?' Something stopped her calling it the *old guestroom*. Was it because she wanted to forget its history? No, she figured she was simply being discreet. There was no reason to let on to Steve that she knew a few things about the Poachers past.

She shivered and caught Clive's frown. It was a sign to leave him to talk to Steve.

It took her four trips from the van, carrying one chair at a time. She set them down in the bar area and stood back while Steve looked at them.

'Good job; the wood looks great,' he said as he picked one up, looked at its underside and set it down again.

'Yes, waxed and polished. We settled on a light base-coat varnish. It lets the natural colour of the elm come through.'

Steve nodded before sitting on one. He leaned forwards and sideways, then let his weight rest back in the way people do when trying out a chair. 'Yes; sturdy, comfortable and traditional. Well done, and thank you.'

She glowed.

'So how many more to repair?' he asked.

'Another eight.'

'Do you want help carrying these through to the back room, Chrissie?' Clive asked. There was something in his tone, an implied *just say yes*.

'Thanks, Clive.'

She couldn't help feeling curious, so much so that it overrode her unease at being close to where Jason had died. It was a relief when Steve tramped upstairs and left them to move the chairs.

'Is this where the fight took place?' Clive asked, dropping his voice as he led the way with a chair.

It seemed poorly lit as she followed with a second chair into the room, almost hidden to one side where the bar extension met the main bar area. The musty smell was strong and claustrophobia threatened, as stacked tables, a bookshelf and piles of sundry items pressed in from the walls.

'I don't know exactly where the fight took place,' she said, the sensory overload combining with her emotions and choking her brain.

'I know I should be asking Ron, but as we're here I thought he might have shown you when you both collected the chairs.'

'And why would he have done that?'

'Because I know you, Chrissie, and you will have asked him.'

The stark, perceptive truth in his words broke the spell. She stood for a few moments and let the old snooping Chrissie percolate as she gazed around the room.

'Ron was reluctant to talk about it, but it was the door into this room,' she said, taking the door handle and swinging the door slowly on its hinges. 'He helped to repair this panel here.' She pointed to one of the upper panels. 'Can you see where there's a piece of wood added? The centre of this panel stands out a few millimetres more than the undamaged panels. And on the other side, the saloon bar side, you'll see the paint helps to disguise any split.'

'Oka-ay….' Clive moved closer to get a better view.

She watched him change into full DI mode as he focussed on the panel, then the doorframe, then the nearby skirting boards and floor.

'Well it's far too late to pick up any blood splatter staining; more than fifty years too late. There've been decades of footfall, mopping, cleaning, and new paint.' His shoulders seemed to slouch with the hopelessness of it all.

'But what about under the repair? This sheet of wood covers the broken panel on one side… at least that's what Ron told me.'

'You mean if you took this off….?'

'Well why not? We know that whatever's under there has been sealed in since the fight.'

'Can you pry it off for me, Chrissie? No, forget I said that. I'll call in the SOC team.'

'I think you need to talk to Ron. He'll be the one to take that repair apart. He'll be able to confirm it's his repair from years ago and… well, has anyone in your SOC team got carpentry skills?'

'You could be right, Chrissie. I'll see if the SOC team can work with Ron on this. Yes, that's the way forward.' He reached into his pocket for his phone.

CHAPTER 29

'Are you coming to the open mic night? It's down the Nags Head. Starts eight o'clock,' Nick asked.

His question was directed at Dave, who had stepped back from the workbench to eye a length of wood. The other carpenters had already left the Willows workshop. Nick couldn't blame them, hell - it was after four o'clock, it was Friday and they wanted to get home. They certainly weren't going to risk getting dragged into helping with the Poachers windows. Bad luck could be contagious. Just by association.

'I'm starting to think we might've bitten off more than we can chew, with these windows.'

'I know, Dave. There's six panes of glass in each of the sashes. Two sliding sashes per window – it could add up to a load of grief.'

Nick stood, reading the dimensions on the construction drawings 'Yeah, twenty-four panes! It'd make more sense if we made both front windows for the main bar at the same time. What d'you say, Dave?'

'Seems sensible.' Dave walked over to look as the drawings as well. 'Yes, same size. It'll be less hassle in the long run. Eight o'clock, you said?'

'Yeah; does that mean you're coming?'

'No, just wondering how long you've got before you slough off from here.'

The barb struck home. Nick knew he'd been distracted, not quite himself over the past few weeks, but he'd thought no one had noticed. It was this ancestry business. It had got to him, crept under his skin and niggled, making him unsure of his past and set him wondering, always wondering.

'Yeah, OK Dave. No need to get all hostile. I'm giving my free time as well.'

When Dave didn't say anything, Nick added, 'I'll be here for a couple more hours, OK?'

Dave nodded. 'Right, well let's get some of this stock through the thickness planer, and then cut into strips for the sash rails, stiles and mullions. We can work on the box frames later.'

'Yeah – sounds like a plan.'

'If we get a real move on, we should have time to start on the mortise and tenons for the rails and stiles,' Dave added.

'Do you reckon we'll get to set up the window-sash router bits today, then?'

'No, but if you hung around longer, we might.'

'I've already said I can't, Dave.'

'OK, OK!' Dave held up both hands in an I-give-up and you-calm-down gesture. 'But I know how you lurve working with the router. I thought a little temptation, a little incentive, might persuade you to stay on?'

'But I'm singing with Jake. As I said, it's open mic. Come along; you'll see it's more fun than watching the router bit cut,' he slowed for emphasis, 'even if it cuts *both* the coving and the rabbit for the glass *at the same time*. There's cool and there's supercool, you know.'

'Maybe, but I reckon making sliding sash windows is carpentry's equivalent to re-setting a Rubik's Cube. That's pretty smart.'

Nick felt the tension between them ease with the banter. Further conversation died when they passed lengths of wood through the thickness planer and the motor roared and the cutting blades shrieked. Left to his own thoughts, Nick couldn't help wondering where Dave's resentment towards him had come from.

He knew Dave hated being on the wrong side of a secret, and he supposed his great-grandfather's past was the secret. So, was this about his great-grandfather? Jeeeez, he thought, Dave is like Chrissie; not knowing makes him more inquisitive. But there was another thing they had in common. They both liked working with things from the past. With Chrissie, it was furniture, but with Dave it was old buildings; he liked to know their history. Could this be the sticking plaster to mollify Dave? Nick's thoughts gave way to an idea.

'If you're interested in the history of the Poachers Basket, you know we can go and see the archivist?' Nick said when there was a lull between runs through the thickness planer.

'Archivist? I didn't know the pub had one.'

'Yeah, it's George Lamanby's wife.'

'How'd you know that?'

'He told us when Tim an' I were fitting their stable doors. He said people keep giving him old photos and memorabilia connected with the pub.'

'Because he's the chairman of the Friends of the Poachers?'

'Yeah. So his wife's ended up looking after it for the Friends. Nice place they've got, by the way, at least judging by the stables.'

'So how does it work then? You just turn up?'

'No, she said to ring and arrange a time.'

Nick was rather pleased with Dave's reaction and he

wasn't going to spoil it by saying he didn't actually have Mrs Lamanby's number. He could get it from Tim or via Pat, the middle-aged secretary and receptionist; the public face of Willows when she manned her small front office. If all else failed, he reckoned he could ring George Lamanby.

'So what do you say, Dave? Do I ring her? Make us an appointment?'

Dave grinned. 'Yes, fix something up for after work or maybe at the weekend?'

'Cool.' Nick basked in the moment.

CHAPTER 30

Open Mic Night down the Nags Head started at eight o'clock.

Megapixels! Matt was running late. He had hoped to get back to Stowmarket with plenty of time to pick up Maisie, down a lager with her in the bar, and bag a table near the microphone - all before the singing kicked off. But Damon had kept him late tracing contact details for more card companies' lists of names. And then finally out on the street, his mobile leapt into life, just as he was zipping up his denim jacket ready to mount his Vespa.

Beep-itty-beep! Beep-itty-beep beep! He pulled off his helmet, fumbled for his phone and read Clive's caller ID.

He bit back the *Mega Blog! What you want?* and whispered 'Yeah?' into his phone.

'Matt? Is that Matt?'

'Yeah.' He waited.

'It's Clive. You left a message with Chrissie. Something about meeting me at the Open Mic Night this evening.'

'Yeah.'

'Well I'm not going to make it. A lot's come up. I'm very busy.'

'Oh yeah?'

'Yes. What did you want to tell me?'

'Well... you've kinda caught me, but....' He squared his shoulders and took on his special status code name – lager & a wedge of lime. 'It's OK to talk now, is it?'

'Yes, Matt. That's why I'm calling you.'

'Right well... I were wonderin' if you got all them

phone records for Jason Brookford and Caleb Coddins?'

'And what's made you wonder about that? More to the point, what have you got for me?'

'On me searchin' I found a death announcement for Caleb's dad, Amos.'

'And?'

'He died back in 2005 on September 1st. Then Caleb lost them boots in the Poachers Basket September 13th 2005. So I'm sayin' them two dates are connected.'

'Why? How are they connected?'

'Coz when I went searchin' on one of them central databases for UK burials and cremations, it turned out Amos were buried the same day them boots went missin'. The 13th September 2005. Now just supposin' there were like a wake for 'im in the pub after... then it has to be someone at the wake stealin' them boots, right?'

'Maybe, but so what?'

'Yeah, but how about his family? They'll 've been at the wake, an' judgin' by his death notice, they don't sound close.'

'How do you mean, *don't sound close*?'

'Not on first name terms.'

'And because of that you're saying they stole his boots? This was back in 2005. Now there aren't any of them around to be on first name terms. At least not locally. You're making connections where there aren't any and wasting my time, Matt.'

'No-no, Clive,' Matt wailed, 'Raelynn Harris were connected to Caleb or them boots back in 2005. She were the one settin' up a notice wantin' 'em found. She's still around. So 'ave you looked to see if her number is on them phone and text records you got for Jason and Caleb?'

'You mean the recent records? We don't have any-thing going back to 2005.'

'Yeah, recent.'

'They're being looked at. What's her number... no, just text it to me, OK?'

'Right.'

'Was that it? Anything else for me?'

'No.'

'OK, thanks for that, and text me the number. Bye.' The call went dead.

Matt blinked, collected his thoughts and pulled Raelynn Harris's number from his visual memory.

He felt good as he texted it to Clive. 'Might order m'self a wedge o' lime in a bottle of lager tonight,' he breathed and then remembered his secret status. Lager came in pint or half-pint glasses down the Nags Head; best to stay under cover. And blogging hell, now he was running even later.

His journey back from Bury St Edmunds to Stowmar-ket was fast. He took the A14 and twisted the scooter's throttle as far as he dared. The speed made him feel weight-less, and like a superhero, he could have been flying. For once he was at one with his body, unaware of his stomach and proud of his search capabilities. By the time he coasted into Stowmarket and pulled up next to the bollards stopping vehicle access to the old market place, he was fired up and ready for the Open Mic Night ahead.

He spotted Maisie carrying a large carrier bag. She swung it as she walked, her poncho cape-wrap flapping, and her ankles and lower calves bare below pale, cropped trousers. Her usual punch of colour struck him as strangely muted, the pinks dull in the fading light and her linen hair braids veiled by shadows. He sat with his legs astride the scooter and waited, only pushing up his visor and waving when she got nearer.

'Hi, Mais!'

'Hiya! Cor; the pointy bits don't half catch,' she said breathlessly, and thrust the carrier bag at him.

'What you got?' he said as he fielded it loosely between the windshield and his chest and thighs.

'The crate from the States arrived today.'

'The one you been talkin' about?'

'Yeah.' She leaned across the bag and kissed him. 'I've been helpin' sort out the new stock. That's why I were a bit late. Thought you wouldn't mind waitin' if I were bringin' you these.'

'So are they–'

'Yeah, you bet they are. They're them cowboy boots you wanted.'

'Cool! Thanks, Mais!'

'Well aint you goin' to look at'em?'

'I will, but we're runnin' late, Mais. I want a good table close to the singers. I'll look at 'em when we get to the pub.'

'Yeah, but Matt....'

'We gotta get movin'.'

Seconds later, Matt accelerated away with Maisie riding pillion and the carrier bag wedged between them. Angular edges dug into his back. Trojan bot! Was it a Fort Worth heel or toe? Worse still, had Maisie brought him ones with spurs? He recalled the Fort Worth boots he'd viewed on the internet. He hadn't seen spurs, and Raelynn Harris hadn't raised the subject either. A hard edge pressing against his spine focused his memory... *yeah, that were it.*

Them spurs were a separate item, somethin' to strap on his inner voice reassured. Spurs were removable. It was going to be OK.

***

Matt knew it was busy in the Nags Head as soon as he rode into the pub car park. Every space was taken, but luckily the area behind the waste bins was still free. He slipped the Vespa safely out of view and anchored the antitheft chain to a concrete post in the fence close by. Maisie adjusted her poncho wrap, tossing the fabric back from one shoulder to reveal folds of the vibrant pink lining.

'I s'pose I'll 'ave to carry this,' she said, scooping up the cumbersome carrier bag threatening to spill off the saddle.

'You look like a superhero, Mais.'

'What you on about?'

'Your cloak's kinda cool.'

'Ta.' She smiled and added, ''Cept it's a poncho wrap.'

'What?'

'It aint a cloak. It's too short.'

He slipped an arm around her and they walked, feet crunching on gravel as they left the bins and wove a path out through the car park. The pub's exterior was stuccoed, disguising its age. It seemed plain and stark, and was set only a few feet back from the road. There was no space for tables, chairs or parasols to grace its frontage outside. An A-frame noticeboard stood at the entrance into the main bar and announced *Open Mic Night 8 o'clock Friday.*

Matt pushed the heavy door. The smell of sweat and stale beer filled his nose. A barrage of sound hit his ears.

'You go an' bag us a table near the mic, an' I'll get the

drinks,' he shouted, his excitement rising with the tide of voices and the nineties hit belting from the jukebox.

He was jostled and pushed at the bar. Lager slopped from his glass when he threaded his way back through the crush.

'Over here, mate,' Nick called.

'Got you a rum n' cola, Mais' he shouted.

The small table looked crowded. Chrissie sat on a chair next to Maisie, who was perched on a tall stool. Jake had parked himself and his guitar on a narrow bench seat and Nick stood leaning against the wall. The carrier bag occupied the greater part of the scrubbed pine top; the rest was taken by glasses. Lager dripped from Matt's as he set the drinks down.

'Watch out!' Maisie yelped.

'She's being very mysterious about what's in the bag, isn't she, Chrissie?' Nick said.

'Yes, so now you're here Matt, can we see what's in it? And maybe free up some space on the table while you're about it?'

A surge of curiosity and excitement gripped Matt as he reached for the bag. He peered inside and gazed at the cowboy boots. The faintly sweet smell of soft, brown, Texan leather wooed him.

'Hackin' dongle! They're bloggin' amazin',' he breathed. He pulled out a boot and ran his hand over the squared-off pointed toe, the wooden heel and thick leather sole. He supposed the leg would reach to mid-calf, although the front and back were shorter; cut away in the shape of a V. It added to the cowboy look. 'An' there aint no spurs!'

'Are they from your retro shop, Maisie?' Chrissie asked, watching his face.

'Yeah.' Maisie frowned. 'Pity there aint much fancy stitchin' on 'em. Did you want spurs, then?'

'No, but they're.... What size you got, Mais?'

'US 10s; that's what you said. There weren't no others that size in the crate. Aint you gonna try 'em on, then?'

'Yeah, try them on,' Nick hooted.

Matt hesitated. The boot looked huge; far too big for him. When he'd asked for a US 10, he'd imagined he could get away with pretending it was his size. But how the blog was he going to fool Maisie now? In desperation he nodded towards the microphone stand in the empty corner, less than a metre away.

'How long we got before you two start singin'?' he asked.

'Long enough for you to try on the boots. That's both boots, Matt,' Chrissie said.

For a split second he hoped she was implying the second boot might be smaller, but he couldn't read her face and Maisie's cheeks had turned rosier than the pink of her hair braids. Blogging hell! He'd just have to pretend they fitted. After all, they were only for *in case* Raelynn tipped up at the B&M office.

'Yeah OK.' He put both boots down on the old floorboards and kicked off his trainers. Now his feet looked even smaller and resembled stubby flippers next to the one-and-three-quarter-inch heeled boots. He slipped his foot into the right boot.

The old leather forefoot was loose before shaping inwards to hug the intended-size-10 wearer's toes. Except Matt's foot had started to taper in the boot's forefoot region. His toes ended short; at least an inch or so before the squared-off tip. He wiggled them without coming into con-

225

tact with the leather upper. He stood and bent his foot, as if to take a step, but the boot failed to grip his heel or move with him.

'How do it feel?' Maisie asked.

'Course I'll be wearin' more socks.'

'But you're always outa socks....' Maisie's voice morphed into a tearful howl as Matt slipped his other foot into the left boot, took a step and nearly toppled into the table.

'You'll break your neck in those,' Chrissie said, rescuing her ginger beer.

'Well, if they aint right I aint carryin' them back to the shop, Matt. I'm tellin' you; I aint.'

'Slow a minute, Maisie. They're cool boots. Can I try them on?' Nick asked.

Matt blinked as he took in Maisie's heated face. Memories of Raelynn's threats still burned his ears. He had to keep the cowboy boots, otherwise Damon might sack him. What was he going to do?

'Come on, they're too big for you, let me try them,' Nick coaxed.

'Yeah Matt, let Nick try 'em. At least he seems keen on 'em. You didn't even want to look at 'em 'til now. You said they aint got spurs.' Maisie voice rose tremulously.

'OK, OK! But they're still mine; right, Nick?' Matt stepped out of the boots.

He watched as Nick put them on, took a few paces, shifted his weight from one foot to the other and finally grinned at him.

'They're cool. How much do you want for them? Come on, what d'you say Matt? Or is it Maisie I'm paying?' Nick asked.

She laughed gleefully and clapped her hands, 'Oh just take 'em for twenty quid, Nick. An' Matt – if you want cowboy boots, you drop round the shop an' try 'em on first. An' you can pay for 'em yourself as well. I'm done with them boots.' As if to make the point, Maisie folded her arms.

'Right, we're on in five,' Jake said as he stood up to carry his guitar to the microphone stand.

'Sorry, mate, but they're a perfect fit. Like Maisie says; go and get some your size. Can't stop... we've a few numbers to sing.' Nick winked and headed for the microphone and his guitar, ready in its case in the corner.

Matt felt gutted. He'd lost the boots, Maisie was cross, and Damon might sack him - and kill him as well. He listened to the dying notes from the jukebox and sipped his lager.

'Psst. Matt. Was there something special about those boots?' Chrissie whispered, as Nick and Jake fine-tuned their guitars.

'Yeah an' no.'

'Like what?'

'Sorry, Chrissie; I can't say. Clive 'd understand, but he don't want me talkin'.'

'Then you'd better put your trainers back on before you get splinters from the floorboards.' Chrissie's frown was aimed at her glass.

Was she telling him she understood his Lager & Wedge of Lime special status? All he knew was that the evening had turned upside down and his best mate was out in front of a microphone, making the Fort Worth's look awesome.

Jake played a few guitar phrases and fiddled with the

loudspeaker while Nick adjusted the microphone height and strummed a few notes on his guitar. The babble in the bar ebbed. The atmosphere became expectant.

Nick spoke into the microphone; 'Hi everyone! So it's Jake and me to get things going this evening! We're starting with an old favourite and then we'll play a new song.' He cast a smile around the bar.

Matt looked pointedly at the cowboy boots. It hurt.

Nick caught Matt's eye and grinned more broadly. 'There's a person instrumental to one of the songs in the bar tonight. Yeah, so I'm going to ask him to help lead the chorus from the floor. Hey Jake; let's play the new one first, OK?'

Jake laughed and plucked a sequence of different chords.

'OK, are we ready now? Matt, are you ready? So it's called *I Broke the Code*.'

Matt felt the glow of acknowledgment. It dulled his pain.

Maisie whooped and clapped.

CHAPTER 31

Chrissie had thoroughly enjoyed the evening at the Nags Head. Nick had been on good form and several of the girls in the bar had been eyeing both Jake and Nick with interest; so much so that when later Chrissie stood up to leave, her place at the table was quickly taken by a stunning girl who'd introduced herself as Sarita.

Of course, Chrissie had been amused by Sarita's obvious attraction to Nick, but the real consequence of the evening was that her own curiosity had been triggered, and now it smouldered. What was so important about the cowboy boots? She could understand that if Clive was involved, he might not want Matt shooting his mouth off about it. But why was Clive involved in the first place?

As she drove home, she replayed the scene with Matt and the cowboy boots. Maisie had told her she'd got him to play ten-pin bowling, so soft Italian boots for playing bocce volo would have seemed more Matt's style... and consistent with his love of all things Italian. But cowboy boots from Texas? It all jarred.

She slowed the TR7 as she approached Woolpit, her pop-up headlights reflected in the glinting eyes of a cat in a hedge. But dare she ask Clive about his connection with the boots? She suspected not.

Clive's car was parked in the lane outside her end-of-terrace cottage. Its black paintwork merged with the night until her full beams caught it. Only then did the Mondeo take shape, its reflectors and number plate dazzling back at her. She smiled. It was understated, a bit like its owner.

So what did her bright yellow TR7 say about her, she

wondered as she parked it. All show and no content? A peacock? No; it was a classic car with age and design, a fun drive and a diversion. She liked its colour, but there was a downside; people sometimes expected her to be an extrovert or dizzy blonde, an assumption based on the yellow paintwork. And she had to admit that if she'd wanted to have a dizzy-blonde day, then it would be easier to drive her yellow car than go through all the effort of glamming up her naturally blonde hair.

However, she figured it must be obvious to most people who met her that she was a million miles from the clichéd Marilyn of the 1950s. Yet, when it suited her, the car became her construct of a disguise - the ubiquitous private detective's raincoat, but designed to confuse rather than hide. And besides, she had the Clegg & Jax Citroën van to drive whenever she wanted.

***

Chrissie had a troubled night. The *I broke the code* chorus ran on a loop through her restless mind while Clive slept the sleep of the exhausted, barely moving from his back and snoring gently. In half dreams she drove her TR7 through the hours of darkness, past reed beds and shorelines. Cats' eyes morphed into Polyphon discs and glinted at her while waves crashed over seawall defences, all with the slow rhythmic sound of Clive's snoring. Finally she fell into an exhausted, dreamless sleep. When she woke up, it was well after nine in the morning and a mug of tea sat next to her mobile phone on her bedside table.

She rubbed her eyes and focused on the tea. She couldn't recall bringing it up to bed with her. She glanced around the bedroom. No Clive... his trousers and shirt weren't on the chair in the corner and... silence. The cot-

230

tage felt empty.

'Clive?' she called with sudden anxiety. And then she remembered it was Saturday and Clive was working. He must have brought her the mug of tea before he left for work, only she'd been too sleepy to drink it.

She reached out and touched the mug. Yes; it was cold and full. She'd solved that puzzle and it was exhausting. She closed her eyes and drifted.

Brrring brrring! The urgent ringtone pulled her back with a jolt. She fumbled for her phone and blurrily read Clive's ID.

'Hi?' she said, her voice full of sleep, 'What time did you leave this morning?'

'About eight. I had to interview someone just before nine. Did you stay awake long enough to drink your tea? You sound pretty sleepy.'

'Hmm, dropped off. But I'm awake now.'

'Sorry, I should have let you sleep on.'

'No, no. I must get into the day. I want to take a shot at another module.'

'Ha; let me guess - more about fraud?'

'Yes, Fraud Risk Assessment.'

'Well that sounds like fun.'

'Hmm, I've got to do a case study. I thought I'd use the Friends of the Poachers Basket booklet as a framework.'

'Careful, Chrissie. You can't identify the Poachers Basket.'

'I know, but the booklet's got loads of information persuading people to buy community shares in the pub. I can play with the figures and give it a different name.' She felt sleepy, but she'd still caught something in his tone. 'Is there something wrong with that?'

'No, but….'

'But what, Clive?'

'Hmm…well keep this to yourself. It looks as if Caleb and Jason did some thatching for the chairman a couple of years ago.'

'You mean George Lamanby? Back in 2012?'

'Yes, May or June, I think.'

'OK, but does it matter?' When he didn't answer she added, 'Fine, I'll keep that in mind and shy away from it! I guess George must've been happy with them.'

'I assume so, otherwise he wouldn't have asked them to work on the Poachers roof. Right then, I'll ring later.'

'That'll be nice. By-e-e.' She ended the call, but her curiosity had been triggered and her thoughts raced on.

'So if Caleb and Jason did some thatching for George Lamanby back in the summer of 2012,' she murmured to the empty bedroom, 'then there'll be a payment from him into their business account… unless it was in cash.'

She pictured the files on Clive's encrypted memory stick. She saw headings and some of the spreadsheet information, but her mind's eye couldn't summon everything. Oh, to have a photographic memory like Matt's.

'I can't even check on the memory stick,' she sighed. It was back with Clive.

She racked her brains. There'd been two payments into the business account during the early summer months of 2012. The amounts had struck her as being a few thousand pounds less than for their average thatching jobs. 'May and July 2012,' she remembered telling Clive. And if those two payments stood out on the balance sheet, then they warranted more probing. Hadn't Clive just given her the hint?

As if on a mission, she threw back the duvet and sprang out of bed. She hurried across the old floorboards, hardly noticing the cold on her bare feet. She showered and dressed quickly, pulling on clean undies, a polo shirt and jeans before rushing downstairs to the kitchen and her laptop. All the while her mind buzzed with questions.

'Now be logical and write a list,' she told herself. She ignored the *feasibility & business planning*, *community share options* and *financial forecast* headings she'd previously scribbled on her note pad under *Fraud Risk Assessment case study*. They could wait. Instead she wrote *George Lamanby* and *thatching job*. This was far more interesting. But where to begin?

'George Lamanby's on the top of my list. I'll start with him.'

She booted up her laptop and typed his name along with *chairman of the friends of the Poachers Basket* into her browser's search. Moments later she was on the Friends of the Poachers Basket website and a photo of the smiling chairman filled her screen. He stood casual-smart against the backdrop of a woven-willow fence that partially obscured the frontage, but not the roof of a thatched house beyond. The picture oozed the reassurance of a mature man grounded in the local Suffolk countryside; a chairman you could trust.

Chrissie zoomed in on the thatch. It looked neat, clean and relatively new. But was it reed or straw? She'd heard that reed was sometimes wrongly used where the traditional Suffolk style and listed building regulations stipulated straw. So did it matter? More to the point, could she even tell from a photo?

She concentrated on the image. What had Ron told

her?

'Reed is often fixed to the rafters, whereas straw is usually attached to an underlying layer. So a straw thatch roof looks thick. A reed thatch roof can look thinner and less rounded,' he'd said.

'But the payments into Jason and Caleb's account were less than expected for an average thatching job. So where was the scam or fraud in that... unless there'd been large cash payments as well?' she asked herself. 'And why would there have been a reason to make large cash payments?' She went back over her discussions about thatching with Ron.

'Traditionally, coastal areas would've used water reeds,' he'd told her.

'And inland, they'd have used straw?'

'That's right, but reed thatch lasts longer. There's a shortage of Norfolk reed.'

'So is reed pricier?'

'It's more likely to be, but it lasts longer. Some say it's better value for money. I've heard they're importing from abroad.'

'Undercutting the price?' she remembered asking as she recalled that Caleb had died in estuary reed beds.

Ron hadn't answered.

'So round here, people use either reed or straw,' she'd said.

'Unless it's a listed building. Then the thatch has to be traditional to the area; straw inland and water reed for coastal properties. The authorities are strict on that.'

Ron's words swirled in her mind and threw up a question. Was George's home a listed building? On a whim she opened the Historic England website. She'd learnt on her carpentry course that it was the go-to site for a rapid listed-building check. Simply key in the postcode of the property in question, and the site showed all listed buildings and monuments in that postcode.

It didn't take her long to find George Lamanby's post-code amongst his chairman's bio details. She keyed it into the site's search box.

'Yes!' There were three Grade 2 listed buildings in his postcode area. So which one might be his? All she had to go on was the thatched roof showing in the background of a photo on the Friends website. She knew it was a long shot as she worked her way through the features listed for each of the three properties

She read one of the entries again: *Farmhouse, c.1600. One storey and attics with a 2-storey cross-wing to the left. Timber-framed and roughcast. Thatched roof....* It went on to catalogue the 19th and 20th century additions and embel-lishments. The implied roof shape might possibly fit the Friends photo, but however many times she read the entry, she still couldn't find a mention of the type of thatch.

'And to re-thatch a listed building, surely George Lamanby would have had to request listed building plan-ning permission?' she murmured. And then realisation struck. If this listed building wasn't his home, he didn't need planning permission to re-thatch. So if she didn't find a record of the planning application on the council's public access site, it could mean one of two things; either his house wasn't a listed building or if it was, he may simply have re-thatched without putting in a planning request.

Her scalp tingled. She knew she might be on to some-thing, but she had no idea what exactly. Should she delve deeper or hand over to Clive? The old Chrissie would have started digging, but today's Chrissie was on parole to become a part-time forensic accountant. She'd have to tread with care if she was going to stop Clive thinking she was interfering in his case.

It was time for a mug of tea and a pause for reflection.

When Clive rang mid-afternoon, she was immersed in her *Fraud Risk Assessment case study.*

'How's it going?' he asked.

'Better than expected. I've had some fun with my fictional community pub. I've made up some balance sheets for the costs and estimated returns of buying and running it. And then I've set a price for the community shares in the pub.'

'And you've completely made it all up?'

'Of course, and I've made the dividends sound wildly optimistic and not given any substantiated evidence to base the forecasts on.'

'And that's fraud?'

'It is if you're deliberately setting out to deceive people. It's about trying to sell shares based on inflated and false growth predictions.'

'Difficult to prove.'

'Yes, I suppose so, unless you've shown your fabricated evidence for your forecasts. Then there'll be a trail.'

'Right' He sounded weary.

'And then there's a risk of fraud if there are no controls in the system to stop someone making off with the money.' She sensed he was starting to get bored and his guard would be dropping.

'Sounds like old-fashioned theft to me,' he murmured.

'It's about deception; financial deception.'

'Hmm.' He sounded thoughtful.

She kept her tone neutral. This was her moment. 'There's something that's struck me and I've been wondering if it might be worth you checking it out.'

She waited, hoping it sounded as if this had simply popped into her head out of nowhere; nothing to suggest she'd been meddling in police business again, as he called it.

'What's that?' He sounded interested.

'Does George Lamanby live in a listed property?'

'Whatever makes you ask that?'

'I'm just curious to know if he had listed building permission for his re-thatching?'

Clive didn't answer, and she knew better than to repeat the question. In fact she was happy with his silence; it was a sure sign he was taking it on board. Instead she changed subject with a breezy 'How's your day going? You haven't said.'

'Ah, busy. Actually I've just heard from the States.'

'How exciting! Some information on missing Americans at last?'

'Not really. They don't have a centralised record going back far enough to help us. They only set up NamUs in 2009.'

'NamUs?'

'Yes, short for National Missing & Unidentified Persons System.'

'Since 2009? But you want to know about forty years earlier than that, right?'

'Yes, 1957 to 1963; all twenty-five to fifty-year-old men reported missing.'

'So are they saying they can't help you?'

'Kind of, but they were trying to be collaborative.

They came up with a suggestion.'

'Oh yes?'

'They asked if our cesspool skeleton could be military, because if it is, they keep federal records for the military which date back earlier than 2009. They're the United States Military Service Records and are held at the,' he paused as if reading from his notes, 'the National Personnel Records Center in St Louis. They'll have army pension and death records, etcetera.'

'But Suffolk, all East Anglia, had loads of the American Army Air Force stationed over here. There'd be hundreds of them.'

'Yes, I said as much. We'd already told them where the skeleton had been found, but I did happen to mention that the American Army Air force had been stationed at Wattisham Airfield.'

'And?'

'Apparently the Maxwell Air Force Base in Alabama holds records for all who served in the Eighth and Ninth Air Force.'

'Meaning?'

'They may have names of the Americans stationed at Wattisham Airfield.'

'But how does that help? They left at the end of 1945.'

'I suppose they were suggesting some might have stayed in the UK or returned to visit.'

'Wow – now that really is a long shot!'

'I know.'

'It'd be a case of cross-referencing names from the Maxwell Air Force Base records with the United States Military Service Records and seeing who had died or stopped drawing a service pension, and fitted the profile,'

Chrissie said, her accountant's brain gearing into action.

He laughed. 'It's a big ask and I'm not holding out much hope. And it's not up to us. We don't have access.'

She felt as if her brain was about to burst with all the information she'd taken on board; her course project, George Lamanby and his thatched roof, and now the suggestion of a link between the cesspool skeleton and the Wattisham Airfield.

'You know, I think I've sat at this computer for long enough today. I'm going to take out the TR7, top down, and blow the cobwebs away. I'll drop by the farm shop and get something nice to cook for supper. I might even call in to say hi to Sarah, maybe grab a coffee with her. How does that sound?'

'It sounds good.'

'Right, then I deduce work won't keep you from supper!'

CHAPTER 32

Nick drew up alongside the Willows secure parking area for the vans. He had arrived a few minutes early, so he sat letting his mind wander back over the weekend. Sarita had proved a bit of a distraction, a curious mix of playfulness and intense seriousness; one moment touching on her training programme in Ipswich to become a radiographer, and the next giggling about lyrics and Bollywood movies. She'd even talked with a blend of wit and gravity about her family's Indian cuisine catering business. 'It's all down to the tomato ketchup in the masala sauce,' she'd said and then smiled.

Secretly, he was also rather pleased with the Fort Worth cowboy boots. He was convinced they'd helped attract Sarita at the open mic night and given him the edge over Jake. He figured they were lucky boots.

And Maisie had been adamant that he should keep them, so when he'd asked Matt to lead the *I Broke the Code* chorus at the open mic night, he was relieved it had gone some way to smoothing Matt's ruffled feathers. His invitation had been a stroke of genius. He knew Chrissie wouldn't have called it genius. She would have said it was down to his intuitive people skills.

He'd have said, 'I was looking out for a friend.' A mate who was also a bit like a younger brother; someone he and Chrissie had helped get through the bench carpentry year with them at Utterly Academy.

'Yeah,' Nick sighed, 'sometimes you don't choose your friends, they just happen. Ha, or your family. I didn't choose my great-granddad Harold, but he's still my great-grandfather.'

His words pulled together two thoughts – Matt and Harold Bertram Roan. One was his friend and the other was his great-grandfather. Nick knew he needed one to find out more about the other, but could his purchase of the Fort Worth boots have thrown a spanner in those particular works? His stomach twisted. He wanted reassurance and on a whim, he pressed Matt's automatic dial number.

'Hi Matt,' he said when Matt eventually answered with a yawn.

Nick waited but there was nothing more from Matt.

'How're you doing, mate?' Nick prompted.

'Yaahhhn. It's a bit early, aint it?' His long yawn and sleepy voice oozed lethargy.

'Ah sorry, mate. I thought you worked Mondays.'

'Yeah, Mondays…. Pixel! Is it Monday?'

'Yup, and it's eight thirty. I've just arrived at work. I was literally about to get out of my car, and… well I wanted to check you're still OK about me keeping the cowboy boots.'

'Bloggin' hell! How'd you know I'd slept through me alarm?'

Nick didn't bother to answer. Instead he repeated, 'Are you still OK about me keeping the cowboy boots? I did pay Maisie for them.'

'Yeah, sure.' The words were almost lost against the sound of what Nick assumed was Matt throwing back a duvet and leaping out of bed.

'And you're still checking out my great-granddad, right?' He had to know.

'Yeah, yeah. Damon's goin' to spammin' kill me. Ta for the cool alarm.' The call went dead.

Nick laughed. What had he expected? A lucid conversation with Matt about the finer points of hurt feelings, disappointment, and fashionable boots? Or maybe a solid timetable outlining further searches into Harold's life? It wasn't Matt's way and deep down, Nick understood this. But then, the phone call hadn't been about Matt. Well it had been, but it was also about…. 'Hell, it was about me. It was reassurance for me!' Insight felt starkly uncomfortable.

And then he remembered something Chrissie had once said. 'Don't spend all your time navel gazing, Nick. Get on and live; sometimes it's the best plan.'

Thud! The sound resonated through the roof of the Fiesta. Instinctively he ducked.

'What the hell…?' Nick cast around.

'Ha – woke you up, did I? Heavy weekend, was it?' Dave beamed at him through the open passenger-side window, one hand still on the roof of the car.

'No Dave, I was thinking.'

'Come on,' his tone spoke disbelief, 'you didn't even see me drive past and park just now. You look like you need a strong coffee.'

Jeeeez, Nick thought - it was like talking to Matt; half the time it was easier not to explain.

'Well don't just sit there. Get yourself out of the car, Nick.'

'Are you offering to make me coffee, Dave?'

'Cheeky beggar. Have a bit of respect for your old trainer, thank you.'

'Sure thing. Hey, I was going to ring Mrs Lamanby today and arrange a time to see the pub memorabilia. Any evening work best for you?' Nick asked, grinning as he got out of his car.

They walked companionably past the locked gates of the secure parking area.

'Wednesday, Thursday, Friday are OK. The wife'll be away visiting her sister in Peterborough for a few days. She's had to bring it forward from the weekend.'

'Right,' Nick chuckled, 'Does that mean we'll be working on the sash windows evenings *and* this weekend? You know I've got a social life as well?' His thoughts drifted to Sarita as they headed through the side entrance into the modern single-storey industrial unit that was Willows & Son.

***

'Well that was a ruddy waste of time,' Dave said as he gripped the steering wheel.

Nick sat in the passenger seat and looked through the van's windscreen. If he kept his eyes fixed on the road ahead, the churning in his stomach might settle and the rising nausea subside. Nick swallowed back some bile as Dave threw the van around another tight bend on the route back from Dunwich.

'It's a completely wasted Thursday,' Dave shouted.

'I don't get why they wanted a firm from Needham Market. It's miles away,' Nick mumbled.

'Word gets around. Willows is good. So why the hell didn't someone tell us they'd changed their minds and settled for a joker with the lowest estimate? We've driven halfway across Suffolk for nothing.'

'Yeah.' Nick could only manage the one word. That last bend had been a white-knuckler. He moved his legs to brace himself better.

'Ruddy cowboys calling themselves carpenters!' Dave boomed.

They drove in silence for a few miles. Nick glanced away from an oncoming car, and focused on the footwell. Hell, he was still wearing the Fort Worth boots! He'd worn them yesterday to impress Sarita again, and this morning he'd put them on without thinking. They were amazingly comfortable, but just wait till Dave spotted them. He inwardly cringed as he imagined the string of cowboy-carpenter jokes Dave would hurl at him.

'So who pays for the stock?' Nick asked, grittily hoping to distract Dave from noticing his boots.

'You mean all the wood we brought with us in the van?'

'Yeah.'

'I expect old Mr Willows'll charge'em for late cancellation. That'll cover it.'

'Yeah, of course.'

They had joined the A12. The road was wider, straighter and the bends less acute. As Nick's motion sickness eased, so his brain geared into action. 'Today isn't completely wasted, Dave.'

'Oh no?'

'We've still got the memorabilia visit. Mrs Lamanby was expecting us this evening, but we could try dropping round now?'

'What? Actually now's not such a bad idea. If the office can't be arsed to pass on a cancellation message, why should we rush back? Yes, give her a call.' Dave's shoulders visibly relaxed.

Nick checked through his phone's call history.

'Ah, this'll be the one I used to organise the visit.' When a female voice answered he launched into his ready patter; 'Hi, it's Nick from Willows. We'll be passing your way earlier than we'd expected. Is it OK if we call in to look at the memorabilia when we pass?'

'It's rather short notice. I thought you were coming at five thirty. Do you want lunch laid on as well?' He caught the sarcasm in her voice.

'No, no, Mrs Lamanby. We don't want to be any trouble, it's just that a few things have happened today and we've had to alter our schedule.'

'I have to say it's a bit inconvenient, but… OK, I'll expect you at about two thirty.' She ended the call before Nick had a chance to utter another word.

'What's the verdict?' Dave asked.

'She's kind of OK with it. Two thirty, so we've some time to kill.'

'Well there's no point in upsetting the woman by arriving too early,' Dave said, his shoulders still relaxed. 'Let's take the back route.'

'Yeah, plenty of time for packed lunch and the scenic route.'

Dave swung off the A12 and headed along a meandering B road.

***

They took their time and for once Dave drove slowly while Nick gave directions.

When Nick recognised the automatic gates set back from the road and the hawthorn hedge visible beyond, he tapped his side window. 'This is it! Turn in here, Dave. The intercom got the gates opened last time.'

Dave pulled up and Nick jumped down onto the gravel driveway. The stony grit and chippings crunched under his cowboy boots. He winced, trying not to draw attention to his footwear as he strode to the gatepost on the driver's side. He pressed the intercom button and spoke loudly; 'It's Nick and Dave from Willows.'

Silence stretched before a metallic voice crackled back at him. Was it Mrs Lamanby? He reckoned it sounded so distorted, that if reality had flipped into a sci-fi parallel world, then she'd got herself trapped inside the intercom casing. Thankfully *take the left fork to the house* was clear enough to make sense of.

The house, when they reached it, looked picture-postcard pretty. It was typical of the old two-storey, timber-framed farmhouses of the area. Pink limewash gave the plaster an idyllic Suffolk touch and tiny windows high in the end gables promised cobwebby attic rooms. The thatched roof dominated the farmhouse; the L-shaped lay-out giving rise to a beautifully cross-gabled expanse of newish-looking thatch.

Mrs Lamanby came out to greet them, nodding a wel-come as Dave parked the van on driveway to one side of the house. Nick found his eyes drawn to the thatched roof as they followed her through a gate in the woven-willow fencing and along a path to the kitchen door.

'It's a magnificent thatched roof, Mrs Lamanby,' Nick said to her receding back as she stepped into the kitchen.

She stopped and faced Nick with a look of surprise, 'What's that you said about the thatch?'

'They did a good job of your thatching,' Dave said cheerily, as he pushed past Nick to enter the kitchen. 'I hope the Poachers Basket eventually gets as good a job done on it.'

She frowned and Nick sensed her tension as he filed in behind Dave.

The kitchen felt cosy and snug despite its generous

size. Oak beams crossed the low ceiling, and warmth radiated from the cast iron AGA cooker with its classic custard-yellow tints.

'I've put everything over here for you.'

She led the way to a large pine table almost filling one end of the kitchen. Five plastic stacker boxes had been placed in a row on its worn surface.

'Wow, you've got loads of stuff. Can you talk us through some of it?' Nick said, instinctively treading lightly to minimise the clip-tap sound his cowboy boots made on the tiled floor.

Nick settled next to Dave on a bench seat drawn along one side of the table, while Mrs Lamanby stood on the other side, opening a box and pulling out photos and sketches of the old pub.

'This is probably the earliest picture we have of the Poachers Basket.'

It was a sketch in pencil on paper, dated 1910 and showed the pub's front aspect. It looked smaller than Nick remembered, but of course it was before the more recent washroom and toilet addition.

'The photos date from the 1930s onwards.' She opened another storage box.

They bent over the photos, passing them to each other, concentrating on the images and lost in thought. The pub tended to feature as a backdrop, the real focus of the photos being on figures in the foreground.

For the most part, small groups of young men smiled at the camera and held up pints of beer. Some were dressed in old style Royal Air Force uniforms, or off-duty clothes. The American Army Air Force men smiled with shorter cropped hair and more informality. They wore tee-shirts with their uniforms, slacks or shorts.

'They look happy,' Dave said, 'Do we know the names of any of these men?'

'Sometimes there's a name or date scribbled on the back, but mostly there's nothing.'

'That's kind of sad,' Nick said.

'Yes, it was. I mean is.' She moved her hand over a mound of photos, 'So this pile is early second world war up through 1942 when the airfield was still Royal Air Force.'

'But it was handed over to the Americans sometime in 1942, wasn't it?' Dave said.

'Yes, they were there from October. That's why there are some American Army Air Force photos in amongst the 1942 ones.'

'Right,' Nick murmured.

'And the runway was extended for what they thought would be heavy bombers. It went across the lane the Poachers is on. That's why the lane stops dead at the airfield boundary fence. The Americans stayed 'til the end of 1945,' she added in a dry monotone.

'You sound as if you know a lot about the airfield,' Nick said.

She looked away.

'So the photos for 1943 to 45 are where?' Dave asked.

'In this pile here. And this box is for the Cold War years, and then these are more recent, dating to the present.'

'And what's in the other boxes?' Nick willed her to say *Polyphon discs*.

'Newspaper cuttings, beer mats, some old sets of darts, tea towels… that kind of thing.'

'Cool,' he murmured, mildly disappointed, 'Do you know if they used to hold music evenings in the pub?'

'What? No. I mean, I don't know.'

'Nick's into music in a big way, aren't you Nick?' Dave spoke in an off-hand manner as he studied a photo, 'Country & western, I believe.'

'So that's why you're wearing cowboy boots; I wondered why,' she said.

'What? Because I like country & western music? You must be kidding; I'm not into that. The boots are cool, and retro is very now, that's all.' He shot a warning look at Dave.

'OK, then I'll leave you with the things on the table. Ask if you need anything explaining.' She nodded again brusquely and retreated to perch on a tractor-seat barstool near the Aga.

Time seemed to lose meaning as Nick looked methodically through piles of old photographs.

'Here, take a shufty at these,' Dave said and handed him a couple of photos.

It took Nick several minutes to work out what was meant to catch his eye. And then he spotted it. Dave was obviously still pursuing the cowboy-boot theme, because one of a group of American air force men sat with his knees crossed in front of the fireplace in the Poachers bar area. The shot was busy with airmen standing behind and to the side, everyone crowding in on him so that his booted foot was lost against the fabric of someone's trousers. But the one-and-three-quarter-inch heel and pointed toe were unmistakable.

'He's wearing cowboy boots, Dave!'

Nick knew he'd made a mistake as soon as he'd said it.

CHAPTER 33

Matt sat at his favourite computer station in the Utterly Academy library and waited for inspiration. Slices of pizza and a double helping of fries had mushed into a warm poultice in his stomach; it was both comfort food and his Thursday lunchtime reward for the last three hours he'd spent with the students in the computer lab. He'd promised Nick on Monday that he'd keep researching his great-grandfather, but he'd run out of threads and he needed a new lead. So, loaded with calories, he closed his eyes and waited for a brainwave.

It was unusual for him to simply let his mind drift. Free-rolling thoughts were by definition disorderly and un-invited. They were likely to be unsettling, and thus something to avoid. Life was more comfortable when his mind centred on what he was researching or an algorithm. Even his daydreams generally followed a well-trodden path, transporting him into the comic-strip world of his childhood books.

He focused his mind on Harold Bertram Roan, Nick's great-grandfather. But Matt wasn't good at thinking of people in an abstract way; he needed solid facts about them or a representation of their appearance.

An image slowly formed in his mind. He identified it as the newspaper picture of Harold, his wife Alice and the fourteen-year-old crossword competition winner. It had been 1962. Matt let his thoughts swirl around the image.

'Hi, are you OK?'

'What?' He recognised the voice, opened his eyes and smiled. 'Oh hiya, Rosie. I were waitin' for inspiration.'

She didn't say anything, but fingered a wisp of hair that had escaped her ponytail, and frowned.

He had no idea what she was implying, but there was something about the way her hair famed her face. It reminded him of… yes, Alice. And then a thought struck. 'Hack! I aint done a reverse image search on 'is face.'

'What? You can't look up students; you'll get yourself banned.'

'No, I aint talkin' 'bout students. It's me mate's great-granddad.'

'Well I'm still not sure it's—'

'He's long dead.'

'Oh.'

He worked in silence, unconcerned that Rosie was standing watching. He pulled a memory stick from his backpack and slipped it into one of the computer's USB ports. A few moments later he'd opened it and found the file with the newspaper article.

'There's several faces in that picture. They're all a bit grainy,' Rosie said.

'Yeah coz it's a newspaper from 1962. Lucky I only need the bloke's face.'

'Then I'll leave you to it.' Matt barely noticed her drift away.

It took him longer than he'd expected to edit out the other figures in the picture. He wasn't even sure if Harold's image would be pixel-rich enough for a reverse image search, but at least now it was only Harold in the frame. 'Spect I'll either get loads of results or nothin'.'

By the time Rosie walked past again, his screen was filled with a myriad of potential matches. They'd been thrown up by the poor specificity made inevitable by the granular quality of Harold's image.

'Well choosing between them isn't going to be easy,' Rosie said.

They both stared at a countless number of grainy faces shown against different backgrounds.

'What about the backgrounds? There could be something distinguishing about them,' Rosie said slowly.

'How'd you mean?'

'Well, like this one. The man's standing in front of a house.'

'Like it could be 'is house?'

'Or somewhere he's visiting. Or that one there is on a horse? Or….'

'Yeah, I get it.' He scrolled through the images.

'Hey stop!' Rosie whispered, 'That one there. The building looks familiar.'

'Scammin' hack, Rosie. Them houses with fancy red bricks an' them pale stone window frames an'….'

'Mullions?'

'Yeah, them mullion things. They all look the same.'

'I'd guess it's a kind of late Victorian style… or maybe Edwardian?'

'Tell you what; I can reverse search the buildin'.'

'Really?'

'Yeah, cool aint it?' He was surprised how much he liked it when she seemed impressed, and his cheeks flamed under his scrappy beard.

'Well I haven't got time to stand here while you edit the images again. I'll be over by the photocopier. Give me a wave if you find out where that place is.' She smiled and moved away.

The reverse search for the building took less time than

for Harold's face, and came up with only a handful of results. He waved to Rosie.

'See, I told you it'd come up with stuff!' he said, and grinned when she hurried over and peered at his screen.

'Bletchley Park? I thought I recognised the house.'

'How's that?'

'I had a great day there when I went with my cousin. Yes, it must have been last Easter. My aunt and uncle live out that way.'

'What? Milton Keynes?'

'Yes.' She smiled and added, 'It's time I got on with my work.'

'But killer app! It were the Secret Intelligence Service's code-breakin' centre durin' the second world war.'

He watched her walk back to the photocopier. Her movements seemed slower and more peaceful than Maisie's. Was it because Rosie was taller? Or was it because she was a library assistant? He'd heard Chrissie describe people and things as elegant; he'd supposed she'd meant tall and thin. Yeah, and Rosie's legs looked like they went on for ever. If it meant she was elegant, then he'd try and use the word next time she walked past.

Matt turned his attention back to Bletchley Park House, and sucked air through his teeth.

So how to follow this particular thread, he wondered. And more to the point, was this clue from one of literally dozens of reverse image search results even relevant? None of them had come up with Harold's full name or a reasonable variation fit, and a fair number were images without full name - or names, at all.

On the spur of the moment he typed in the search box, *how to find out if someone worked in the Secret Intelligence*

253

Service. For the next thirty minutes he lost himself in articles on suggested methods of searching. 'So, it's down to the National Archives, an' mainly them physical records held at Kew,' he murmured.

It didn't take him long to learn that the Freedom of Information legislation didn't apply to MI5 and MI6 records. 'Hah, *not for your eyes, Matt Finch*.' And as any searches would pretty much have to use original documents, it wasn't going to be something he could do from a computer in the Utterly Academy library. Bloggin' hack! He'd have to visit the home of the National Archives in Kew.

'Get a load of this,' he breathed as he scanned through the eye-watering list of various departmental names and section codes in the Archives' catalogue.

'So it's *KV* for MI5; *HD* for MI6 an' also *HD* for SIS, the Secret Intelligence Service. An' them's just for starters.'

His photographic memory made the reference codes less confusing when he scrolled through more section codes listed on the online catalogue denoting British Army intelligence, Naval intelligence, or Air Ministry intelligence.

'Yeah, but them ones only go up to 1964.'

The First and Second World War subject matter was split into subsections such as; Bletchley Park, Signals Intelligence, Cyphers, Enigma, and Special Operations Personnel Records. Spamming Trojan! It might be less impenetrable, but it was still a whirlpool of code combinations he'd have to come up with if he wanted to request the relevant file material to search.

Something leapt off the screen. 'Blog almighty! Nick can write to the *MI5 enquiries team* an' see if his great-granddad worked for MI5. It says you're allowed to do that if your reli's dead. Now that'd be spammin' easier.'

Matt closed his eyes. The effort of coming up against no-entry signs and cul-de-sacs was exhausting. Was there any mileage in searching another background thrown up on the reverse image results? The horse, another house…? It was all so tenuous and the odds were stacked against him picking a background leading to Harold.

'Bored or waiting for another brainwave?' Rosie's voice pulled him from his sense of hopelessness.

He opened his eyes. 'Oh hi, Rosie. I were thinkin'… yeah, I were thinkin' elegant!'

'Elegant?'

His face burned. 'Yeah, I were thinkin'.' He wanted to add, *you're elegant* but only one word came out. '… Elegant,' he faltered.

'You mean Enigma if you were thinking about Bletchley Park.' She shook her head and moved away to a bookcase further down the library.

He felt stupid. And worse still, Rosie had shaken her head. He pulled at a few hairs in his beard to distract from the humiliation. Did she really think he didn't know the correct name of the most famous code machine in the Second World War? Or was there something else wrong about the word elegant? He never felt like this with Chrissie or Maisie, but then he didn't try to tell them they looked elegant… or Nick, for that matter.

But at least now he had a plan. He decided to text Nick and ask if his mum remembered hearing her family use the shorthand names for Bletchley Park? It could add to the list of coincidences; it might make sense of something.

He pulled his mobile from his pocket and sent Nick a text.

Hi – done more research like you asked. Bletchley

Park came up. Does your mum remember Harold, Alice or Louisa talking about Bletchley Park or Station X, Station ten, or Room 47 the Foreign Office?

He pressed send.

'DOS-in' hell! I aint told 'im to write to 'em.' He fired off another text.

Also - write to MI5 enquiries team and ask if Harold worked for them. He has to be dead for them to answer. And it has to be your reli if U R asking.

As he slipped his mobile back into his pocket, he re-membered he hadn't sent the PO Box address for the MI5 enquiries team. Blog! He fired off a third text message with the PO Box address for Nick.

CHAPTER 34

'What did you say?' Mrs Lamanby fired the question at Nick.

'It's this photograph of... I guess they're American airmen. They look kind of cool.'

She frowned and slid gracefully off the stool where she'd been sitting close to the AGA cooker. 'I thought I heard you say something about cowboy boots,' she said.

'Well, one of them's wearing some supercool boots, Mrs Lamanby.'

'You're only saying that, Nick because they're like the ones you're wearing.'

'No, Dave I–'

'Let me see.' Her words were a command.

For an instant Nick was transported back to school and a teacher was demanding to see his footwear. Should he play deaf or comply?

Mrs Lamanby held out her hand.

Dave passed her the photograph.

Nick let his breath escape slowly while she focused on the picture. He'd been so close to making a fool of himself. What if he'd stuck his foot out or pulled a boot off to show her when all she'd wanted to see was the photo? He glanced at Dave, but Dave was busy watching Mrs Lamanby.

Ping! A text alert broke the moment. Nick grabbed his mobile from his jeans pocket before it could repeat its alert and attract more attention. But what could Matt want? He opened the message. *Done more research... Bletchley Park came up....*

Ping! Matt again? He frowned. What the hell had Matt

found? He scanned the new message. *Also - write to MI5 enquiries team and ask if Harold worked for them....*

Ping! More from Matt! Now a PO Box number?

'Is something wrong?' Her voice cut into his confusion.

He frowned. 'What did you say, Mrs Lamanby?' He pulled his mind back to the kitchen and the Poachers.

'You've had a string of messages. What's going on?' Her words came in a rush.

Nick looked up from his phone into Mrs Lamanby's unsmiling face. The blood seemed to have drained from her sun-damaged skin. Her eyes spoke cold suspicion. A sudden twitch of her lips might have been an attempt to smile, but he guessed it was nothing to do with him. Something much deeper was stirring within her.

'Are you OK, Mrs Lamanby?' Nick asked before he'd had time to think better of it.

'Why shouldn't I be?' She dropped her gaze back to the photo.

'Sorry, it's just that....'

'I'm fine. I hadn't noticed he was in this, and then with all those *Pings!* I mean... I hadn't realised the man was wearing....' Her words petered out, and a distant look followed.

The atmosphere felt heavy. Was she being brave about someone or something? Judging from how edgy she'd been with him so far, Nick figured it was best if he left her to compose herself. He bit his lip and waited.

'So,' she said, at last breaking the silence, 'tell me; why did you move today's appointment?' She appeared to aim her question at a point just above Dave's head.

'Um,' Nick murmured and nudged Dave to answer.

'Ah yes, our schedule. Clients sometimes change their minds; you can imagine how it goes, and when wires also get crossed… let just say we didn't get the message until we'd driven out to Dunwich.'

'Dunwich? What was the job?'

'Building wooden stiles,' Dave said smoothly.

'I thought regulations specify kissing gates, not stiles, these days.'

'Yes, but the equal access regs are for footpaths. If it's not a footpath and it's private land, then as long as the owner and his dog can climb over the stile, it's no one else's business.'

'And it's cheaper,' Nick chipped in.

She nodded slowly.

'I guess you use the field gates to reach your horses, Mrs Lamanby. You've no need for kissing gates or stiles,' Nick said, in what he hoped was an easy manner.

'And anyway, you wouldn't be riding through… what did he say it was, Nick? A field of the old square head master wheat?'

Mrs Lamanby stiffened.

'I thought he said it was a wildflower meadow,' Nick murmured, recalling the rather awkward exchange with the client that morning.

'Really? Are you both saying you can't tell the difference between a harvested field of thatching wheat and a wildflower meadow cut for hay?'

'There were several fields with different crops and four stiles to build,' Dave said evenly.

'But you were experts about my thatched roof when you arrived.'

'Hardly experts, Mrs Lamanby. But we could see the

thatch. The Dunwich fields have been harvested,' Dave countered.

Nick caught the disbelief in her eyes.

'Hmm, maybe a mug of coffee will sharpen the pair of you up?' She smiled a rather tense smile.

'Coffee? Oh thank you, Mrs Lamanby. I like mine milky and Dave–'

'White and one sugar, thanks.'

'Ha, don't thank me. I want you to do something.' She must have caught Dave's frown because she added, 'One of the stable doors has dropped a fraction on its hinge. It needs adjustment. And while you're about it, you can give me a quote for a wooden stile from the back field into my stable yard.'

'No problem,' Dave said, visibly relaxing as he reached to take a pile of newspaper cuttings from one of the plastic boxes on the table. Nick guessed he was thinking *if there's trouble from Willows for dropping round here during work, well hey; we came to give a quote*.

A blanket of domesticity descended as Mrs Lamanby opened cupboards and jars, poured milk into a pan and set it on the AGA to heat. Clicks and clunks sounded as she loaded a silver-looking espresso machine and set mugs ready on a kitchen counter.

'I only buy the dark roast. It can be too bitter for some people's taste, so I'm heating your milk. I'm told it helps take the edge off the bitterness.' She smiled when she caught Nick's glance.

He breathed in a rich nutty aroma drifting down the kitchen. 'We can always add sugar.'

'Y-e-e-s, but I've always found it pays to watch the sugar carbs.' She straightened her back, somehow accentuating her trim torso and muscular thighs.

Was she flirting, Nick wondered. He couldn't help noticing her fit-looking body and supposed it was from handling the horses and riding; pretty impressive for an older woman.

When she finally set the mugs of coffee on the table, Nick focused on her hands and wrists. They looked strong… yes, strong was definitely how he'd describe them. Strange that he hadn't noticed when Tim and he fitted the stable doors, but then why should he? He'd been in professional carpenter mode. Today felt different.

The first sips were bitter, so they stirred spoonfuls of sugar into their milky coffee while Mrs Lamanby watched and smiled. The aroma sent Nick's taste buds into a frenzy of anticipation as the sweetened, bitter blend smoothed across his tongue.

'Just what I needed,' Dave murmured, but grimaced an aside at Nick.

The coffee wasn't overly hot and Nick gulped down mouthfuls of the slightly nutty flavours while he sifted through the pile of newspapers and cuttings.

'This one is interesting,' Dave said, pushing an old sheet of newspaper across the table so that Mrs Lamanby could see it as well. 'It's more about social history than the pub.'

Nick peered at the yellowed paper with its faded photograph. It showed workmen digging a trench in what appeared to be the lane running through Wattisham village. He read out the headline, '*Main Sewer Comes to Wattisham Village.*'

'That will have been around 1960, I think,' Mrs Lamanby said.

'Yes Nick, it's a piece of social history. Hey look; the Poachers.'

'Yeah, the thatched roof's always been a bit dodgy,' Nick laughed.

Mrs Lamanby smiled, but it didn't reach her eyes.

For the next half hour Nick and Dave flicked from one cutting to another as the mellow comfort of the coffee waned. Nick began to feel agitated and jumpy.

'Right; we've spent long enough on this. It's time to take a look at your stable yard and door,' Dave said and smacked his hand down on the table for emphasis.

'Good, then I'll show you.' There was no mistaking the command in Mrs Lamanby's bearing as she led the way.

They followed, but this time, Nick hurried through the kitchen. He didn't care if his cowboy boots clipped and tapped on the tiled floor. The thought of fresh air drove him forward. His stomach felt uncomfortable and a faint nausea hovered in his throat.

'Take your van. You'll need your tools. My husband will be home soon and I don't want you blocking where he likes to park. I'll lead the way on the ride on.' She tossed the words over her shoulder as she headed off to the right.

'The ride on?'

'I guess she means the ride-on mower, Dave. Her husband was using it like a buggy last time I was here.'

They traced their way back down the garden path and through the gate in the woven-willow fence. By the time they'd climbed into their van, the sound of a two-stroke engine popped and rattled in the distance.

'I'm feeling a bit odd, Dave. I don't think I should have drunk all that coffee.'

'But it was made from ground beans, Nick. The real

essence of coffee. Nothing lost between roast and cup - none of your instant rubbish! I expect you're not used to drinking decent coffee.'

'Well, if it was so good, why didn't you drink all of yours, then?'

'I like my coffee hot and... I don't know what she'd done with the milk, so I left mine once it'd gone cold.'

'Then you missed out on all the coffee bean goodness you're banging on about.'

'And it was a pretty strong brew. The caffeine's probably gone to our heads. Ah, here she comes.' Dave started the van and crawled in low gear behind Mrs Lamanby. She led them on the mower back along the track and down the fork to the stable yard.

Dave champed at the enforced slow speed. He slapped the steering wheel with his open palm and cursed under his breath. Nick tried to keep focused but he figured he'd drunk twice the amount of caffeine as Dave. And if the caffeine had cranked Dave up enough to swear and clout the van, then what the hell was it doing to him? His agitation spiralled. The nausea took a firmer hold. Shite, was he going to throw up?

They stopped with a jolt when they'd reached the stable yard. Nick flung the van door open and leapt out.

'What the hell are you doing, Nick?'

'I'm gonna be sick,' he yelped and clapped a hand to his mouth.

'What's going on?' Mrs Lamanby shouted as she jumped down from the mower.

'He's going to vomit.'

'What? Don't you dare throw up all over my yard. Use a bucket!' she yelled.

'What bucket?' Nick moaned as his stomach threatened to contract. He clamped his jaws.

'The horse trailer. You, Dave! Open the groom's door. There'll be an empty bucket inside. Hurry!'

Mrs Lamanby closed in on Nick. Her vice-like grip tightened on his upper arm. Knuckles pressed into the small of his back.

'Move!'

Powerless to resist, he was propelled towards a blur of green in the open-fronted barn. Like a film in slow motion, he watched as Dave unfastened the groom's door, reached inside and retrieved a wide black bucket.

He shoved it at him. 'Here throw up in this.'

The groom's door swung. *Wham!* It smacked into Dave's head and shoulder. Dave staggered as the door bounced off him.

Nick lost view as he retched into the bucket. He glanced up to take breath, but his world spun and Dave went fuzzy. The band of steel on his arm eased… then vanished. He blinked and concentrated on Mrs Lamanby.

She grabbed the door. *Wham!* It slammed into Dave again, this time faster and with more force. It didn't bounce away; her hand braced it. Dave buckled over and crumpled into the horse trailer.

Ughhh. Nick vomited uncontrollably. Curdled brown liquid splattered into the bucket. It was foul, bitter and acidic. His sides and stomach ached. His throat burned. How could he have so much inside him?

'Keep it down,' she barked, as if her command could hold back the tide.

'I-I can't,' he groaned as more foulness rose in his throat.

'Sit down,' she commanded.

'But....'

She dropped out of view. Nick swayed.

'Sit down. I've moved his legs out of your way.'

'What?' Nick's bottom hit the trailer floor hard. Dave was somewhere behind him in a heap. Motionless.

'Tell me who to ring to fetch you.'

'What?'

'Give me your phone!'

Nick fumbled in his pocket. His head ached and his hands were like clay.

'Unlock it. I can't get your contacts if it's still locked.'

'But my fingers... they're....'

'Oh give it to me. Tell me your code. And while you're about it, you'd better give me Dave's phone as well.'

'But...?'

The foulness began to erupt again. Nick dropped his phone and hugged the bucket. Helpless, he retched and spat into its rank depths.

Mrs Lamanby leaned in close, snatched up his phone and dug an elbow into his ribs.

'OK, OK,' he spluttered as she shoved past him to wrestle Dave's mobile from the heap behind.

'The code,' she shouted as more vomit hit the bucket, 'tell me the code.'

'Four... three... two... one,' he coughed. He needed someone to get him home, and fast. His world swirled and rotated. Was he going to die?

'Ha! You didn't fool me!'

He opened his eyes and strained to focus. She stood in the stable yard directly in front of the groom's door where he sat, slumped in the trailer with the bucket. She held his phone and read out snippets of his messages.

'*Bletchley Park*? *MI5*? And it seems *Harold worked for them*. Who the hell are you? And who the hell is Harold?'

Nick tried to say something, but his throat burned and the words came out as a croak.

'So how long have you been watching me... taunting me with my own cowboy boots?'

He couldn't answer. His headache throbbed and his eyelids weighed heavy.

'Give them back!' she yelled, grabbing one of his boots and yanking it off his foot.

He had no strength to resist. She pulled off his other boot.

'And this is for all your talk about the thatch. Dropping hints like you know, but pretending you don't. Were you going to blackmail me as well?' Her eyes blazed and a sudden judder seemed to galvanise her. She leapt at him where he sat on the floor in the groom's entrance to the trailer. Her knee connected with his chin in an upward thrust, smacking into it and snapping his jaw shut and... blackness.

CHAPTER 35

Nick groaned as consciousness seeped back.

'Nick, wake up. Nick!'

Had a voice whisper-hissed his name? Was he dreaming? He struggled to open his eyes but his lids were leaden. And pain... an ache, somewhere deep in his head and behind his eyes. He opened his mouth; it felt parched. He tried to swallow but moving his tongue was torture.

He coughed. 'Argh....' His ribs hurt.

'Come on, Nick, wake up.' The whisper hiss again.

With a Herculean effort he opened his eyes. Darkness surrounded him. He blinked.

'Nick, are you OK?'

'Wha's...?' It was more of a croak than a whimper. His tongue hurt too much to say more.

'That ruddy woman's locked us in the horse trailer. I can't get out. I've been trying for hours.'

''Railer?' he echoed as memory flooded back. Hadn't she...? Hell yes, she'd kneed him! Gingerly, he checked his jaw. It was sore. And his tongue...? He must have caught it between his teeth when she'd landed the blow.

'I bi' m' tongue,' he moaned and let his arm flop back, exhausted. His hand rested on textured floor matting. Realisation dawned. She'd kayoed him.

'Shi',' he breathed.

'Is that all you can say, Nick? That bloody door didn't put my lights out by itself. She... she damned well knocked me out with it!'

'Bof of uf.'

'What?'

'She hi' me.'

'She hit you? So you weren't out cold from vomiting? Thank God. I thought you were dying.' His voice cracked.

Nick wanted to say *dying'd be a relief*, but his tongue hurt too much. 'Phome,' he mumbled.

'Yeah, good idea – like I wouldn't have been yelling and shouting for hours if I'd remembered I had a phone. She's taken our bloody phones, Nick!'

'Ugh?' Nick reached for his pocket and then remembered. 'Four… free… ou… one,' he groaned.

'What the hell are you on about?'

'She 'ook my 'ode.'

'What? She took your code? She's got your code lock as well as your mobile? What the hell were you thinking?'

'She 'ricked me.'

'She bloody tricked us both. What I don't get is why.'

Dave lapsed into silence and Nick tried to elbow himself into a semi-sitting position. Dave grabbed his shoulders.

'Back-to-back. If we lean back-to-back, we share our body warmth. And we'll lose less heat through the floor when we're sitting. Pull your legs up. Hug 'em. It's going to get cold tonight.'

A groan escaped with the effort.

'Ha, Nick! It's like a foetal position, but we're sitting. I read it somewhere in a survival manual, but I never imagined I'd use it in a horse trailer in Suffolk.'

The sharp smell of vomit and the sweeter, earthy scent of horse dung pervaded the air.

'I'm going to keep talking, Nick. It'll help us hold it together while you recover a bit. OK?'

'Hmm.' He nodded, knowing Dave would pick up his

movement.

'OK, we need to get out of here. The back ramp and the front side ramp are both closed and secured from the outside. We came in through the groom's door, and that's been locked and bolted from the outside. I figure the trailer's made of aluminium coated panels. They're built to withstand a horse.' He laughed. It was humourless.

'I've tried to break the inspection window but it's toughened glass and I can't kick that high. And anyway, it's too small to climb through or even use to reach the outside door locks. And now it's getting dark.'

'Shi'.'

'The woman's crazy. And dangerous - I reckon she's poisoned us, or rather, tried to.'

''Oisoned uf?'

'Yes. I don't know what she gave us, but it must've been in the coffee or that milk. Lucky I didn't drink much of mine and you've chucked up most of yours.'

An acrid smell already hung in the air, and Dave's words conjured the black bucket swirling with vomit. It was a vision of hell; hell on earth.

***

Ping! The text alert woke Matt. He'd been dozing; floating in the zone somewhere between total awareness and dreamy sleep. He fumbled around, searching for his mobile. It had been in his hand. He remembered looking at Maisie's goodnight emoji; a little yellow disc of a face with closed eyes and zzZ across it.

'Thank hack!' His fingers connected with his phone lying next to his pillow.

He rubbed his eyes and yawned. Yeah, he thought, Nick's got back to me at last. The time on his phone was

22:00. It was still Thursday. He opened the message.

Confirm Harold has to be dead. U R

'What? What's Nick on about?'

He read the message again, but it still didn't make sense. He scratched his head and scrolled back to the two earlier messages in the chain, the ones Nick was responding to. There'd been the PO Box number for MI5 enquiries, and before that his message telling Nick to write to MI5.

He scanned through it: *Also - write to MI5 enquiries team and ask if Harold worked for them. He has to be dead for them to answer. And it has to be your reli if U R asking.*

'But Nick knows Harold were born round the turn of last century. And 1900 to now is.... Do 'e think Harold's one hundred and fourteen-years-old?'

Course Harold got to be dead by now! he texted back.

He expected to slip straight into a dreamless sleep but the oddness of Nick's message unsettled him. He chewed it over, and instead of making more sense of it, his confusion grew. It made him anxious and in turn, hypersensitive to every thought and sensation, even pitching the sounds in the bungalow super loud against the quiet of the night. His mum's footsteps thumped like a drumbeat down the hallway. The bathroom door closed with a knockout slam and the toilet flushed with the roar of Niagara Falls.

He buried his head under his pillow.

When morning dawned, it was a relief. He was awake before his phone alarm rang, and after he'd silenced its shrill notes, he pressed Nick's automatic dial number. He waited but Nick didn't answer. He tried again, but still no answer. He sent another message.

Ring me. It's urgent.

***

Chrissie was surprised by the earliness of Matt's call. He was by habit more of an afternoon or night person. So when her mobile's *brrring brrring* cut through the Friday-ten-o'clock calm of the barn workshop and she put down her mortising chisel, she was fully expecting it to be a customer or the auction rooms.

'Hi, Chrissie,' the familiar voice breathed.

'Matt? Is everything all right?'

'Yeah look, can you do somethin' for me? See I can't speak easy from work. Damon don't like it; 'e gets cranky.'

'OK, but what do you want me to do?'

'Nick aint right. He's sent me a weird text and he aint answerin' me calls. I dropped round 'is flat when I got to Bury this mornin' but 'is car aint there.'

'But he'll have left for work. And if he isn't answering calls, it could be girl trouble, or maybe he's hungover.'

'So you think he were pissed or it were the latest bird. DOS-in' hell.'

'No... I mean I don't know what to think. What was the message? No, better still, why don't you send it to me?'

'Killer app!' The call ended.

Before she'd had a chance to put her mobile down, a series of text alerts *pinged*.

'Is everything all right, Mrs Jax?' Ron asked.

'I don't know.' She didn't look up. She was too busy opening the messages.

'Then I reckon it's time for a break and a mug of tea while you're deciding. I'll put the kettle on, Mrs Jax.'

While Ron limped across the workshop, filled the kettle and dropped teabags into their mugs, Chrissie read the chain of emails. 'But I had no idea Matt's been digging into Nick's great-grandfather,' she breathed.

'So, Mrs Jax?'

She sat down and collected her thoughts.

'I don't know, Mr Clegg. It seems Matt has found out things about Nick's great-grandfather and I don't think Nick's taken it too well.'

'Well you've lost me, Mrs Jax. How d'you mean he's not taken it too well?'

'He isn't answering Matt's texts or calls.' She pressed Nick's automatic dial number and waited. It rang but there was no answer. 'And he hasn't answered mine just now.'

Ron didn't say anything, and for a moment Chrissie wondered if he'd heard her. But then, not everyone was as nosey as her, she reminded herself. Ron would be waiting to be told more and if nothing was forthcoming, she guessed he'd assume it wasn't his business. But what about Bletchley? He'd want to know about that. He was the one who'd found the coded message.

'Matt believes Nick's great-grandfather Harold, at least I guess that's who Harold is... might have had a connection with Bletchley.'

'You mean Bletchley Park? The place for code breakers? You know, that could make sense.' He nodded slowly, as if something was slotting into place. 'If Nick isn't answering his calls, well, it's his business and perhaps we should respect it. But Willows'll know if he's called in sick, or not turned up for work.'

'You're right, Mr Clegg. Why didn't I think of that? I'll call them now.'

CHAPTER 36

Nick opened his eyes. He was lying on his side, still curled in the sitting-foetal position he'd adopted for warmth, except he'd capsized in his sleep. The minutes stretched as he reconnected with his body. The textured, rubber-composite floor matting pressed hard against his cheek. Tingling needles shot like bolts through his hand when he tried to move his arm; the one his knee had pinned against the matting. He started to straighten his legs, but his hips and knees complained. He felt cold and stiff.

'You've decided to wake up, have you?' It was Dave's voice.

Daylight filtered into the gloom through the high inspection window. Nick lifted his head to get a better view of the inside of the horse trailer.

'Ow!'

'It still hurts?'

'Yeah.' He raised his hand, the one that didn't feel like a block of prickling lard, and touched the back of his neck. Memories of the previous day flooded back. 'Oh Gog,' he groaned. At least his tongue didn't sting too much when he moved it.

'Take it easy, lad. I'm afraid you've missed the bacon, sausage, eggs, beans and toast.'

'What?'

'Ha! You didn't flinch so I guess your stomach's on the mend.'

Ugh, his stomach! It was a sore, empty void, but so long as the nausea didn't come back, he'd be OK. His foggy brain struggled with the gallows humour, or rather,

Dave's take on gallows humour. From past experience he knew it meant things were really bad. Anxiety took a firmer hold.

'What's... what's the time?'

'They've stopped serving breakfast so....' He checked his watch, 'it's just after ten.'

'OK, Dave; I got the joke. What the hell's going on?'

'Well, I was waiting for you to wake up.'

Nick gazed at Dave's face. It was shadowed by a day's worth of stubble. It gave him an air of gritty toughness, but the habitual bonhomie was failing and his voice sounded rough. His ex-trainer appeared more like a nightclub bouncer than a carpenter. Nick hoped his own unshaven look conjured an aura of hard-edged resilience. He squared his shoulders and winced.

'So... so has she...?' He was going to ask if Mrs Lamanby had made any contact or demands, but Dave's withering look stopped him.

'I've been shouting and yelling and kicking at the doors. Someone, I guess Mrs Lamanby, came on that buggy thing yesterday evening and again at about seven o'clock this morning to see to the horses. It sounded as if she brings them in from the field behind the stables and then turns them out again in the morning. And then she rides the buggy away.'

'And that's it? How about Mr Lamanby? He seemed quite a nice bloke.'

'I wouldn't know. I've never met him and I don't think he's come out here. But someone drove our van away.'

'What? When?'

'Around three this morning.'

'Shi'e!' Nick's guts twisted. 'We… we need–'

'Yeah, we need to get out of here before she hooks her car exhaust into the trailer and kills us. I reckon I've made enough noise to know she's ignoring us.'

'But why'd she want to kill us?' Nick tried to control his spike of panic.

'I don't know but I reckon she's waiting until we're almost dead before she dares open the trailer.'

'So… so should we play dead and then jump her?'

'That's maybe not such a bad idea. It could take eons before anyone thinks to look for us here. Well done; I knew you'd come up with something more than vomit.'

'Yeah thanks. But it's not much of a plan.' He wondered if anyone would miss him for another twenty-four hours or even try and track him down when he didn't turn up for band practice on Saturday morning. And stupid, stupid, stupid! Why hadn't he been definite about a Friday night date with Sarita, instead of just hinting?

'No, I reckon I've done my shouting, Nick. Now we try dying to tempt her in.'

Nick cast around. This time his neck didn't stop him. He felt more determined, or was it just desperation? He made mental notes. The walls were constructed from aluminium-coated panels with waist-height, plastic kickboard linings. One of the interlinked floor mats had been lifted, he guessed by Dave to check out the floor underneath – more aluminium. It smelled of horse. Everything was essentially flat or gently curved with no projections or edges for a horse to damage itself. There really was nothing to rip from the structure and use as a makeshift weapon or tool. And the roof? Not only was it aluminium, it was seven and a half, no… eight feet high. Hell, she must have emptied the trailer. There were no breaching or breast bars, no partitions or lengths of rope; only the black vomit bucket. His heart sank, and then he had an idea.

'How about my belt, Dave? The buckle prong might work as a screwdriver?'

'The panels are riveted, floor, roof and sides. It's a friggin' aluminium strongbox on wheels.'

'So, do horses like it this dark?' He focused on the small inspection window; the single, non-opening sheet of toughened glass fitted high in one of the front aluminium panels.

'I don't know, but those half doors above the back ramp can be swung open. They'll be how most of the light normally gets in.'

'Have you tried?'

'Yeah. They're bolted closed from the outside. But at least those air vent slits let in some fresh air. The smell from that bucket....

'Hey but when she comes in, a bucket of stale vomit in her face might take her by surprise.'

Dave smiled. 'True. And if she tries the car exhaust trick, we can... use your shirt to block across the vents.'

'Oh thanks! So it's my shirt, is it?' Nick's thoughts slipped sideways, 'Why'd she take my boots?'

'Probably didn't like the pointy toes.'

'No, I meant there must be something important about them. Maybe I can trick her into coming in if I say I know stuff about them.'

'Then you'd better think up something fast, otherwise we need to get on with pretending we're dying, before we actually do.'

CHAPTER 37

Chrissie's mid-morning Friday break was proving to be stressful. She was determined to exude an air of calm authority and spoke slowly and evenly when she rang Willows & Son. She glanced at Ron; he was the one who'd suggested she made the call.

'Good morning. My name is Mrs Jax. Please may I speak to Nick Cowley? He's not answering his phone and it's important.'

'Hold on a moment. I'll see if he's in the workshop.'

Her anxiety grew as she listened to the silence on the line. Pat, Mr Willows' secretary, seemed to take forever.

'He's not here, but we'll try to let him know you wanted to speak to him,' Pat said before explaining his car was at Willows but he was out on a job in Dunwich with Dave. 'I'll leave a message with the customer.'

'Thank you, yes please ask Nick to ring me. And also, would you let me know if you can't locate him. It's important. You've got my number.' Chrissie ended the call.

'What did Willows say?' Ron asked.

'Pat from the office said Nick is working with Dave over in Dunwich.'

'So is Nick's car at Willows, Mrs Jax?'

'Yes, and so, I presume, is Dave's.' She looked at Ron, as if seeing him for the first time. He appeared more hunched, and his forehead more creased than usual.

'What? What are you thinking, Mr Clegg?'

He took a deep breath. 'If Nick didn't call in sick then he'll be with Dave over in Dunwich. But….'

'But what, Mr Clegg?'

'You told me Nick isn't answering Matt's calls or texts this morning… or yours. And you seemed to think it's because Matt told him about his great-grandfather being connected with Bletchley Park.'

'Yes, he thinks Harold might be connected. But Matt isn't sure yet.'

'So don't you think Nick might need time to take it in? And if he's not ready to talk about it yet, then could it be why he's not answering your calls?'

'Yes. And I can believe some of Nick's reaction might go over Matt's head, but even so, judging by the text messages, they look rather exciting - not shocking.'

'Can I see the messages, Mrs Jax?'

She was surprised. This was most unlike Mr Clegg. 'Yes, of course. I'll get them up for you.' She walked over to his stool. 'Just scroll them like this,' she said and handed him her mobile.

She waited, watching his face, her eyes darting to the small screen with each new message.

'MI5? And what, or who is *U R*, Mrs Jax?'

'Oh, that's just text speak. It's a kind of phonetic shorthand. The letter U represents the sound of the word *you* and the letter R is for the word *are*. It saves spelling everything out.'

'And is this text shorthand always capital letters?'

'No. It's about speed, so it's even quicker to use lower case.' She frowned. 'Why? Do you think the capitals are significant? Like it's someone's initials?'

'I wouldn't know, Mrs Jax.' Ron frowned and then added slowly, 'The bit about Harold having to be dead seems a bit odd. It's almost like Nick isn't sure his great-grandfather is dead. Is there a photograph of Harold -

Nick's great-grandfather, Mrs Jax?'

Brrring brrring!

She snatched the phone from Ron. 'Yes?'

'Mrs Jax? This is Pat from the office at Willows & Son.'

'Yes, yes. Have you managed to contact Nick, yet?'

'No. He's still not answering his phone and neither is Dave. I've called the customer in Dunwich and he says Nick and Dave left there yesterday morning. But the van is still out and it seems no one signed for the van to stay out overnight.'

'What? So where are they now?'

'I don't know, but I'll keep trying to contact them. And I've informed Mr Willows. He wants to speak to the police.'

'The police?'

'Yes, they could have had an accident. It's all very unusual. I mean it's not unusual to keep the van out over-night if the site's a long way away and the job's going to take a couple of days or so. But this client had cancelled and failed to tell us. There'd been nothing for them to do over there. I'll let you know if there's any news.' The line went dead.

'Oh dear,' Ron said softly, 'did you just say *the po-lice*?'

Chrissie's guts twisted. 'Yes, Willows think Nick and Dave may have had an accident. I-I'm going to ring Clive. He'll know what to do and how to find out.'

The rest of the day turned into a blur as Chrissie's thoughts kept drifting back to Nick and Dave. Try as she might to focus on replacing a drawer front and fit the origi-nal lock, images of a crumpled Willows van kept flashing into her mind. It was a relief when Clive called to say he'd drop by the Clegg & Jax workshop on his way back to Ipswich from Bury St Edmunds.

'This'll be him now,' she said at a little after three o'clock, when an engine purred and stones crunched on the concrete outside. A car door slammed and she hurried out into the courtyard.

'Clive!' She almost flung herself into his arms. 'Any news? Have you found them?'

'Wooah, settle down. It's less than five hours since they've been reported missing. Stickley's checked with Traffic, the ambulance control centres and the local hospitals. There've been no reports of the van being involved in an RTA over the last twenty-four hours, or of either of them being admitted to a hospital in East Anglia.'

'Thank God for that. But where are they then? I've a really bad feeling about this. It's like–'

'OK, OK. But try to keep a lid on it; your brain works better that way.' He smiled and his face softened as she grabbed his hand.

'Come in. It's warmer.'

'Hello, Ron.' He nodded a greeting as he stepped inside.

Chrissie got out her phone. 'I think you should look at the last text Nick sent to Matt.'

'OK.'

She handed him her phone and watched as he scrolled through the text messages. 'Well? What do you think, Clive?'

He frowned 'Have these been forwarded to you from Matt's phone?'

'Yes, it was easier than him trying to explain them.'

'Hmm, they're… do Nick and Matt have some kind of matey code speak they use?'

'I don' know. Why?'

'OK, the last message from Nick was sent yesterday at 22:00, and his last definite sighting was yesterday morning when he left Dunwich in the van with Dave. So, there've been no actual sightings of Nick or Dave since around 10:45am yesterday.'

'So you're saying they've been missing for more than twenty-four hours.' Panic rose in her throat.

'The late-night text implies it's not twenty-four hours yet. Look, Willows have reported a van and two of their employees missing, so a file's been opened. It's being treated as theft at this stage.'

'What? Theft? You think Nick and Dave have stolen the van?' Her voice soared.

'No, but at least it allows us to search for them straightaway. Remember, none of this might have reached me yet, or even at all, if you hadn't called. I've set Stickley on making those preliminary checks. We're ahead of the game if it's a missing person's case.'

'Right,' she said, unconvinced. 'So what happens next?'

'The traffic cameras on the A14 and A12 will have recorded the van's number plate. We can check their route with the ANPR database.'

She frowned.

'ANPR – it's Automatic Number Plate Recognition. The cameras should have tracked where the van went.'

'Unless it's on the small B roads and lanes.'

'True. But let's see what the traffic database comes up with first, before we get defeatist. You could help by finding more contact numbers. Willows gave us the next of kin. That's Nick's parents and Dave's wife. But friends - we don't have their numbers. They might know something.'

He handed back her phone.

'I've an appointment about listed building planning permission with someone in the council offices in Ipswich, so I need to go or I'll be late. We've put out a call to the patrol cars in the area to look out for the Willows van and I'll give you a call if I've got any news, OK?'

'Thanks, Clive.'

She barely had a chance to smile before he'd gone.

***

Nick licked his lips, but it didn't make them feel any less dry or assuage his thirst. He checked his watch. It was four o'clock. 'She's not come back yet,' he whispered.

'She's got to when she stables the horses for the night. She'll be here by seven. You'll see.'

Nick didn't know if he *wanted* to see.

If only the nightmare could end when he closed his eyes; if only he could hold up his hands to fate and say, 'I quit.' He'd drift from his aching head, the creeping cold, his parched throat and gnawing guts... away.... drift away.

'Hey Nick; hang in there, mate.'

'Yeah... yeah 'course,' he said with a start, 'I've been thinking... what if she won't come inside coz we're too... alive?'

'Then make it sound like you're almost dead. But don't overdo it for now, mate.'

***

Matt slumped onto Chrissie's comfortable sofa. 'Thanks for askin' me round.'

'Well it makes sense for us all to be here together.'

282

She handed him a can of lager and sat in the armchair, perched on the edge of her seat.

'Yeah, 'cept Clive aint here.' He glanced round her cosy living room, his mind running through his news and added, 'Jake reckons Nick were with his new bird last night. Least that's why he thought Nick were out all night.'

'And we can't check because no one seems to have Sarita's number. And Dave's wife is visiting her sister in Peterborough, so no one knows if Dave came home last night.'

Matt swigged a mouthful of lager direct from the can. He didn't know what to say, so he waited for Chrissie to say something.

'Do you think the last text, the 22:00 text, was Nick speak? The U R letters; what do you think Nick meant by them?'

'How'd you mean, Chrissie?'

'Well, he used capitals, like they're important or it's someone's name.'

Brrring brrring!

She grabbed her mobile off the coffee table. 'Clive? Any news?'

Matt watched her face but couldn't hear Clive's words. He knew her frowns meant bad news. Trolling bad. He swigged more lager and anxiously flipped between trying to read her face and fretting about the U R. Wasn't he the one who'd first used capitals when he'd sent the message to Nick? It was… like for emphasis; like louder. Is that what she meant by Nick speak? 'Hey, Chrissie–'

'They've found the Willows van,' she said putting her phone down on the coffee table.

'Great! An' Nick an' Dave?'

'No news. Someone's reported a van left on a bridle path near Priestley Wood. Seems it's the Willows van. He doesn't know how long, but it wasn't there yesterday.' She held up her hand; Matt guessed a gesture to stop his questions. 'The van was locked and there was no one inside it.'

'What? Like they've gone walkin' in the woods?'

'I don't know. But where the hell's Priestley Wood?' She stood up and hurried to a wooden box on one side of the fireplace. She pulled out some Ordinance Survey maps.

'Clive said east of Barking and west of the B113.' She selected one of the maps. 'Here, it'll be on this one,' she said, unfolding it and laying it like a paper tablecloth across the coffee table.

Matt checked his phone. The time was 17:40.

***

Nick heard footsteps outside the trailer and looked at Dave. 'Now?' he mouthed.

Dave nodded.

'Water!' Nick moaned, turning the word into a reedy croak. He waited, watching Dave for a signal. He caught his half shrug.

'I've… a… message. Your boots,' Nick rasped, 'please w-a-t-e-r.' He hoped he'd got it right; pathetic and too weak to be a threat, but loud enough for her to hear. His heart raced. He checked his watch. It was six thirty.

***

Matt let his head rest back against the sofa and closed his eyes. All he saw was the map printed in his memory.

'D'you s'pose they're lost in the wood, Chrissie?'

'I've already said I don't know, Matt. Don't keep asking. I can't think why they'd park there in the first place.'

Her voice sounded sharp. Was she cross with him? He

retreated into his comic-strip world. His heroes would have followed the rivers, sensed magnetic north and harnessed the help of an eagle.

'It's my fault Nick's gone missin'. It's all the U R, MI5 stuff in me texts,' he groaned.

'Don't be daft, Matt. Why would any of this be down to you?'

Spammin' malware! Even Chrissie was cross and thought him daft.

In a flash he got it. 'Flamin' malware! I shoulda left Harold alone. Nick writin' U R in capitals weren't right.'

His guts twisted, but he knew what he had to do. He stood up.

'I gotta go, Chrissie. I gotta check out round Barkin' on me scooter.'

'What? Have you gone mad? It's seven o'clock. It's getting dark. You're not thinking straight. Leave it to Clive and the police. Please, Matt!'

He didn't wait to hear more. He rushed down the narrow hallway and out to his scooter.

***

An engine started after the clatter of stabling the horses finished.

'What's going on out there?' Nick mouthed to Dave.

It sounded a little distant at first. Was it the ride-on buggy? No. It definitely sounded like a car.

Dave signalled to stay quiet and to take their positions.

Nick nodded. It was almost seven thirty.

They listened as the car drove towards the trailer. It stopped. A car door opened, slammed, and footsteps approached.

Nick rested his head on the floor and resumed his *al-*

most dead sprawl in front of the groom's door. He was close, but not close enough to stop her coming in.

Dave pointed to the high inspection window at the front of the trailer and crouched, as if he'd collapsed into a heap against the side. Nick had watched him practise the move earlier - crouch as if dead, then quickly stand up. It was a bit like the pre-ski exercises he'd once seen a past girlfriend work out to music. But this had a different intent; when Dave stood up, he'd be tight against the side wall and initially hidden from view through the outward opening door… and ready with the bucket of vomit.

The footsteps slowed, and then thudded softly onto the tow-hitch framework at the front of the trailer. It was how she got height to look through the inspection window. Nick tensed and held his breath.

Crunch! She'd jumped down from the framework. They'd passed the dead test. He took a breath. His pulse thumped in his ears.

He watched Dave silently stand up.

Clunk! *Bang*! Metallic sounds vibrated along the trailer's steel framework and aluminium floor. This was new.

The floor tipped down and lurched.

'What the hell's she doing?' he croaked at Dave.

'She's hitching up the bloody trailer.'

'What?'

Seconds later the engine revved. The trailer jolted forwards. They were on the move.

Dave lost his balance and stumbled across Nick. The bucket slopped vomit.

'Ugh!'

'Get up, Nick.'

'I'll be all over the place, like you.'

'Yeah, but at least I'm not rolling in your sick.'

'You're going to hurt yourself.'

'Grab me a rubber floor mat. No, a clean one!'

'But....'

'Stand up, Nick. She won't have adjusted the tow settings. Our combined weight - we're lighter than a horse.' He flung himself across the trailer and shouldered the side. It swung a fraction and steadied.

'It nearly snaked. You'll kill us.'

'Yeah, Nick. So pull up another rubber mat. We can protect ourselves.'

'Do we want it snaking? It'll turn over, Dave.'

'Yeah, but it could be our best chance of getting out of here. Have you got a better plan?'

Nick's mind felt numb. He freed up another rubber floor mat.

'Good! Now you're on my wavelength, lad. So, both of us together and keep your centre of gravity high. Aim at the sides, but towards the rear.'

Staying close, they flung themselves at the side of the trailer. The mats protected their shoulders. It was their body armour as they hit the aluminium wall. They bounced off, launched back and thudded against the opposite side. They ended in a heap.

'OK, Dave; but we need to stay on our feet. A rhythm will help get the snaking really going. How about a bit of Queen? *We Are the Champions*. It'll keep us in time.'

They struggled to their feet.

CHAPTER 38

Matt rode as if on a mission. An Ed Sheeran sound track pounded inside his head as he leaned with the scooter. He was a low-flying bird. A jet fighter. He didn't have a plan; he simply knew he had to find Nick. Guilt drove him. It was all his fault. Even Chrissie thought he was a fool; she'd as good as told him.

He visualised the map and sped along the lanes from Woolpit to Onehouse. He cut southwest of Stowmarket and raced at fifty-five miles an hour along a stretch of Battisford's Straight Road. He was heading for Barking. He joined the B1078 and slowed, scanning the road for turnings to Priestley Wood. The light was fading as he pulled off the tarmac and onto a rough track.

The Vespa complained. It wasn't an off-roader. It didn't like the ruts or clumps of coarse grass. The scooter jolted and skidded into a furrow, nearly throwing him. He stopped, pushed up his visor and yelled, 'Nick? Dave? Where the frag are you?'

He listened for a voice or sound, anything to suggest Nick was somewhere out there.

The silence almost crushed him. 'Nick? Dave?' he shouted again. But there was nothing. He pulled his visor down and manhandled the scooter around. Sweaty and breathless, he rode back to the road.

Right or left, he wondered, his angst growing. The map had shown several tracks and footpaths wide enough to be bridle paths. But which one was he on? Which one to try next?

He watched an SUV towing a horsebox trailer as it

approached along the main road. He waited for it to pass and pulled out behind. He rode slowly, scanning for bridle paths and tracks towards Priestley Wood. A sharp bend loomed and he shifted his view back to the road. In front, the trailer swung from side to side as it disappeared round the corner. Killer app! He'd heard about snaking, but he'd never seen it before.

He accelerated to keep up. He leaned into the corner, drawn to see more and ready to brake if the trailer had flipped. And then he was round the bend. But there was no debris and no carnage. The SUV drove on, the trailer swaying behind it.

'Spammin' hell! Don't the driver see what's happenin' behind 'im?'

In a flash Matt knew what he had to do. If he accelerated and overtook the SUV, he could flag the driver to slow down and warn him before disaster struck. He might have messed up with Nick but he wasn't going to get this wrong. It was his chance to make amends, like a comic-strip knight of the road.

He steadied the Vespa. He'd need a clear view and straight section to get past the horsebox trailer if it was swaying like a pendulum.

Minutes passed as they sped towards Needham Market; the SUV leading, the Vespa tracking. The SUV slowed, and turned right. Matt switched on his hazard lights and followed. He waved and pointed at the trailer. The SUV braked, and then took another right, accelerating onto the road to Great Blakenham.

'He's seen me an' he's goin' even faster!' Matt howled.

The SUV was gaining distance. He followed, hazard

lights flashing. What the blog was the driver playing at? Matt waved and pointed again at the snaking horsebox trailer. Was the SUV rear-view blind? But the evening was drawing in, and the speed demanded Matt grip both handlebars. He quit his frantic signals and concentrated on catching up.

Ahead, the trailer's brake lights flickered and the SUV swung across the road. The trailer swayed violently, twisting on its tow point. Matt gasped. The tow rig held. Matt, a few seconds behind, watched the SUV and trailer rock and bob out of sight down a track.

'Pixel!' Matt hissed. Now what? It looked as if the SUV had driven onto private land. Matt rode slowly into the entrance of the track and sat astride his scooter. Should he go any further?

Thud! Crash! Thud! The sudden noise freaked him out. It was brutal, like something heavy smashing into the ground close by. Metal screeched as if twisting on metal. A softer *thud* followed. 'What the frag was that?' He pushed up his visor and listened, straining to pick up the faintest sound. There was nothing bar the idling from his engine, and he wasn't prepared to take off his helmet to catch more.

His pulse raced, fired by the chase and tweaked by fear. If there was an overturned horsebox, then… could he be sure the screech he'd heard was metal? What if it was the scream of an injured horse? His stomach twisted. He knew he had to find out. He eased the scooter forwards.

The uneven track was made up of powdery grit. It looked eerily pale in the beam of his headlight. His tyres kicked up white dust as he followed the trail. Was it chalk? A few yards on, it curved into the gloom. He followed the bend.

'Blog almighty!' he breathed as his headlight caught a large angular shape.

***

Nick opened his eyes. It was pitch black and he was curled into a ball. Where was he? He bent his elbow and found he was gripping a rubber floor mat. His hand hurt like hell. He moved his leg. Another mat shifted and Dave groaned.

'Dave? Are you OK? I can't see you. Where are you?'

He felt something budge near his leg.

'I'm here. We flipped it, Nick. We are the champions, mate!'

It came flooding back - the jolt and the epic lurch. There'd been a split-second while time stood still; the moment they'd almost clambered up the wall of the horsebox, walking it like the inside of a giant rolling ball. They'd crouched like limpets as it finally went over. Loosened floor mats flipped and fell, but their rubber shields held. The side of the trailer became the floor, the floor and roof became the sides. They'd overturned it, all right.

'Yeah, but I can't see a bloody thing in here. Let's get out.' Nick moved his fingers, 'Youch! I think I've bust something.' The flash of pain was nauseating.

'Be quiet! The mad woman may be out there. She could be waiting for us,' Dave hissed.

'But if we don't hear her, how do we get out?'

'We hope help arrives.'

'Jeeeez,' Nick breathed.

***

Matt took a deep breath and rode slowly towards the angular shape. It blocked the uneven track and extended into the crushed and broken shrubs on either side.

He knew at once what must have happened. It was ob-

291

vious. The SUV headlights were still on full beam; one shafted into the ground, the other streamed into the foliage at the side of the track. It caught the slope of a pale mound of rubble.

'They've spammin' flipped! First a hard right an' then a sharp bend in the track,' he gasped, awed by a force capable of overturning both a vehicle and horsebox trailer. It felt raw and violent. Shocking.

His Vespa front light played across the exposed underbellies. They looked dark and threatening. Their wheels cast shadows and projected off the ground like the limbs of bloated animal carcases. It was sickening. Matt's stomach turned. He slowed to a halt. He felt sick.

Where the spam was he? What was this place?

Beep-itty-beep! Beep-itty-beep beep!

He almost spun out of his skin. He pulled off his helmet and grabbed his phone from his pocket 'Yeah?' he panted.

'Matt, it's Chrissie. Where are you? Any news?'

'Thank blog it's you! An SUV and horsebox trailer 've just flipped.'

'What? Are you OK? Where are you? Have you found Nick?'

'No, he aint here. I'm down a track off the Great Blakenham road; the Needham Market end. It's kinda chalky.'

'Hang on, I'm looking at the map. Hey, are you at the chalk quarry? There should be some old quarry buildings and some water or... a lake there.'

'What? I aint seen none of that. It's just weird here.'

'Has anyone been hurt?'

'I don't know...'cept yeah, they must've been.'

'Stay put; I'll call Clive and an ambulance.' She rang off.

Her voice had steadied his nerves. She may have said *stay put*, but she'd also asked if anyone was injured. It spurred him on. He dug deep for his tattered courage.

'Hello? Anyone there?' he tried to shout, but his voice failed, then cupping his hands like a loudhailer, 'Hello – anyone need help?' All that came out was a hoarse whisper.

Heart pounding, he got off his scooter and pulled it onto its parking stand. He left the front light on. He wasn't risking total darkness.

He walked slowly, squeezing past the front of the SUV, taking care not to get snagged by the broken shrubs or twist his ankle on the white rubble. He couldn't see through the windscreen. Limited light and the inflated air bags hid whatever horrors were inside. He worked his way on round, but the roof was in darkness. It faced him like a metal wall, shielded from the Vespa's full beam. He tapped and banged the roof, passing his hands over it as he searched for a sunroof; some kind of way to get inside the SUV. But there was nothing.

The rear door appeared to be a hatchback design. He tried to get closer, but the tow gear and horsebox trailer blocked his progress. DOS-in' hell!

He thumped the uppermost surface of the trailer and waited, listening for sounds of life.

***

'Nick,' Dave hissed, 'did you hear that? Something banged on the trailer.'

'Shite, it's the mad woman.' Fear squeezed Nick's throat as he raised his head off a rubber mat. He caught the sound of sliding and a rustle. *Swish!* The noise was close, only centimetres away. It came from the other side of what had been the roof but was now a side. She must be very near to be brushing against the horsebox. Was she about to open it to check if they were dead, or kill them? Please, God they had enough strength to overpower the mad woman.

***

Matt caught a sound. It might have been his heartbeat, but could it have come from inside the horsebox? He thumped the trailer again and shouted, 'Is anyone in there?' And then more softly, 'Good horsey.'

'Help! Help!'

He almost choked on his heart, 'Flamin' malware! Is someone in there with them horses?'

'Matt? Is that you, Matt?

'Nick? Nick? Thank blog! Are you OK? What you doin' in there with them horses?'

'There aren't any horses. Just get us out of here.'

'What?' He'd recognised Dave's voice, 'You got Dave in there as well?'

A siren wailed in the distance.

'There's help comin',' he shouted, finding his full voice and punching the air.

CHAPTER 39

Chrissie sat in her cosy living room and stared at the map. 'Priestley Wood is barely a mile from the chalk quarry, as the crow flies,' she murmured, 'and that's assuming it flew in a straight line. Hmm, it's quite hilly between the B1078 and the chalk quarry near the Great Blakenham road.'

Without thinking, she held a hand to her mouth and nibbled her thumbnail while she studied the terrain. She checked the time. Was it only half an hour since she'd phoned Clive and called an ambulance? It felt like a lifetime. Was it too soon to ring Matt again? She stood up and paced around the room. Clive would be mad with her if she drove there. And it would be impossible to pretend it wasn't her nosiness getting the better of her. But what if…? A plan took shape in her mind.

She forced herself to wait another fifteen minutes. 'Right,' she whispered and pressed Matt's automatic dial number. He answered on the second ring tone.

'Chrissie?' His voice came across thin and reedy.

'Are you OK, Matt?'

'Yeah. We got 'em!'

'What d'you mean? Got who? Has Clive found you? And the ambulance? Has it arrived?' She was bursting to know.

'Yeah, yeah. But–'

'But what? Come on; it's horrible this end not knowing what's going on. I mean, there's been an accident, right?'

'Yeah. They're still gettin' the driver out.'

'And the horses?'

'Yeah well, I were tryin' to say. There weren't no horses. It were Nick and Dave.'

'What?'

'Yeah, see we've found Nick an' Dave.'

It took her a couple of seconds to grasp his meaning. Relief almost swept her away. It certainly loosened her tongue.

'Thank God! Are they OK? Did you just say they were in the horsebox? But why? Why were they in the horse-box?' And then she stopped. Shooting her thoughts at Matt in a volley of rapid-fire questions wasn't going to work. He'd be grappling with either the first or last question, while she wouldn't know which he was answering. *Slow down*, she told herself.

She waited a second, and when he didn't say anything, she added, 'Hey sorry, Matt. Just tell me; is Nick OK?'

'Yeah, kinda. He's been knocked about, an' so 'as Dave.'

'Oh no! But will they be OK?'

'I s'pose, but I aint been allowed near since them am-bulance and heavy cuttin' lot arrived. It's spammin' weird here. I keep thinkin'; what if I hant followed the horsebox trailer?' His voice wobbled.

She bit back her *but why were you following a horse-box trailer* question. He didn't sound good and it could wait. 'Do you want to come back here?' she asked instead, and added, 'I can rustle up jacket potatoes with cheese, and there's more lager in the fridge.'

'Really?'

'Yes, of course. You sound as if you could do with some, and anyway, I want to hear all about it. Hey, but tell me again; Nick and Dave are going to be OK, yes?'

'Yeah, I s'pose'

'Take care. Ride safely.'

Cooking hadn't been exactly part of her plan but she figured the smell of jacket potatoes baking would be comforting. And comfort loosened tongues. It might even dispel any accusations of nosiness on her part. Yes. It might just be the answer.

***

When Chrissie flung open her front door, mouth-watering aromas seeped from her hallway and out into the dark Friday night chill. Matt pulled off his helmet and breathed in the smell of baking potato.

'Spammin' Trojan,' he murmured, and then unable to hold back his grin, 'We got Nick and Dave; we found 'em!'

'It's the best news ever. Well done you! And well done everyone! Now don't stand out in the cold; come in. Leave your helmet on the table here.' She pushed Bill's photo frame and her car keys to one side to make some space.

'Thanks.' He followed her into the kitchen. He hadn't realised how hungry he was. The earlier lager had taken the edge off his appetite, and the fear and angst had cramped his stomach. The small kitchen felt nest-like and safe.

'I've never seen the old chalk quarry. What's it like?' Chrissie asked, as she tipped a tin of baked beans into a saucepan. 'The potatoes are crisping in the oven. I've used the microwave to speed things along.'

His ears went buzzy when she opened the oven door. He could barely hear her; she seemed distanced, as if he was viewing her through plate glass. Silently, she got out plates and cutlery and grated cheese. Was this happening in real time? If he blinked, would it all black out? But worse still, could the quarry reappear; a colander of darkness, pale cliffs, white powdery dust and the smell of fear?

She took his arm. Her voice floated on the air.

'Matt, are you OK? You've gone a bit pale. Hey, come and sit down.'

She led him out of the kitchen and into her living room. He sat heavily on the sofa.

'Stay there. I'll bring the food in on a tray.'

'An' a lager, Chrissie.'

He sat quietly, trying to process what had happened. It had felt unreal at the quarry. How could he possibly explain it? But if he simply said what popped into his head, then maybe he could leave Chrissie to make sense of it for herself.

'Clive called her Mrs Lamanby,' he said when Chrissie set a loaded tray down on the coffee table.

'Mrs Lamanby? You mean George Lamanby's wife?'

'I dunno. 'Cept I heard Clive say *we'll get you out of there, Mrs Lamanby.* He were talkin' to the driver.'

'The driver?

'Yeah, s'pose so.' He dug into the baked potato on his plate.

'So why were Nick and Dave in the horsebox trailer?'

'I dunno. I couldn't get it open. The cuttin' team had to use a crowbar... an' then they wouldn't let me talk to 'em.'

Chrissie didn't say anything while he ate. She seemed absorbed in her own thoughts, and anyway, she was eating as well. It gave him a chance to let the buttery, cheesy flavours and the sweet tomato sauce sooth him, and begin the repair of his world.

He swigged back a mouthful of lager. Yeah, his systems were being restored.

'Where d'you suppose they've taken Nick and Dave? The hospital or the investigation centre?' Chrissie asked.

'There were more than one ambulance,' Matt murmured, remembering the scene.

She must have been satisfied with his answer because she switched to an unrelated topic.

'Ron asked if he could see a picture or photo of Harold. I got the impression he was rather interested in the Bletchley Park and MI5 connection.'

'Do he read comic-strip?'

She laughed. Matt wasn't sure why.

'So, do you have a picture of Harold I can show Ron?' she asked.

He still had no idea if Ron was or wasn't a comic-strip reader. 'Yeah, I got a newspaper one, an' a possible from a reverse image search. I'll email you the file.'

'Thanks.'

Matt let his head rest back against the cushions. He was safe, warm and comfortable. He shut his eyes and drifted... drifted into deep nothingness. The next thing he knew, someone was shaking him.

'Hey, wake up!' a familiar voice boomed.

'Oh, just leave him, Clive. He's been like that for a couple of hours.'

Matt recognised Chrissie's voice immediately. Pixels! He'd fallen asleep on her sofa. He groaned. Couldn't they just leave him to doze a little longer? He kept his eyes firmly closed but let their voices drift into his ears.

'You know it's almost midnight, Chrissie?'

'Yes; Matt fell asleep and I've been waiting up for you. There's no way I'd have been able to sleep until I knew what had happened to Nick.'

'No, I guess not.'

'Would you like baked beans with your cheese and baked potato? There're a few left.'

'That'd be… real comfort food. Thanks.'

Matt listened to what he guessed was Chrissie going out to the kitchen and Clive sitting down in the armchair. He concentrated on keeping his breathing slow and even… slow and even. Pixels! He was dropping off again. Would sleep morph into a quarry? If he kept listening, then he'd stay awake enough to stop the darkness taking him.

He stirred a little as he heard Chrissie's footsteps return, the sound of Clive shifting in his chair, cutlery being picked up from a tray and the first mouthfuls being eaten. Matt conjured the mouth-watering tastes and tried not to swallow. He was supposed to be asleep.

'So come on Clive; tell me what's happened to Nick and Dave. Matt had no idea.' The sofa cushions moved a little as Chrissie sat down next to him.

'We wanted to take them straight to the investigation unit, but on balance it's best they've gone for a check-up in A&E. It's turned out they're being kept in overnight.'

'What?'

'Calm down, Chrissie. It's precautionary. You see, Dave is sure they were both drugged by Mrs Lamanby yesterday afternoon. He said she got them to the horsebox trailer on some pretext and then knocked them out. That's how she managed to lock them in.'

'What?'

'I know; it's almost unbelievable. But, there's vomit in the horsebox. I figure toxicology on it will tell us what she drugged them with.'

'But why were they with her in the first place?'

'They're both working on the Poachers Basket and she's the archivist. They went over to look at the collection.'

'It sounds harmless enough. So why'd she want to drug them?'

'Dave thinks it's because of a photo. Something they remarked on but she hadn't noticed was in the collection until they pointed it out.'

'Really? So you're saying she drugged them? Locked them in a horsebox trailer? All because of something they'd seen?'

'Yes, and I don't think she was going to stop there. I believe she planned to kill them.'

'Kill? Oh my God!'

'We're getting a warrant to search the place. Hopefully we'll find the answer.'

'But won't George Lamanby, or his wife, have got rid of what Dave and Nick saw?'

'It depends what it is. Dave didn't think Mr Lamanby was involved.'

'You keep talking about Dave. Are you sure Nick's OK?'

'Nick was in a worse shape than Dave. But he'll be OK.'

'Oh no. Poor Nick.'

'We'll have to wait and see what the doctors say, but I'm guessing some fractured ribs, and broken fingers and toes, along with bruising; basically, lots of minor injuries. They were both tossed around in the horsebox trailer before it fell on its side.'

'What? So how come their van was found near the

woods?'

'I think Mrs Lamanby wanted their deaths to look like an accident. Something on the lines of - they go for a walk in the woods, lose their sense of direction, it gets dark and they stumble down the chalk cliffs and perish in the lake in the chalk quarry.'

'But....'

'And you know the oddest thing about this? Mrs Lamanby took Nick's shoes, or rather his cowboy boots.'

Clive's words shot through Matt like an electric shock. He opened his eyes. 'Did you say cowboy boots?'

'I thought you were asleep.' Clive had an edge to his voice.

'Yeah, I were sleepin'.' Matt yawned for good measure and added, 'I bet them boots are the ones Maisie got for me.'

'Yes I remember; the open mic night in the Nags Head. They were too large for you, but they fitted Nick perfectly. Are we meant to believe Nick walked all this way in socks or bare feet?' Chrissie drew her finger across the map.

'Except it might've been difficult to tell. Chalky water is strongly alkaline. It would have macerated his skin. I don't know how long it'd take to start breaking down leather... but if he'd been in the quarry lake long enough before he was discovered... then, who knows,' Clive said.

'That's horrible.' Chrissie held her hand to her mouth.

'Yeah, but how'd the van get to Priestley Wood?' Matt asked. He was remembering the rough track. He'd almost fallen riding his Vespa out that way.

'The forensic team are working on the van.'

'Do you think someone else drove it there?'

'I don't know, Chrissie. Look. It's been one hell of a long day, and tomorrow… or rather it's now today, is going to be even longer. Time we got Matt off home.'

'No – it's OK, Matt. You can spend what's left of the night in the spare bed. I'm sorry Clive, but we almost lost Nick today. I'd never forgive myself if Matt had an accident on his way back to Stowmarket.'

'Cool,' Matt breathed. He'd found his friend, knocked back a couple of lagers, eaten baked beans and now he was as good as staying in a hotel. Things were looking up… so long as the dark quarry didn't return.

CHAPTER 40

Two weeks had passed since the Chalk Quarry Reckoning, as Nick liked to call it. He had wanted to write a song about it, but Chrissie said, 'There's a case looming. You can't go round all the pubs and nightclubs singing about the evidence.' She had a point.

However nothing could stop lyrics popping into his head and weaving through his thoughts, nor block the rhythm of the snaking horsebox from breaking into the beat of his life. Simply catching sight of his strapped broken fingers on his left hand triggered *We Are the Champions*. And as for his footwear – he'd exchanged his trainer for a boot walker from the hospital fracture clinic. At least it hid his fractured toes, strapped together for support while they healed.

The Chalk Quarry Reckoning had hit the news and although names had been withheld, word on the street had whipped up enough interest to make his next gig with the band a crowded triumph. He might not be allowed to drive yet, but he could sit on a stool and sing. And he didn't even need to hold the microphone; he could fix it to a stand. His real nightmare was being off work, bored and alone with his thoughts. So he was pleased when Clive dropped by to see him in the St Andrews Street flat.

'Do you want a coffee?' he asked Clive, as he led him into the living room.

'No thanks. I don't want to put you to any trouble. I've a few things to go over with you and... well I wanted to see how you are.' He smiled, and Nick caught a glimpse of genuine concern.

Nick slumped onto the futon couch while Clive adopted the higher sofa. He suspected Clive had instinctively taken the position of advantage; a habit born of years interrogating suspects. Nick sensed the danger and determined not to let his guard down.

'OK, so what do you want to know?'

'Well firstly I should say we've charged Mrs Lamanby with poisoning with intent, grievous bodily harm with intent, kidnap and now… murder.'

'Murder? Dave's OK, isn't he?'

'Yes, yes. Calm down; I'll explain. We've discovered a lot more about Mrs Lamanby over the past couple of weeks and… I'd like you to go over all that was said when you and Dave visited her on Thursday October 16th.' Clive sounded mellow and relaxed.

'You mean the Thursday we went to see the archives?'

'Yes.'

'OK, let me think. She got funny about her thatched roof when we admired it.'

'How'd you mean?'

'Dave said something like *they did a good job of your thatching. I hope the Poachers Basket eventually gets as good a job done on it.*'

Nick watched Clive nod slowly.

'She didn't say anything, but I could tell she didn't like it. And then she got funny when Dave mentioned square head master wheat. It's an old wheat variety; taller than the modern strains. It's still used for thatching. The client who turned out not to be a client over in Dunwich had grown some for thatching.'

'OK… and did you tell her you'd just come from the Dunwich client who grew it?'

'Yeah.'

'What else do you remember?'

'She was a bit odd about my cowboy boots. Dave was making fun of me wearing them. He was kinda drawing attention to them, and she got a bit weird when I pointed out an American airman wearing cowboy boots in one of the photos.'

'Yes, we know about that from Dave.'

'But then I got three text messages from Matt all at once, and it really freaked her. Yeah, I'd forgotten about that.' Nick found Clive's relaxed, non-probing manner strangely soothing.

'How'd you mean?'

'She seemed to change. Yeah, she came over all nice and offered us coffee. Earlier, she hadn't offered us anything. She'd even joked about supposing we'd want lunch as well, you know, as if we were taking advantage of her hospitality.'

'And were you?'

'No. All I'd done was ring and ask if we could come sooner than we'd planned. Then she went all iffy on me when I said a few things had happened and we'd had to alter our schedule.'

'That's interesting.'

'What did she put in the coffee? No one's told me yet.'

'As we suspected, it was poisoned.'

'But with what?'

'Cytisine; it comes from laburnum trees. It's a bit like nicotine and in large quantities it'll kill. In this case it was homemade and high dose.'

'So has it... damaged me?'

'I'm not a doctor but lucky for all of us, you vomited most of it. And that has cracked the case.'

'What?'

'It's been analysed. We've found cytisine in what you vomited into the bucket and splattered inside the horsebox. When we searched the Lamanbys' place we found evidence that Mrs Lamanby had made cytisine from laburnum seeds. And this is the clincher; the composition of her homemade laburnum poison, with all its impurities, matches what was in your vomit and what we found in Caleb Coddins' hipflask.'

'Bloody hell. Wasn't he the bloke caught in the reed beds a month or so ago? He died, didn't he?'

'Yes. So you were lucky. Can you see we have a theme? Thatch, or should I say thatchers, and cytisine poisoning.'

'Jeeeez. So you think Dave and me talking about thatch made her turn on us?'

'Possibly, but from what you're saying it wasn't just the mention of thatch. You wanted to look at the pub memorabilia sooner than planned because *a few things had happened*. Then there was what you saw in the old photo, your cowboy boots and your text messages. I think she thought you'd discovered whatever it was that made her kill Caleb Coddins.'

'What? You're kidding? But what made her kill Caleb Coddins?'

'We're working on a blackmail theory.'

Nick pulled a face. 'Why would anyone want to blackmail Mrs Lamanby? My texts weren't about blackmail. It was only Matt telling me about my great-grandfather, Harold Roan. Although… that's right… it's coming back to me now. After she tricked me into giving her my phone, she read out the text messages. She thought *U R* was someone's name, you know, their initials. She went very strange. That's when she knocked me out.'

Clive was about to say something, but seemed to change his mind and stared at the worn carpet.

'I never answered Matt's text. I could hardly text while we were in her kitchen; after that I was sick. Then she had my phone.'

'Yes, the time the text was sent fits your version of events. I think the *Confirm Harold has to be dead* text was her way of trying to find out if someone was after her. And Matt's reply - *course Harold got to be dead by now!* was....'

'Dave and my death sentence?'

'Something like that.'

'But George Lamanby seemed like a nice bloke.'

'We've no evidence he was in on it. We only found her DNA in the Willows van, not his. She loaded her bicycle into it. So I figure she was the one who drove it out to Priestley Wood and then cycled home.'

Nick sat for a few minutes letting everything sink in. 'You know this kinda makes it feel better. I thought it was some random hate thing. But you reckon she thought we were onto her and it was a case of either her or us?'

Clive nodded.

'But there has to be more to it. I saw it in her eyes when she looked at the photo. It was physical, like a feral response. There's something tied into the past.' He let his voice trail as his thoughts moved forward. *Don't chalk over the past*, the potential lyrics ran in his head.

In all honesty it was a relief. Believing someone hated

308

him enough to kill him had been the worst kind of under-mining, nightmarish experience of his life.

'So I was a threat, not a figure of hate.' His emotions flew. *Caustic feelings* and *chalky water*; hmm… *chalky water* would make a good title for the song.

'I'll post the letter to MI5.' He held up his hand to show his strapped broken fingers; a visible excuse for his delay.

'Good; and I hope my visit has helped. We'll need you to pick out the photo with the airman in the boots. Lucky for us, she didn't destroy it. Dave's identified it amongst some photos we found she'd hidden away.'

'But Dave didn't tell me.'

'He's been instructed not to discuss it with you, or you with him. We don't want the defence crying witness associ-ation and influence.'

'Oh.' Relief washed through him. 'That's why he's been distant with me.'

'I don't usually say much around a case, but… be-cause it's you, I figured letting you in on a few facts might help you come to terms with what happened to you. But keep it to yourself. Understand?'

'Yeah, I've got it. And… thanks, Clive.'

'I tell you what.' Clive stood up. 'I'll drive you down to the station. You can add what you've just told me to your statement. And while you're about it, you can identify the photo. It might trigger more memories.'

'Yeah, OK. And I'll post the letter.'

***

Nick sat opposite Clive and studied the photo on the desk. The room was starkly functional with plain, pale-wash walls, sash windows, filing cabinets, a modern table desk with drawers, and of course, a computer and monitor taking pride of place on the desk.

'So she didn't destroy it,' Nick said as he gazed at the faces in the photo.

'No.' Clive appeared more formal now that he was in the police station.

'Can you make the cowboy boots larger?'

'Yes… I'll do it on the screen.'

'Thanks.' Nick stood up and limped round the desk to view it. He didn't know what he was expecting to see, but if the cowboy boots had helped to destabilise Mrs Lamanby then he reckoned they deserved a closer look.

'Do you think they could be Justin Boots made in Fort Worth, Texas?' Clive asked.

Nick frowned. He had no idea of the different makes of cowboy boots. 'I wouldn't know.'

'Matt told me about a missing pair of *Justin Fort Worth Boots*, but they'd have been more recent than this photo.'

'Really?' Something clicked into place in Nick's mind. Of course, Matt would have researched retro cowboy boots. That's why he'd wanted Maisie to get some for him. He'd probably told Clive all about the different labels. 'What make were mine? I assume you found them when you searched the Lamanbys' place.'

'No, we haven't discovered them yet. If the brand is important, we can ask an expert to identify them in the photo.'

'Matt or Maisie should know the make of mine.'

They lapsed into silence as Nick scrutinised the image and wondered what it must have been like for those American airmen arriving in October 1942.

'Yes?' Clive's tone pulled Nick back to the present. He dragged his eyes from the monitor and gazed at a familiar-looking plain-clothed man in his late twenties who stood in the doorway.

'Something's come through from the States. I think you should take a look, sir.' The cheese-grater voice sounded harsh against the blandness of the room.

'Thanks. Oh and Nick, this is DS Stickley. Sergeant, Nick Cowley here has remembered a few more things from the poisoning and attempted murder.'

DS Stickley nodded. 'I think we've already met. How're the fingers?'

'Sore; I can't play my guitar.'

Clive tapped on the keyboard and opened a document on the screen.

'What?' Clive barked, 'It's a miracle! The Americans have possible IDs for some of the airmen in the old photos we sent. And they've got a potential name for the one you're looking at now!'

'Really? But how does it help anything?' Nick asked.

'You're forgetting the cesspool body. It could be American. And the one with the cowboy boots is,' Clive leaned forward to read from the screen, 'called Harris... yes, first name Hubbard but also known as Fort Worth or FW.'

'Hub Harris – it has an American ring to it,' Stickley's voice grated, 'They've asked if they can have the DNA analysis. They want to try matching it with living relatives in the States.'

'Good, get on with sending it. Tooth pulp, wasn't it? And we asked the lab to look at the DNA from the blood behind the door panel. Chase it up. And while you're about it, ask if there's a match with our cesspool man's DNA.'

Nick realised he'd been forgotten in the burst of ex-citement. It was a good feeling. He felt safe, above suspi-cion. And like a fly on the wall, he opted to stay silent.

'Hmm… Harris; I've heard that name before. Hell, it's Matt again. I wonder…. It could be the link to the past we've been looking for. Get Matt Finch in now, Stickley. And tell him to bring his laptop and memory stick with him.'

'Right, sir.'

'Harris… Harris,' Clive murmured, eyes closed and frowning, 'of course – Raelynn Harris! My god! Is there a connection?'

CHAPTER 41

'You never told me how Mrs Lamanby reacted when you challenged her with being Raelynn Harris,' Chrissie said, tossing the words over her shoulder to Clive.

It was a Sunday morning, and she sat in her small kitchen. Open recipe books covered the table. She faced her laptop, its screen filled with glossy images of savoury finger food for parties.

Clive didn't answer immediately, but finished rinsing his coffee mug under the tap. She knew he'd heard her because he walked across the kitchen, rested his hands on her shoulders and lightly kissed the top of her head.

'Now what made you suddenly ask?'

'I've wanted to for ages and now that you've more or less wrapped up the case, I thought you wouldn't mind.'

'Is that why you're looking at party menus? To celebrate it's over?'

'Ha; ever the detective!'

'Well, if you're inviting Matt, I think you'll need something more substantial than....' He leaned in to read the screen, '*Smoked salmon on cream cheese blinis.*'

'I know. Hey, you haven't answered my question.'

'OK, then. You need to remember Mrs Lamanby's been charged and she's in custody, so by the time we interviewed her about her alter ego, Raelynn Harris, she was under caution with her solicitor present. But we still got quite a reaction from her, despite her solicitor trying to get her to play the *no comment* card.'

'Wow, so tell me; was she upset or angry or... I don't know, indifferent?'

'She started off denying it in a rather cold way. Then we faced her with what she didn't know – her DNA has a close familial match with the blood under the door panel at the Poachers Basket, and with the tooth pulp from the cesspool body. That's when she broke down.'

'I'm not surprised. So are you saying she's the daughter of the bloke in the cesspool?'

'Yes.'

'So the photo of the American airman was of her father? And he's the one dead in the cesspool. Wooah! I think even I would have broken down if I'd been told all that.'

'Well she knew her father was an American airman called Hubbard Harris. She told us he met her mother, Marylou, while he was stationed at the Wattisham Airfield during the Second World War. Marylou was a local Suffolk girl and country & western fan, but at the end of the war Hubbard returned to the States leaving Marylou behind, pregnant and with his cowboy boots as a memento. Raelynn was born in 1946.'

'So you're saying the cowboy boots were her dad's?'

'Yes, I think she glamorised and fantasised about him, and they represented a link with him.'

Chrissie nodded as the boots' importance sank in.

'Matt told me about a connection between Caleb Coddins, Raelynn Harris and some cowboy boots that Balcon & Mora had been asked to trace and find. But we didn't know who Raelynn Harris was. She didn't seem to exist.'

'Really?'

'Yes, Raelynn Harris only existed for a newspaper advert she placed, years ago. She co-opted her father's surname for it. But Raelynn was real. Her stepfather never adopted her, so she kept her mother's maiden name. It was on her marriage certificate to George Lamanby. Then after she married George, Raelynn morphed to Rosalind or Roz.'

'But the laburnum poison connects Caleb now, right?'

'Exactly! We suspected from Matt's research, that Caleb's father might have been Raelynn's stepfather.'

'And was he?'

'I suppose we could check her DNA against Caleb's to see if they have the same mother; Marylou.'

'So how did she react when you suggested Caleb was her half-brother?'

'She lost control. Resentment, hatred; it all poured out. Amos her stepfather sounds like he was a hard, bigoted man. He took Marylou's daughter in when they married, but he barely acknowledged Raelynn and wouldn't let her join the family thatching firm.'

'Why? Because she wasn't his child?'

'Maybe, but Raelynn believed it was because she was a girl. Amos took on a male apprentice instead, who later joined the firm.'

'Oh no, don't tell me it was Jason Brookford?'

'You've got it. And of course, he was a slippery opportunist with a cruel streak.'

'Well I'd already guessed about him blackmailing the Lamanbys. All that business of no listed building permission and thatching with reed instead of straw. But sadistic?'

'Jason knew the cowboy boots were important. Raelynn said she hadn't been allowed to wear them. After all, they were men's boots, therefore Caleb had them. And Jason knew Raelynn hated Caleb for it.'

'Ah.'

'Exactly. So when they disappeared from the Poachers Basket after Amos' funeral wake, Raelynn suspected Jason had nicked them. At least that's what she told us.'

'I bet she blamed Caleb for losing them as well.'

'No doubt. There's nothing like stirring up trouble between a half-brother and half-sister.'

'So much hate!' Chrissie needed a few moments to take in the enormity of it. She almost felt sorry for Raelynn. Being passed over for simply being a woman was something she could relate to. It wasn't unknown in the world of carpentry.

'Now I get why Jason was left without his shoes when he died in the Poachers Basket,' she sighed. 'We said at the time it was like a message. She'll have tempted him in with a promise of vodka and…. Was her husband involved?'

'She says not, although she used his keys.'

'I bet her solicitor was upset she talked so freely!'

'Yes and no. I expect all the psychological trauma will be used in her defence in court.'

'But she won't get away with it, will she?'

'It's only circumstantial evidence in Jason's case; her number on his various phone records won't be enough to charge her with his murder. The CPS will decide. But Caleb's murder and Nick & Dave's attempted murder should stick.'

'I blame the Poachers Basket for all this. Just think, if she hadn't been the archivist collecting all those old photos last year, she might have been able to bury the past.'

'Chrissie, you can't bury that amount of hate and resentment. Not unless you come to terms with it. And anyway, you're forgetting her father. What was he doing over here, we're guessing in 1961, to get killed and dumped in the pub's cesspool? I think he was involved in American Intelligence.'

'That's crazy. How can you say that?'

'Just some hints we've had from our colleagues in the States. Remember it was the time of the Cold War. Hub Harris will have been familiar with the Wattisham Airbase. No doubt he had old contacts; possibly even some Russian dealings.'

'So you don't think he was here visiting his daughter?'

'Raelynn denied having ever seen him, and I believe her. Hub was far too hardboiled for emotional baggage. There's no evidence he even knew he had a daughter.'

'Oh no,' she breathed, as thoughts of the Polyphon and its secret messages surfaced. 'But the Polyphon disc, Clive! Hub was killed with the disc cutting into his neck. You don't think... you can't think Nick's great-grandfather was involved?'

'I don't know what to think, Chrissie, and sometimes it's best not to dig. We're in the realm of classified material and the Intelligence Services. At least I can give the cesspool man a name. I reckon the coroner will pass a verdict of unnatural causes and anything further will be held in closed session or not at all.'

'Right,' Chrissie murmured. Clive's manner told her he didn't want to say more. Was he under orders to tread no further or did he know but it was classified information? She sensed not to push her luck and ask.

But it couldn't stop her thinking about the LEAVE NOW message, scrolled up inside the Polyphon's keyhole as if unread. If it was meant for Hub, it might explain why he hadn't escaped with his life. But the Polyphon belonged to Nick's great-grandfather and something didn't sit right.

'Don't fret about food for the party,' Clive said, interrupting her worried thoughts. 'Sausage rolls will be fine.'

CHAPTER 42

'Are you sure you won't join us all this evening, Mr Clegg?' Chrissie asked as she swept up wood shavings around the wood lathe. 'I know you don't normally come along to American Thanksgiving celebrations down the Nags Head, but it's an excuse to unwind.'

'No thanks, Mrs Jax. I think I'll pass on this one.'

'I know, it may get a bit lively. I was thinking of throwing a we-have-survived-it party, but I haven't found the energy and it's the fourth Thursday in November already!'

'And soon it'll be Christmas. Time flows like a riptide when you're old.'

'Don't say that, Mr Clegg. You'll get me all maudlin and this evening I want to be happy.'

She tipped the shavings into the sweepings bin and carefully propped the brush and pan back in their place.

'I don't remember you saying anything about the photo printout I gave you of Nick's great-grandfather at the prize giving.'

'That's because I didn't say anything, Mrs Jax.'

She searched his face. 'Come on, Mr Clegg; what aren't you telling me?'

'Some things are best not said, Mrs Jax.'

'Now you've really got me wanting to know.' She waited a moment, and when he didn't add anything, she asked, 'Is it because the picture was too grainy?'

Clive had once explained the technique of suggestive questioning. She watched Ron's reaction to see if she was close to the mark and when he shook his head, she launched in with, 'But you've seen the face before, haven't you?'

He set his jaw. She knew she was bang on target.

'So, it has to be a while ago,' she murmured, thinking aloud. 'Oh no, it wasn't when you were a kid was it?'

He nodded.

'Oh, Mr Clegg. Was it at the Poachers Basket? Was it the time of the fight when you helped mend the door panel?'

He didn't answer but the weariness in his face spoke volumes.

'It's not beyond reason he might have been there and that you might have seen him. We know Nick's great-grandfather was involved in codes and probably the Intelligence Services. Nick's waiting to hear back from MI5, and he's expecting them to confirm it.'

'Your instincts are as right as ever, Mrs Jax. But I hadn't told you because… what good can come of it? Nick might not take it too well knowing his relative was mixed up in someone's disappearance.'

'Death, you mean. Unless he was there to sort it out and clean up afterwards?'

'You're right, Mrs Jax. It doesn't have to mean the American died by his hand. And it can't tell us who had to LEAVE NOW.'

'No, because the title on the disc in the fireplace wasn't Loves Old Sweet Song.'

'What was it, Mrs Jax?'

'Clive isn't allowed to say. So I want, no I'm *going* to believe, Nick's great-grandfather tried to warn the American that he wasn't safe, his cover was broken and he should LEAVE NOW. I guess it went wrong. I hope he was only there to clean up afterwards.'

'I think, Mrs Jax, it's best not to say more. Some things are best left unsaid.'

***

The Nags Head was buzzing with people. The jukebox belted out Bruce Springsteen's *Born in the USA* at full volume, while people jostled at the bar to order Suffolk's answer to American Thanksgiving Day – turkey rolls with cranberry sauce, creamed corn soup, and of course, slices of pumpkin pie and pecan pie. A list of American lagers was chalked on the blackboard propped behind the bar. Smiling faces were everywhere.

Chrissie quickly found her group of friends near the fireplace.

'Hi, Dave! Great to see you. All good now?'

'Hey Chrissie! Yes, if it's done one thing for me it's… well I don't mind being in a crowd like this. In fact, I feel safer.'

'And of course, you're sticking to beer, not coffee!' Nick chipped in.

'Yes, that as well. Hey Matt, I think I owe you another pint for saving us.'

'He's been dining out on a lot of lagers recently. Yeah, you're a hero, mate!' Nick clapped Matt on the shoulder.

Chrissie noticed the finger strapping had gone and his hand looked back to normal.

'And,' he added, 'I've heard back from MI5.'

'Are you allowed to tell us?' She waved at Maisie, who was weaving her way to them through the crowd.

'Probably not, but their answer explains a lot. It's what we all expected.' He smiled and Chrissie saw the pride in his face.

'Good, it gives closure,' she said and then added, 'Is

320

Sarita coming?'

'She's working, but she'll be at the gig on Saturday.'

'I heard some of them Utterly students are designin' a computer game – *Escape the Horsebox*. Pretty cool, yeah?'

'Awesome, Matt.' Nick gulped more beer.

'But I dunno 'bout the spammin' name.'

'I'll drink to *Chase the Horsebox*,' Dave laughed.

'Or something like *Mattzo GoGo*?' Chrissie smiled. She knew they were all going to be just fine.

The End.

Lightning Source UK Ltd.
Milton Keynes UK
UKHW020640140322
400024UK00006B/189

9 781912 861156